"Lovers,"

Zach said softly. "That's the word I'd use."

"We're hardly that," Leah retorted, managing an uneasy laugh.

"We were exactly that once."

"Once. It's been over for a long time now."

"Nothing is over until it has an end. You and I, we never really had an ending."

"Yes we did, Zach. It just wasn't the ending you wanted."

"No, it was the one you wanted, remember? The one you chose."

"Look, this is ridiculous," declared Leah, shaking her head. "I have no intention of standing here, arguing with you over something that was over and done with years ago."

"That's just it," he countered, emotion permeating his low tone. "It's not over and done with."

Dear Reader,

Welcome to Silhouette **Special Edition** . . . welcome to romance.

Last year, I requested that you send me your opinions on the books that we publish, and on romances in general. Thank you so much for the many thoughtful letters. For the next couple of months, I'd like to share some quotes from these letters with you. This seemed very appropriate now while we are in the midst of the THAT SPECIAL WOMAN! promotion. Each one of our readers is a special woman, as heroic as the heroines in our books.

This September has some wonderful stories coming your way. *A Husband to Remember* by Lisa Jackson is our THAT SPECIAL WOMAN! selection for this month.

This month also has other special treats. For one, we've got *Bride Wanted* by Debbie Macomber coming your way. This is the second book in her FROM THIS DAY FORWARD series. *Night Jasmine* by Erica Spindler—one of the BLOSSOMS OF THE SOUTH series—is also on its way to happy readers, as is Laurie Paige's *A Place for Eagles,* the second tale in her WILD RIVER TRILOGY. And September brings more books from favorite authors Patricia Coughlin and Natalie Bishop.

I hope you enjoy this book, and all of the stories to come!

Sincerely,

Tara Gavin
Senior Editor
Silhouette Books

Quote of the Month: "All the Silhouettes I've read have believable characters and are easy to identify with. The pace of the story line is good, the books hold my interest. When I start a Silhouette, I know I'm in for a good time."
—P. Digney,
New Jersey

PATRICIA COUGHLIN

MY SWEET BABY

Silhouette®

SPECIAL V **EDITION**®

Published by Silhouette Books New York
America's Publisher of Contemporary Romance

For my son, Billy

SILHOUETTE BOOKS
300 East 42nd St., New York, N.Y. 10017

MY SWEET BABY

Copyright © 1993 by Patricia Coughlin

ISBN: 0-373-09837-5

First Silhouette Books printing September 1993

Printed in the U.S.A.

PATRICIA COUGHLIN

is also known to romance fans as Liz Grady and lives in Rhode Island with her husband and two sons. A former schoolteacher, she says she started writing after her second son was born to fill her hours at home. Having always read romances, she decided to try penning her own. Though she was duly astounded by the difficulty of her new hobby, her hard work paid off, and she accomplished the rare feat of having her very first manuscript published. For now, writing has replaced quilting, embroidery and other pastimes, and with more than a dozen published novels under her belt, the author hopes to be happily writing romances for a long time to come.

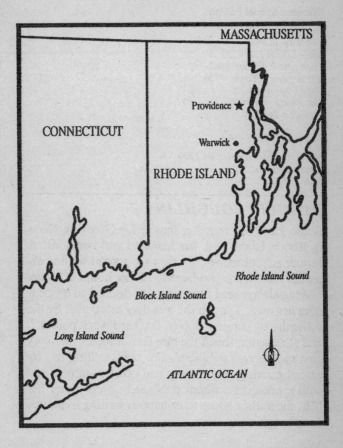

Chapter One

The last time she'd seen Tiger Blackmore, Leah had been seventeen years old, pregnant with his baby and scared as hell.

Now she was just plain scared.

Only a moment ago she'd been settled in her favorite chair, looking forward to the six o'clock news and the dinner of Low Mein she'd picked up on her way home from work. Keeping up with current events was crucial to her job as a features writer for *Rhode Island Monthly* magazine and the local news often inspired ideas for future pieces. Leah was an observer, an expert at dissecting events, putting a new spin on them and packaging them for consumption by the magazine's readers.

In fact, she was much better at observing than doing, more at ease chronicling the action than being part of it. Not that she wasn't moved by the people and events she covered. She often was, with stories about children in particular finding their way to a dark, private place buried deep inside her. That's why she never chose to write stories about young children. As much as possible, she liked to keep the heartache that flickered across the television screen each night from touching her directly. She felt safe here behind the locked door of the sprawling stone-front ranch house with its cobalt-blue shutters and awnings.

The house was much too big for one person, which was one of the main reasons Leah had bought it. Growing up in a large family crowded into too few rooms, she understood the luxury of space. Along with a great many other things that had once been beyond her means, she could now afford extra room, and she took comfort as well as pride in that fact. This house, on a sheltered cul-de-sac in a good neighborhood was her haven, her oasis, her reward for all her hard work and sacrifice. Until a few moments ago she had been snug in the belief that nothing bad could touch her here.

Then the doorbell rang.

Fidgeting with the tie of the dark green velour robe she had changed into when she arrived home, she stared at Tiger across the threshold, the way she had done dozens, no, more like hundreds, of times before.

He stood framed in the open doorway, a sight worth seeing in tight jeans and a well-worn brown leather jacket. In the background, a killer Harley, just like the one he used to ride, was leaning against her curb, enshrined in a pool of white light from the streetlight above.

As the silence between them pulled tight, a broad, familiar, one hundred percent lethal smile spread across Tiger's face. It had been fourteen years since she'd been on the receiving end of that smile. His face was different, older, lined around the eyes and mouth, and harder in a way she found difficult to define. It didn't matter. When he smiled at her,

her pulse and equilibrium responded as if it had been only yesterday. In spite of the winter night cold, Leah's skin felt warm all over.

"Hello, Leah."

"Tiger," she said, amazing herself with her lack of eloquence. His name was about all she could manage until she found a way to moisten her tongue, and the word came out sounding more dazed than she would have allowed under ordinary circumstances. She could use a sip of water... and a shot of hundred-proof oxygen wouldn't hurt, either.

"Tiger," he repeated, as if experimenting with the sound of his nickname. "Do you have any idea how long it's been since anyone has called me that?"

Leah shook her head in true dimwit fashion.

"Too long," he said softly. "But it seems a little pretentious for a thirty-two-year-old. These days, I answer to Zach."

Zach. Short for Zachary Owen Blackmore, the name he had detested growing up. Even in the yearbook, he had insisted that Tiger appear in quotation marks beneath his picture. And no one seeing that picture, with his straight black hair falling to his shoulders and framing a lean, darkly handsome face, his expression caught somewhere between defiant and mischievous—just like Tiger himself—would ever doubt the appropriateness of the nickname he had first earned on the football field.

Leah was surprised to see that his hair was nearly as long now as then. Most guys his age had long ago surrendered to haircuts and three-piece suits. But not Tiger, evidently. Thinking it over, Leah realized that really shouldn't surprise her at all. His unconventional haircut wasn't the only reminder of the old days; his expression was still just as bold, his posture just as lazy, his eyes just as blue, and when they looked straight into hers, the way they were doing now, Leah felt the same old thrill.

She had to get a grip on herself.

Giving the belt of her robe another tug, she smiled at him. "Well, it certainly is a surprise to see you...Zach. You look wonderful."

"So do you. Better than wonderful." His gaze roamed over her unhurriedly. "Your hair's different."

She shrugged, uncertain whether that was intended as a compliment or a complaint, and ran her fingers through the short, light brown curls that were regularly permed and clipped to carefully tousled perfection at the best salon in town. "I cut it. Years ago actually."

He nodded.

"It's a lot easier to take care of this way. Just wash and go, and that's usually all I have time for in the morning. I mean, trying to get to work on time and all."

God, why was she babbling this way?

Zach nodded again. "Yeah, I can see how short hair could have real advantages."

Again his gravely drawl left Leah wondering if he meant to be flattering or facetious and she had to stop herself from toying nervously with her hair.

"It usually looks better than this," she offered. "I'm afraid you caught me off guard."

He eyed her coolly. "That was my intention. I was afraid if I called and warned you that I was coming, you wouldn't see me." Leah, trapped between the truth and good manners, was left without a response.

"Would you have?" he pressed.

"I...I don't know. Maybe. I probably would have asked what you wanted to see me about first."

"What if I said that I just wanted to see you? Nothing more. What then?"

"I don't know," she said again. "Is that why you came? Just to see me again?"

"No." He reached into his pocket and pulled out something, holding it up for her to see the gold tiger charm she'd given him over fourteen years ago, swinging at the end of the solid chain he'd worn it on.

"I came to give this back to you."

The sight of the charm ripped opened a door between Leah and the past. A door she'd thought had been sealed shut and which she'd desperately wanted to leave that way. On the other side of that door lay heartache and misgivings and danger, all swirling around the memories of that year or so when her life and Zach's had seemed to be utterly and permanently entwined. A time symbolized by the gold charm in his hand.

She'd bought it for him after spotting it in an antique store window. The sleek aggressive lines of the casting, which made the tiger seem to be moving even when standing still, had reminded her of Zach. It was a one-of-a-kind piece, the shopkeeper had told her, and that reminded her of him, too. It had also been recklessly expensive, she recalled, costing more than three months of her salary as a part-time grocery clerk. But back then Zach had inspired her to do all sorts of reckless things.

She'd been so young at the time, thought Leah with a sudden, aching wistfulness. They both had been. Young and in love and foolish enough not to see how actions taken in the name of that love had the power to change lives forever... their own and others.

Instead of taking the charm from Zach, she instinctively shoved her hands into her robe pockets. Her reaction only drew him closer. He moved up a step so that they were almost touching.

"Don't you want it back?"

She shook her head. "Not especially. Actually I'd completely forgotten about it."

"And me?" His soft, deep voice melted a path through the cold night air, which was all that separated them. "Did you completely forget about me too, Leah?"

"I didn't say that."

"Can you say it? Can you look me in the eye and say it now?"

Leah drew a deep breath and said nothing. When she exhaled, the air shuddered out of her in little puffs of white steam that brushed Zach's face and disappeared.

"What do you really want, Zach?" she asked at last.

His smile flickered. "In general? Or at the moment?"

"From me. What do you want from me?"

"That's easy. I want to come in and talk to you for a while." Somehow even without moving, he seemed to loom closer. "Let me come in, Leah."

Leah hesitated. Inviting him into her house, perhaps serving him coffee and cookies and making small talk while dressed in her bathrobe was the very last thing she wanted to do. It was too awkward, too stressful, too...reckless. And except for that short time with Zach, she had never been a reckless person. Unfortunately she also wasn't a rude person, and short of being rude, she couldn't think of any excuse not to invite him inside.

"All right," she said. "Come on in."

Zach followed her through the front hall, with its polished rose quarry tile and into a living room that Leah knew looked as if it had been lifted from the pages of a Laura Ashley catalog. She liked it that way. Amidst the chintz and fringed toss pillows and delicately framed prints with which she chose to surround herself, Zach looked even bigger and harder and more dangerous than he had outside. Out of place. Sort of like an ink blot on an Impressionist painting.

It occurred to Leah that she would do well to remember that.

Zach glanced around the room without registering any reaction at all until he reached the open container of Chinese food beside her chair.

He frowned. "I'm interrupting your dinner."

"No. Actually I was all finished," she lied. "I was just about to make coffee. Would you like a cup?"

He nodded, casting a skeptical glance at the full container as she hurried to take it away. "Is that how come you're even skinnier now than you were in high school? Because you only eat a bite of dinner and say you're through?"

Leah paused en route to the kitchen, glancing over her shoulder to confront his speculative gaze. "How can you tell I'm skinnier when I'm wearing a robe that adds at least ten pounds?"

His dark gaze held hers. "Easy. I pictured you without the robe."

An old familiar thrill shot through her. And that, Leah thought as she hid it behind a warning frown, is exactly why she should never have invited him in for coffee.

"Look, Zach—"

"Sorry," he interrupted, holding his hands up in an apologetic gesture. "You know me, always saying what I'm thinking, no exits or U-turns between brain and mouth."

Leah had to smile. That was true enough. Zach had been a lot of things—wild, impulsive, and stubborn as sin—but he had also been painfully straightforward. Evidently that hadn't changed, either.

"That's the problem," she told him. "In this case, I not only don't want you saying it, I don't want you thinking it, either."

"Got it," he said with a grin, "no more picturing you naked."

Leah shook her head and withdrew. In the kitchen, she shoved the container of Chinese food into the refrigerator and pressed her hands to her cheeks to see if they felt as hot on the outside as on the inside. They did. This was ridiculous. Zach Blackmore was an old boyfriend, part of her past. Her *distant* past, she reminded herself. In view of all that she had changed and grown and accomplished in the years since, it was really a pretty insignificant part of her life. They had simply shared some good times and had a few laughs.

And made a baby together, Leah thought grimly, *let's not forget that little piece of ancient history.* As if she ever had...or could.

Ancient history, that's exactly what it all seemed like whenever Leah let herself think about it, which was very rarely. There was no sense in thinking about things that couldn't be changed, and she was, above all else, a sensible woman. Far too sensible to let herself dwell on it now, that was for sure.

She couldn't afford to, not if she wanted to hold herself together long enough to make coffee, get through the next hour or so and send Zach on his way again. She suddenly went cold all over. Could it be that ancient history is really what he was here to talk to her about? No, she told herself a little desperately. What would be the point of it after all this time? She was just letting her imagination run away with her.

Turning to the coffeemaker, she paused with the measuring scoop in hand, wondering how many cups she should make. Two, she decided. No sense encouraging him to linger. After quickly measuring water and grinding the proper amount of fresh beans, she flipped the switch to On and returned to the living room.

Zach had tossed his jacket on the sofa, revealing a blue denim shirt as faded and lived-in as the jeans hugging his lean hips and long legs. He was standing with his back to her, studying the framed photographs grouped on the back wall of the room. Most of them featured Leah with famous people she had interviewed for the magazine. For a minute, she stood silently and studied him, remembering little things she thought she'd forgotten.

"Why don't you have a seat," she invited when he turned and met her gaze. "I'm just going to take a minute to change into something . . ." She paused and surrendered to a wry smile. "Less comfortable."

Zach started toward her at an amble. "Why bother? That robe is not what I'd call revealing. And we're hardly strangers."

"Wrong, Zach," she said, responding as much to the look in his eye as his words. "That's exactly what we are, strangers."

"How can you say that?"

"Because that's what happens when you don't see someone for fourteen years. You move on, go in different directions, you change and grow and for all practical purposes you become strangers."

He stopped in front of her.

"Is that really how it feels to you right now, Leah? Like we're strangers?" When she hesitated, he lifted his hands and gripped her upper arms gently, his deep blue gaze challenging. "Tell me that this feels like a stranger's touch."

It didn't, and the shock of awareness that ripped through Leah caused a tremor that she was certain Zach had felt even before his mocking smile confirmed that fact. Part of her wanted to tell him to get out, and part of her wanted to melt against him and see if the magic was still there for them, still as powerful and overwhelming as it used to be.

She twisted from his hold. "What it feels," she said coolly, "is inappropriate."

"You're right," he agreed, with far more grace in the face of a rebuff than Leah recalled him having. "I really didn't come here to upset you."

"No, you came here to return the pendant, right?"

"That's right." He once again produced the pendant, this time holding it out to her in his cupped palm. "Go ahead. Take it."

"Why?"

"Because it's yours. I should have given it back to you years ago, at the same time you sent back all the junk of mine that you had hanging around."

"I meant why now? Why after all these years did it suddenly occur to you to return it to me?"

He shrugged, leaning back on booted heels. "After my father died I went through some stuff I had left at the house. This was with it and I . . . Hell, I don't know, it didn't seem right to just throw it out or leave it there, so I took it."

"I was sorry to hear about your father, Zach."

He nodded. "Yeah, well, he was pretty sick at the end."

"That must have been very hard for you."

"Not really. You want to talk about virtual strangers, that's what we were, virtual strangers."

Leah nodded with understanding and sympathy. "That happens when you grow up and move away. My folks moved to Florida a few years ago, and even though we call and write, it's not the same."

"That's a little different, considering that I only lived an hour's drive away from my father. Not that it would have changed anything even if I'd pitched a tent in his backyard. We were always strangers." As he spoke of his father, his eyes had become even darker and more opaque, but now something flashed in them once again. "That's how I know for sure that you and I aren't strangers. Not by a long shot, Leah.''

"Maybe strangers was too harsh a word," she conceded.

"Give me a better one."

"Oh, I don't know, Zach. Acquaintances."

"Uh-uh. I'm acquainted with my barber and with the guy who owns the liquor store where I buy beer. This is something else."

"Old friends then, classmates, alumni...what word would you use?"

She knew instantly that she had made a mistake.

His eyes heated so that she felt assaulted with intimacy even before he spoke. "Lovers," he said softly. "That's the word I'd use."

"We're hardly that," she retorted, managing an uneasy laugh.

"We were exactly that once."

"Once. It's been over for a long time now."

"Nothing is ever over until it has an end. You and I, we never really had an ending."

"Yes, we did, Tig... Zach. It just wasn't the ending you wanted."

"No, it was the one you wanted, remember? The one you chose. What I wanted didn't matter, as I recall."

"Look, this is ridiculous," declared Leah, shaking her head. "I have no intention of standing here, arguing with you over something that was over and done with years ago."

"That's just it," he countered, emotion permeating his low tone, "it's not over and done with."

"It is for me."

He stared at her hard, making Leah squirm under his intensity. "Yeah, I guess it would be."

"And," she added, "I have no desire to open it all back up again. So if you came here to argue and..."

"I didn't. Come here to argue, that is."

"Right. You came to return the tiger."

"That's right." This time when he held it out to her, Leah snatched it and stuffed it into her robe pocket without looking at it. She didn't want the pendant, a symbol of all they had once shared, distracting her any more than she already was.

"Thanks," she said. "And now, since you've returned it—"

"Actually," Zach broke in, "returning the tiger was only an excuse. I really just wanted a chance to find out how you were doing, to talk with you, and maybe catch up with each other's lives."

"You know, Zach, it's really been a long day for me. Maybe another time we could..."

Leah hesitated. At the realization that she was about to send him away, something unexpected flickered in Zach's eyes. In the past she had seen Zach look angry and amused and frustrated as hell, but she had never seen him look lonely. It occurred to her now that his coming there out of the blue might have something to do with his father's recent death and her heart went out to him in a way that she knew was foolhardy.

"Never mind," she said, "I'll get the coffee and we can talk for a while... That is, as long as you don't insist on talking about anything controversial."

"Controversial?" he repeated, a note of dry humor in his tone. "I'd say that's a matter of interpretation."

"Not in my house," she said sweetly. "How do you take your coffee?"

"Black and strong."

This time when she returned to the living room, carrying a tray with two cups of black coffee, Zach was sitting down. Leah supposed that any man six feet one inch tall would look uncomfortable folded into the low, rose-and-ivory striped club chair, but as she approached from behind, there seemed to her to be something especially tense and uneasy about the way Zach sat with his shoulders hunched forward. He straightened as she placed the tray on the coffee table and watched her curl into the corner of the sofa. His dismal attempt at a smile gave her the impression that she had intruded on some serious thinking.

Leah warmed her hands on her mug as Zach took a sip from his. For a second she wished she had thought to light a fire, then caught herself. This scene was entirely too cozy as it was.

She raised her brows as Zach quickly lowered his mug and grimaced at her.

"I thought you said you were making coffee," he said, his tone bordering on accusation.

"This is coffee. Oh, maybe I should have mentioned that it's an almond-hazelnut blend."

"Why ruin the surprise?" he muttered.

"It was either that or chocolate raspberry and somehow I thought you'd prefer something more subtle."

"You got that right."

"I buy the beans at a small gourmet market here in Providence. I think it's good to be adventuresome now and then."

"Yeah, maybe. Personally I find plain old Columbian coffee plenty adventuresome."

"At least this is decaffeinated," she offered.

"There's that to be thankful for, I guess."

"I take it caffeine keeps you awake?"

"Actually I have no idea. Lately I've got so many other things keeping me up nights, it's hard to tell if the caffeine is kicking in, too."

Leah felt another rush of empathy, wondering if grief was one of the "other things" keeping him awake. "Are these things that keep you awake anything you'd like to talk about?"

He held her gaze for what felt like the longest twenty seconds of her life. "No."

Leah nodded, understanding how painful it was to open up about some things.

"Okay then," she said, smiling at him gently. "Let's catch up. Do you know that I have absolutely no idea what you've been doing for the past fourteen years?"

"Then I have an advantage, because I do know a lot about what you've been up to."

She eyed him quizzically, a faint twinge of anxiety fluttering inside her.

"I've read a lot of your stuff, Leah," Zach told her by way of explanation. "Stuff you wrote when you were with the paper, and now at *Rhode Island Monthly*. It's good. *You're* good. Real good."

"Thank you."

He gave a quick smile. "I guess I should have said I know what you've been up to professionally."

"That still makes you one up on me," she replied. "So what have you been doing...professionally?"

"I'm a cop."

Her eyes widened. "A cop? You?"

Zach nodded. "That's right. In Boston. And don't ask why, because I'm damned if I know. It's just something that happened...story of my life, right?"

"How long have you been a cop?"

"Since college. I started out on patrol, then moved on to detective and...other things."

"You must really like it if you've stuck with it all this time."

"I did . . . do. Much to my old man's disgust. The good doctor thought his only son would choose to do something more prestigious with his time."

"Prestige," said Leah. "Now there's something that's a matter of interpretation."

Zach's faint smile conveyed his appreciation. "Well, my father's interpretation wasn't favorable. If you never heard what I was doing, it's probably because he took pains never to mention it in public."

"Your father and I hardly traveled in the same social circles," she reminded him.

Zach glanced around the room. "I don't know. I'd say that these days your circles weren't all that far apart."

Leah understood his point, that she had come a long way from the days when her family had been crowded into a third-floor tenement in one of the city's rougher sections, while he had lived in a brick colonial on the elite east side of Providence. She acknowledged it with a slight nod. "So exactly what sort of 'other things' have you moved on to doing now?"

He shrugged, staring into his coffee mug. "Undercover stuff mostly."

Leah listened as he briefly recounted his history on the force, from the time he impulsively took the exam for the police academy, mainly because a buddy of his was taking it also, to the present. His tone grew steadily more relaxed as he talked about his work, describing how naturally he had taken to the job, working his way through the ranks to detective and to some of the riskiest undercover work on the force.

Leah could easily believe that. From what she'd seen in her years of reporting, police work was rough and dangerous and not for the faint of heart. That would suit Zach, all right. But it also required a man who was willing to toe the official line and obey orders, and Zach had never been the type to follow rules, never mind enforce them.

When she made a tactful remark to that effect, he shrugged, his expression quickly turning grim.

"Yeah, that's always been my problem, all right." He placed his mug on the coffee table and stared down between his spread knees. When he glanced back at her, it was obvious his smile was forced. "Anyway, that's more or less it for me. The work doesn't leave a whole lot of time left over for a personal life and I don't really have much of one."

"No wife?" she asked, conscious of an absurd little bubble of dread in her tummy, which popped and disappeared as he shook his head.

"Never even came close." His gaze slid to her hands, then back to meet hers. "I'd heard you'd gotten married."

"I did. It didn't work out." Leah tensed, sensing the inevitable question that would come next, knowing it would fall too close to that danger zone around her heart.

"Did you have kids?"

She shook her head. "No. No, we didn't. We were both busy with our careers and . . . we just didn't."

Her hands were trembling. To hide her nervousness from him, she hurriedly placed her mug back on the coffee table and shoved them into her robe pockets, but the sound of the ceramic mug landing on the glass-top table seemed to reverberate in the silence that stretched between them, underscoring her tension.

She felt pinned by his dark, unwavering gaze.

"Leah," he said at last, his voice too quiet. "I have to ask . . . Do you ever think about it?"

"Think about it?" Leah echoed uncertainly. She couldn't breathe, much less think. "About having kids, you mean?"

He made an impatient gesture. "I mean about ours . . . our baby." The word ripped through the room like a gunshot, destroying the illusion of normalcy that Leah had been hiding behind. "Do you ever think about him? Or her? About our baby?"

Reeling inside, Leah stiffened and looked away from him.

She heard him go on speaking, dimly aware that the pain erupting fresh inside her was echoed in his hoarse tone and not caring. Not caring about anything but getting through the next few minutes and getting him out of there so that she could be alone to put everything inside her back the way it should be. The way it had to be if she was to go on getting up each morning and going through each day, living her life with anything close to peace of mind.

"You know," he said, "I think that's the worst of it, not even knowing if you had a boy or a girl. Never knowing. You're the only one who could have told me that and you were too busy getting on with your life. Too busy getting ahead, making it. And you have. This place sure is proof of that."

His tone had grown increasingly taut and now, from the corner of her eye, she saw him take in the exquisitely decorated room with one angry sweep of his arm.

"So maybe now that you've made it," he went on, "you can spare the time to tell me what I need to know. That way, when I think about it, I can get it right. Which was it, Leah?" he demanded, bitterness edging each word. "A boy or a girl? Did you give away my son? Or my daughter?"

"What difference does it make?" she countered frantically. "What difference can it possibly make after all this time...."

"It makes a difference to me, damn it," he retorted, his anger exploding. "I want to know, and I figure that even after all this time, you owe me that much."

Leah struggled to get to her feet, the long robe tangling around her legs, tripping her. Anger and fear and anguish pounded in her head like drums coming closer and closer.

"I don't owe you anything."

"That's not the way I see it."

"That's your problem."

"At the moment. I'd say it's both of our problem."

"I want you out of here. Now."

"Not until I get an answer," Zach replied, still without moving.

"You want an answer?" she shouted. "Okay, I'll give you one. It was a boy. A son. We had a son. Now are you satisfied? Do you really think knowing is going to help you sleep any better at night?"

She took no pleasure in seeing her announcement hit home in the glittering near-black depths of his eyes.

Much more slowly, and more gracefully than she had, Zach got to his feet.

"No," he said, his deep voice absolutely flat. "But it sure as hell will help me to find him."

Chapter Two

An explosive silence filled the room.

"What did you say?" Leah asked, her hushed tone a stark contrast to her angry tirade of a moment ago.

"I said that knowing that I'm looking for a boy should help me to find him," replied Zach. "It's not much to go on, but considering that it's about a hundred percent more than I knew when I walked in here, I'd say I'm already making progress."

She *had* heard him correctly. The stunned surprise that Leah had felt when she opened the door and saw Zach standing there was nothing compared to what swept through her now. "Help you to find him? What are you talking about?"

"I'm talking about finding my son."

My son. Just the sound of the words, coming from Zach's mouth, filled her with fear and pain and confusion.

"I don't understand," she said.

He shrugged. "I don't know any simpler way to put it than that. Maybe it would help if you tried thinking about it as the opposite of what you did to him fourteen years ago, when you gave him away to strangers."

Her anger flared anew. "How dare you say..."

"You'd be surprised at the things I'd dare to say—and do—about now. You've heard the expression nothing to lose? Well, that's me, honey. You're looking at a man with nothing to lose."

Leah shook her head in disbelief. "Listen, Zach, I have no idea what's going on with you, with your life I mean, or what might have prompted you to come here out of the blue, after all this time, and start making wild threats about..."

"I'm not threatening you, Leah. That is, unless you're afraid to find out what happened to the baby you gave away. Our son. Are you afraid?"

"Of course not."

"Good. Then you can help me find him. For starters, I need to know everything you can remember about his birth... where, when... Who was involved in handling the adoption? I don't suppose I'd be lucky enough that you even know the name of the people who took him?"

As he spoke, Leah shook her head back and forth slowly, horrified by what he was proposing. Help him find something she had been trying to leave behind for fourteen years? Help him plow through memories she struggled daily to forget? Help him tear open wounds she doubted would ever fully heal as it was?

"No," she managed at last. "I won't help you."

His mouth slanted in a sardonic smile. "Right. Somehow that's what I figured you'd say. I guess you still don't like having unexpected developments interfere with all your neat plans for the future, huh?"

"You mean do I like having people show up on my doorstep uninvited, dredging up matters I'd prefer to leave alone?" she countered coolly. "No, I don't."

"That's tough. Because I have every intention of dredging deeper, and if it comes to it, I plan to interfere with your life plenty."

Leah shivered, and folded her arms tightly. "For God's sake, Zach, this is crazy. The fact is that even if I did agree to help you, it would be hopeless."

Leah watched him shrug, wondering how such a careless gesture could hold so much determination. "Yeah, well, I sort of have an affinity for lost causes."

"I mean it, Zach, you're wasting your time. I understand better than you do, obviously, how these things work."

"Then why don't you go ahead and explain it to me?" he challenged, folding his arms cross his chest. "Just how do these things work?"

"When you . . ." She paused and wet her lips, searching for the right words, distancing, legalistic words, that would frame this discussion in a way that would make it bearable for her. "When you surrender a child for adoption, you sign forms, official forms, and you surrender all rights to that child. That means that you don't have any right to go looking for him now."

"Why not? I never signed anything. And I sure as hell never agreed to any surrender."

"That's just an expression, for heaven's sake. And you didn't have to sign anything. Have you forgotten that we were never married? Legally speaking, that means you never had any rights to surrender."

"I haven't forgotten anything about what happened back then. For instance, I haven't forgotten the reason we never got married . . . have you, Leah?"

"There were lots of reasons...good reasons, damn it, but you refused to listen to them, just like you're refusing to listen now."

"I couldn't afford to listen...not back then and not now. You're much too good with words, too good at wrapping them around me and making me think that maybe things I know are true, aren't true. That what I know is right, might be wrong somehow. The truth is there's only one reason we didn't get married, and that's because when I asked..." He paused, his expression growing even embittered. "No, when I *begged* you to marry me, you said no."

"No..."

"Yes," he snapped, reaching out to grab her by the arms as she started to turn away, forcing her to confront the anger blazing in his eyes. "That's exactly it. Now who's the one who doesn't want to remember the way things really were?"

"I do remember. And, yes, I remember that I was the one who actually said no..."

"Practically on the courthouse steps," he reminded her harshly.

"I had no choice," she protested. "It was all happening so fast. What matters is that I realized in time that we were making a mistake. We were so young! I was only seventeen, Zach, and neither of us had jobs or educations. You had a motorcycle instead of a car and we didn't have a place to live or the money to raise a baby. And we weren't ready to raise a baby back then. Neither one of us."

"That's garbage. We were old enough to make a baby, and we were damn well old enough to take responsibility for what we did."

"Unfortunately it doesn't take much common sense, or money, to make a baby... And damn you anyway—in my own way I *did* take responsibility for what we did."

"Exactly," he said, his lips curling in accusation. "*Your* way."

"The only way," she shot back, her stiff posture at odds with the tremble she couldn't keep from her voice. "For all of us. For God's sake, Zach, think about the way things really were. Think about—"

"No," he interrupted roughly. "I don't want to think about money and cars and high-paying jobs and all the other things we didn't have, because that's crap. I could have handled all that."

"Oh sure, why not? When you're a rich doctor's son all you have to do is snap your fingers to get what you want." Leah took a deep breath, fighting for control. "But this was different, Tig…Zach. A baby isn't the same as a new stereo or a bigger bike."

He released her abruptly, as if letting go of something too hot to handle, his expression a mingling of sorrow and contempt. "Don't you think I knew that?"

"No," she said, rubbing her upper arms where he'd held her so tightly. "I don't think you ever took time to really think about it at all. I think that getting me pregnant and marrying a girl from the wrong part of town was one more way for you to try to get your father's attention."

His lips thinned with outrage. "You think I did it on purpose? You think I meant to get you…"

"No," Leah assured him quickly. "I don't think you meant for me to get pregnant. But once it happened, I think you only looked on the bright side."

"That's a crime?" He sneered.

"Yes. No… Not exactly. You really did want to marry me, and you truly believed we could have made it—"

"Because we could have."

"But I also think you weren't being realistic…and part of the reason for that is that you relished the chance to rub your father's nose in one more act of rebellion . . . one more way of reminding him that you were alive.''

"You couldn't be more wrong. I'd accepted long before then that most of my father's attention went to his work, and that what little was left over was eaten up by my stepmother and her kids . . . his new family," he added with an undercurrent of bitterness that Leah knew stretched back years. "No matter what I did there was never room for me there. I won't lie to you, one of the reasons I wanted us to get married was so that I finally would have a family where I belonged . . . you and the baby were going to be my family.''

"It would never have worked," she said weakly.

"It would have worked," he countered, each word a gritty protest. "I would have made it work if you'd just trusted me enough to give me a chance.''

"It wasn't a matter of trust. Can't you see that?'' demanded Leah, turning and pacing a few feet away to put some distance between his body and hers. The few feet of neutral space did nothing to calm her nerves. "It was a matter of fear. I had my folks and my friends, everyone, all warning me that I was making a mistake. All I could think was that I didn't want us to end up like my parents, having to get married, saddled with too many kids too soon, always struggling just to make it from paycheck to paycheck, and blaming each other for being stuck. I watched them struggle every day of my life, and I saw what it did to them. I didn't want that for you and me . . . or for our baby.'' Her shoulders sagged inside the heavy robe. "I was just so scared.''

Zach remained silent, his expression closed.

"I know I hurt you, Zach," she went on, wondering if he had any idea of the price she herself had paid, was still paying, for her decision. "And I'm as sorry for that now as I was then, but I did what I had to do at the time."

"Okay, I'll buy that," he said, in a clipped tone that was more suggestive of concession than agreement. "So you should have no problem understanding why I have to do this now."

The implacability in his manner filled Leah with fresh panic. "What I understand is that you can't do it.... I'm not even sure it's legal for you to try to find him," she argued.

Zach smirked. "I'm a cop, remember?"

"Meaning what? That even if it is against the law, the fact that you're a cop and can probably get away with bending the law makes it okay?"

If possible his expression turned even stonier. "Cops don't get away with anything these days," he snarled. "Don't you read the paper?"

"I'm sorry. I didn't mean to imply—"

"Forget it. All I meant is that as I cop I have a pretty good idea of what's legal and what isn't. I'll walk the line with whatever agencies are involved, and with whatever stupid regulations they throw at me, but I'll also use every outside source and advantage I have. I'll follow any lead, pull any strings, twist whatever arms I have to."

He stepped closer, his dark blue gaze resting heavily on her. As a kid he'd been wild and stubborn and utterly confident of his ability to do anything he set his mind to. Leah had no idea what sort of things he had seen and done since, but at that instant she knew that whatever they were, they had simply honed those qualities in him, and a shudder ran through her.

"I intend to find my son, Leah," he said. "With or without your help."

Turning away from her, Zach grabbed his jacket from the chair where he'd tossed it and made his way back to the front door. He pulled it open, pausing only long enough to add, "I'm staying at Sam Costello's place. His number's in the book. Call me if you change your mind."

"I won't," she said, her voice growing stronger as she called after him, "You're making a terrible mistake, Zach."

Zach scowled as he hurried down her front walk. Maybe he *was* making a mistake, but given his track record, what was one more?

Swinging his leg over his bike, he braced himself with his legs spread to yank on a pair of gloves, taking out his anger at himself on the supple black leather. Gloves on, he stepped hard on the pedal, gunning the bike's powerful engine.

With or without your help. Smart, Blackmore, real smart. All in all, a brilliant closing gambit, guaranteed to bring out all of Leah Devane's wariest, most self-serving instincts. What had happened to cool, calm and charming, the approach he'd planned to use on her and had rehearsed all the way here from Boston?

He knew what had happened to the cool and calm part of his strategy at least. One look at Leah had dynamited cool and calm right out of the realm of possibility. Even wearing a robe and without makeup, the sight of her had been enough to make him instantly hot and bothered.

Chalk it up to surprise, he told himself. He had prepared himself to deal with the Leah of his memories, a pretty girl with lots of potential. He hadn't bothered to consider that the years since might have polished all that raw potential he remembered into something much more potent. Leah Devane had grown up to be a very beautiful woman.

That left him with charming, and in his own way he'd done his best to be that. Unfortunately, charm had given way in a flash to fourteen years of bitterness when he realized that she couldn't care less about helping him with his search . . . that she couldn't care less about their son. Time hadn't changed that any.

Oh, sure she'd had the decency to appear…uneasy, when he'd first broached the subject of their baby. But didn't he have firsthand knowledge of how good Leah was at feigning emotion? Once he began pressing the issue, she'd looked just plain angry.

He knew about tracing missing persons, and he knew that without Leah's help, without the crucial bits and pieces of information that only she might be able to supply, his search would be much harder. Maybe even impossible. That was his only reason for going to see her tonight.

Zach flashed a self-derisive smile into the darkness. Clear, cold night air washed his face as he steered the bike onto the main road that led to the neighborhood of tenements where his old friend Sam's apartment was located. He always found it hard to lie to himself under a sky full of stars. So, he admitted to himself now, maybe asking for her help wasn't the only reason he had gone to see Leah tonight. Maybe he'd been itching for this visit ever since he'd cleaned his stuff out of his father's house after the old man's funeral and had come across all those reminders of Leah and the time they had spent together.

Maybe he'd wanted to find out firsthand if he might have misjudged her all this time, if maybe after it was too late, she had regretted . . . How had she put it? Ah yes, *surrendering* their baby, and along with the infant any shot they'd ever had at a future together. Maybe he'd wanted to know if in a lot of small, hidden ways, her life, like his, had never felt quite right after that.

Now he knew. Sitting in her pretty, picture-perfect house, sipping gourmet coffee and watching her eyes shoot sparks at him as he suggested disturbing the tranquillity of the nice,

successful life she'd created for herself, he'd gotten his answer loud and clear. He hadn't misjudged a damn thing.

Realizing that had sent his mood crashing. He cursed
softly now, thinking he should have exerted more self-
control. He'd interviewed enough hostile suspects and reluctant witnesses to know that sometimes you have to clamp
down on what's simmering in your gut, force a smile and get
along in order to get what you want out of them. No question, he could have played things with Leah a whole lot
smarter. He hadn't, however, and he wasn't given to
brooding over things he couldn't undo. Acknowledge and
move on, that was his creed. His grip on the bike's handles
tightened as the familiar words ran through his head. *Acknowledge and move on.* Sometimes that was easier said
than done.

Without Leah's help he would have to fall back on one of
the oldest tenets of police investigations, begin at the beginning. First thing tomorrow morning he would be at the
Providence city hall, hoping to get lucky and find that Leah
had given birth at a hospital in this county and that their
son's birth certificate was on file there. After that... He
didn't even want to think about after that and how the hell
he was going to decide what city in what county in which of
the fifty states he ought to try next.

If only he could recall more of what Leah had said to him
that last night, the night they had planned to meet and run
off to be married. Instead she had shown up to tell him she'd
changed her mind. Zach grit his teeth at the wrenching inside which the memory of that night could still invoke.
There wasn't going to be any wedding, she had told him
tearfully, there wasn't going to be any future, there wasn't
going to be any wife and baby who would need him the way
he'd so desperately wanted to be needed.

They had probably talked and shouted at each other for less than an hour before he'd taken off, leaving her there alone to grapple with his promise that if she went ahead with her crazy plan to give away his baby, that they were finished forever. Less than an hour, but the things she'd said, the things she'd decided, had changed his life forever.

So why couldn't he remember more of it? he thought impatiently. It shouldn't be so hard. The meeting had been typical Leah, with reasons and arguments all prepared beforehand in her usual reasonable and logical fashion. He remembered her going on about money and education and how they didn't have enough of either one, and about how having a baby would ruin all her grand plans to go to college and become a journalist. As if journalists were forbidden to be parents, too, he thought bitterly.

That's basically all he remembered, that and the stifling, overwhelming feeling of powerlessness that he had felt when he finally understood for sure that nothing he could say or do was going to change her mind. It had infuriated him to know that she had the power to dictate the terms of the rest of his life and he had no power over it at all. He'd had that same feeling again a few weeks ago, when he faced the inquiry panel set up by the department, and then, like that night with Leah, he'd finally had to get up and walk away before he suffocated on his feelings of frustration.

Even now, just thinking about it, the same clawing need for air began to build inside him. He took a few deep gulping breaths and pushed thoughts of the inquiry away. The last thing he needed tonight was to get caught in a web of anger and self-pity.

Instead he forced himself to once again think back to that night with Leah, willing himself to recall some small detail she might have mentioned that would give him a better idea of exactly what she planned to do, where she planned to go to have the baby. Nothing came. As he took the turn onto Sam's street, he caught the wink of the neon Miller sign hanging above the neighborhood bar a few blocks from the apartment and he braked sharply.

He could use a drink about now and no matter what his friend said, there was no way he could comfortably sit and have it at Sam's place.

Parking the bike outside, he went in, and ordered a beer. He downed it in two quick gulps and automatically lifted his hand to signal the bartender for another, then stopped.

He really wanted that next beer, and the next. He wanted the mental numbness he knew they would eventually deliver, putting a nice mellow screen between him and his feelings, between him and everything. He really needed that insulation tonight, which was exactly why he couldn't afford to go for it. He'd seen too many cops in trouble go down that road. Hell, he'd been down it himself a few times recently, ever since that night in an alley in Southie. On those occasions he'd told himself it didn't make any difference whether he was drunk or sober, whether he was able to haul his butt out of bed in the morning or spend the whole day sleeping off the night before. And it hadn't made any difference. The police force was his life, and as long as he was suspended pending a ruling on whether that shoot in the alley had been a good one, he had no reason to care if he even saw daylight.

That was no longer true. Taking a couple of bills from his pocket, he dropped them on the counter as he shoved himself off the bar stool. Now he did have a reason to get out of bed in the morning. He had something he needed more than the next drink. He needed to find his son. He needed to know for sure that his kid wasn't squaring off against an armed cop in some stinking alley in some city he couldn't even name.

* * *

Leah had a method for dealing with problems. It was a foolproof strategy for determining what course of action she should take, whether the problem she faced was deciding if she should buy the new red leather boots she'd fallen in love with or wait for them to go on sale, or finding the best slant for a feature story that was giving her trouble.

She had first devised it years ago, when Sister Dominic, her third-grade teacher had read to the class the story of Solomon and the two mothers who had come to him claiming the same child as their own. Some of her classmates had been horrified by the king's apparent coldheartedness in suggesting the baby should be cut in two so that each mother could have half. Not Leah.

She had appreciated his levelheaded wisdom. As the oldest in the family, she was often pressed into service as a baby-sitter for her younger brothers and sisters and called upon to settle their squabbles. From that day on whenever they fought over a particular toy or whose turn it was to go first down the slide, she had simply pretended that she was King Solomon, detaching herself entirely from the emotional elements of the situation and searching for the most equitable solution possible regardless of the consequences.

Of course, these days she no longer actually pretended to be Solomon, but she still used the same approach to problems. First she made a list of all the pros and cons involved, and then she went back over the list and drew a line through any pro or con based on emotional considerations. Finally, with only rational, dispassionate arguments remaining, she would made her decision.

Unfortunately now, when she needed it most, her rational approach wasn't working. And the reason both irked and alarmed her. The fact was that, where Zach Blackmore was concerned, everything she thought or wanted or wished was based in the dangerous, murky world of emotions.

She had been making lists for hours, ever since he had stalked out of her house last night. Handwritten lists, mental lists, lists on her computer here at the office, and when she was done crossing out, the lists invariable ended up the same. Empty. She knew that somehow she had to convince Zach that he couldn't go ahead with this crazy quest of his, but she had no idea how she was going to do it. Judging by his attitude last night, she had a hunch he wasn't going to back off simply because she wanted him to.

The sound of the office intercom distracted her from the intricate doodling she was doing instead of working on the story that was due next week. She leaned forward and pushed the blinking red button and the booming voice of Bud Hirsch, her boss and mentor, filled her office.

"Leah?"

"Right here, Bud."

"Come on in, ASAP, will you? I have something to run by you."

The intercom went dead. Bud didn't expect a reply. He expected her to get to his office ASAP. And with good reason. Usually when he summoned her, Leah was happy to comply.

She loved her job at the magazine and she loved working with Bud—loved the confidence and enthusiasm he projected, which set the tone for the whole operation. She'd learned a lot about writing from Bud, and even more about running a magazine for profit. When Bud finally decided to pack it in and retire to Florida, which as he neared sixty he was threatening with increasingly regularity, Leah hoped to be considered as his replacement.

This afternoon she approached his office with something less than her usual eagerness. Bud was sharp and she didn't look forward to having to explain to him the circles that a sleepless night had left beneath her eyes or the uncharacteristic scatterbrainedness she couldn't seem to shake.

"Come on in," Bud urged when she rapped lightly on his open door. He nodded at the chair across from his. "Take a load off."

Tall and beefy, Bud had an enviable head of thick silver gray hair and a ruddy complexion that was the result of both his love of the outdoors and high blood pressure.

He squinted his ice-blue eyes and took a good hard look at Leah. "What the hell ran over you?"

"Thanks," she retorted. "That's just what every woman wants to hear first thing in the morning."

Bud shrugged. "I call 'em like I see 'em. You look like you tied one on last night."

"Well, I didn't. I just didn't get a whole lot of sleep."

"Why not?"

Good, old, tactful Bud.

"I was up late working on the daycare piece."

"So? You've worked late before. You never came in looking hung over."

"I guess this story is giving me more trouble than I expected. Don't worry, I'll handle it."

"I'm counting on it," Bud replied. Evidently deciding to accept her explanation at face value, he flipped open the file folder on the desk before him. "Maybe I can even help. Take a look at this."

He shoved a newspaper clipping across the desk to her. It was from the Warwick town paper, a story about a sixteen-year-old local girl who had returned to school after having a baby. Bud had circled in red the mention of the school-run daycare center that was making it possible for the girl to keep her baby and attend classes.

"Have you heard of this?" Bud asked when she looked up. "School-run daycare centers for kids raising kids?"

"Yes, I have," Leah replied cautiously. "It's happening in several cities throughout the state."

"So you already have it covered in your piece?"

"Actually, no, I don't."

Bud looked flabbergasted. "Why the hell not?"

Leah shrugged. "I didn't think it fit."

"Didn't fit? This is news, Leah, and when something's news you make it fit."

"Bud, my story is an overview of the availability and quality of child care in the state. These school-run centers are available only to students, and frankly, I don't think they're of interest to most of our readers."

"Well, I choose to differ. I think this whole angle is plenty interesting and I'm betting our readers will, too. I think you ought to get out there and take a look a this place...what is it called? The Happy Days Daycare Center."

"No," Leah replied instantly, her instinctive unease running deep.

Bud's brows shot up. "No?"

"I mean I have the story just about wrapped up."

"I thought you were having trouble with it?"

"I was. But I have it all worked out now," she lied. "And the last thing I need is to introduce an entirely new slant."

"So don't make it a slant. We'll run it as a sidebar. It'll be a hell of a lot more readable than just a rundown of costs and who's got the best sandbox."

"My story's bigger than that," protested Leah, ignoring the fact that she didn't as yet have a slant on the story, bigger or smaller.

"This will make it bigger still. Maybe one of the biggest we cover this year. Child care is a hot issue, Leah, I want to make sure we do it justice."

"What if the school doesn't want publicity?" she asked, grabbing at straws. Programs like this always wanted publicity. "What if they won't agree to an interview? Or don't have the time to see me before my deadline. School vacation begins soon," she reminded him.

Bud gave an impatient wave of his hand. "Charm them."

"Easy for you to say."

"And do." He grinned at her. "It so happens the principal there is an old friend of mine. I already set it all up...you talk to the director of the child care program first thing Monday morning."

The small ember of dread that had been resting in the pit of Leah's stomach ever since he handed her the newspaper clipping suddenly ignited.

"I'm sorry, Bud," she said, leaning forward. "There's no way I can work this in to my piece."

"Why the hell not?"

"For starters I don't have time before deadline. Why not send Danny to the school and let him write the sidebar?"

"He's a guy, for Pete's sake."

"That's sexist."

"So sue me. I'm an old man, set in my ways. Besides, it's your story."

Leah squared her shoulders and met his gaze. "I only agreed to write it in the first place because I understood that it was mostly a matter of compiling statistics and interviewing officials from the state licensing board. I think I've made it abundantly clear that I prefer not to do stories that deal with children directly."

"And I try to give your preferences every consideration. But neither your likes and dislikes, nor those of any other writer on staff, dictate editorial policy around here. I need you on this, Leah. End of discussion."

Leah slid closer to the edge of her seat. "It's just that I don't think I can do a good job with it."

Bud grinned at her and reached for his glasses, a clear signal that he was done talking and ready to get back to work. "You'll do fine. I have great faith in you."

"Fine," she snapped, getting to her feet. "Don't say I didn't warn you."

"Wouldn't dream of it," Bud countered, a hint of the humor that usually existed between them creeping into his voice. "Leah..."

She stopped at the door and turned, her expression impatient. "What?"

"You know I wouldn't be insisting unless I thought it was best for the magazine. If there's something you want to tell me, some reason you absolutely can't manage—" He broke off as she shook her head.

"No," she replied. "I can manage."

"Good. Because you're the best mixture of gut instinct and objectivity I've got on staff. Maybe the best I've ever seen. Get the story, Leah, forget the rest."

She left without saying anything further. What could she say to explain why she was so opposed to visiting the Happy Days Daycare Center without revealing more about herself and the past than she ever revealed?

She shivered, her mind streaking back fourteen years to what was unquestionably the low point of her life. She didn't like to think about those long months when she'd lived in the isolation of the home for unwed mothers. She didn't like to think about the shame and guilt and second thoughts that had become the shadows of her soul. Most of all, she didn't want to have to think about the baby boy whom she had held only a handful of times and yet whose weight and scent and feel were a vivid impression always floating just beneath the surface of her memory, so that all she had to do was close her eyes and...

Leah quickly jerked her eyes open and dropped her arms to her side, glancing around to see if anyone was watching her act like a fool. She never, ever, permitted herself to think about this at work. She seldom allowed herself to think about it at all, but never at work. She wouldn't be doing it now, she assured herself, if not for Zach's visit.

She released a small, disgusted sigh. If he had to reappear and mess up her life, why couldn't he have done it during the summer? Or spring even. Anytime but December when her resistance to remembering was already so low.

Leaning back in her swivel chair, she let her gaze zero in on the calendar on her desk and the red-rimmed blocks that marked the upcoming holiday. For Leah, the Christmas season held a special heartache. For one thing, Christmas itself represented lost milestones, each Christmas holding some new promise or accomplishment she would never share with her son. His first tree, the first Christmas he walked, his first visit to sit on Santa's lap, his first bike. She could tick them off by rote, each passing year another unique facet of the much bigger pain etched in her heart.

Now, in addition to December and Zach, she had this daycare visit to contend with. It was going to mean being around lots of young children, most likely children of all different ages and sizes and with adorable little mannerisms that would give her plenty to wonder and speculate and anguish about. Dimples and scraped knees and cowlicks and dozens of other wonders, each presenting a new question about the little boy she would never know, each adding a fresh note to the sense of loss that underscored her whole life.

But even that Leah could take. She was an expert at dealing with pain, at suppressing her feelings, at gritting her teeth and getting on with things. The pain was the price she paid for making the decision she had. Who knows? If she had made a different choice, abortion or marriage to Zach, perhaps she would be living with a different pain, a worse one, and one that wasn't hers alone to bear. And that thought was what kept her sane.

She had meant it when she told Zach that adoption had been the best thing for their son. She believed that. She had to. God, help her she had to. In the early days, she used to go to sleep each night, her cheek pressed to a tear-soaked pillow, counting all the reasons he would be better off with his adoptive family, all the things they could provide for him that she couldn't. Eventually the litany had become such a part of her that she no longer needed to tick them off individually, but together they formed a tightly braided lifeline that ran through her core, getting her through the days, and the nights alone.

He was better off—he *had* to be. She refused to let Zach stir up those old feelings of guilt and doubt. She couldn't, thought Leah, almost breathless from the sudden tightness in her chest. She had to go on believing she had done the right thing, because she was afraid not to. Afraid of what she might find if she allowed anything—or anyone—to crack the surface of this neat, successful life she lived.

Besides, she reasoned, all the books and statistics she'd ever read agreed with her that children adopted into loving families do better than those raised by teenage mothers. That was even more true fourteen years ago, when there had been no school daycares and other programs to help a pregnant teenager who wanted to keep her baby. And although most experts advised being honest with the child about the fact of their adoption, they also cautioned that the adoptive parents are the best judge of when and how much information a child is ready for.

The adoptive parents. Not the mother who gave him up or the father who, when things didn't go as he wanted—when she had refused to run off and be married—had walked away and never looked back. Who for fourteen years had never even bothered to ask if he was the father of a son or a daughter.

Zach had no right to go stirring all this up again, she thought angrily. Maybe he was suffering the aftershock of his father's death or an early midlife crisis. Whatever the cause, it was wrong. Wrong for her, and more importantly, wrong for their son. Suddenly Leah knew that she had found the sound, well-founded reason she needed to stop Zach.

Their son had his own life, one that didn't include them. And never would, she thought, tensing against the sudden longing that rose inside her. He deserved to live that life without their interference. The only possible purpose that could be served by locating and contacting him now was to satisfy some selfish, belated curiosity on Zach's part. And she intended to tell him so.

Chapter Three

Leah checked the telephone book for Sam Costello's address. She thought about calling and telling Zach what she had to say over the phone, or simply calling to make arrangements for them to meet someplace to talk, but in the end she did neither. She simply drove over to Sam's place after leaving the office around eight.

She recognized the name of the street where Sam lived. It wasn't far from where she had grown up and she found her way there easily. Maybe too easily, she thought as she drew closer. Although she'd thought of nothing but this all day, she still felt as if she needed more time to prepare herself to confront Zach again.

Like maybe another fourteen years.

Most of the houses in this area were two-and three-story tenements, some of them stacked on top of bars and liquor stores and joints with names like Pappy's Variety, the kind of establishments common in neighborhoods where a new winter coat is a major purchase and where folks chase their dreams with lottery tickets. Leah pressed her lips together, thinking how more than the layout of the streets felt familiar here.

A light snow was falling, the tiny flakes swirling beneath the streetlights and neon signs, cloaking trash cans and parked cars with a translucent blanket of white. The effect was similar to filming an aging movie star through a filtered lens, gently deceiving, just enough to hide the harsh signs of reality and make Leah think that just maybe this was all a dream.

She seldom came to this side of the city anymore. There was really no reason for her to. As she'd told Zach, her parents now lived in Florida, in a double-wide trailer in a trailer park shaded with palm trees. It was "only a stone's throw from the interstate" her mother boasted to everyone, and for some reason that seemed important to her. Leah understood that the trailer, the first home her parents had ever owned, was their own version of heaven, and she was happy for them.

Even before her folks moved out of state, her brothers and sisters had scattered. Her two sisters and their families lived about a half hour away, in the southern part of the state, and she had brothers in New Hampshire, Oregon and California. Leah frowned at the thought of her sisters. Christmas was next week, which meant that any day they would be calling, pressing her for an answer about spending the holidays with them and their husbands and children, and she would have to come up with yet another good reason not to.

Since her brothers and sisters were all younger than she was, she wasn't sure exactly how much any of them knew or remembered about those mysterious months she had spent away from home. It wasn't something she ever talked with any of them about, or wanted to. And so each year she manufactured trips or friends or parties that kept her from spending Christmas with them, and kept them from knowing the truth, that she spent every Christmas Eve and Christmas Day alone, remembering what she wished she could forget.

She drove slowly, recalling the weather forecaster's prediction of slippery streets. When she reached Sam's, she parked in front, grabbed her purse and slid from the car before she could have second thoughts. Her designer purse was exactly the same unusual shade of golden leather as her gloves and boots, the perfect accompaniments for the shawl-collared black cashmere coat she was wearing today. If they'd been anything less than perfect, she wouldn't be wearing them. Leah loved clothes and she loved looking good in them.

It wasn't simply vanity or a desire to draw male attention, though she was aware she attracted her share. She hadn't been cheerleader pretty as a teenager and she wasn't a classic beauty now. If anything, her willowy frame, light brown hair and hazel eyes held an appeal that was a blend of mystery and intelligence, a combination a woman had to grow into. At almost thirty-one, Leah figured she was getting there. Men seemed to agree, although she regarded that sort of attention as a distraction at best.

After her divorce, amicable but heartbreaking nonetheless, Leah had vowed that she would never marry again. And since she wasn't interested in either affairs or one-night stands, dressing for male approval seemed rather pointless. She dated occasionally and casually, period.

To Leah, the right clothes and the right image served a much more important purpose. She'd learned that looking good is the basis for other things she considered absolutely crucial... things such as self-confidence and power and protection. In a way, her three-closet wardrobe was her suit of armor, and she treated it as respectfully and lovingly as any knight ever did his.

As she climbed the steps to the porch and checked the nameplates by the front door to find that Sam lived on the third floor, she was aware that all that expensive armor wasn't making her feel quite as invincible tonight as it usually did. Must be the nature of the enemy, she mused. Although why a ghost from her past—from the sounds of it, a stressed-out cop with problems of his own—should have the power to make her palms sweat, she had no idea.

To distract herself from nervous anticipation of the upcoming clash with Zach, she thought instead of the man he was staying with. Sam had been Zach's best friend in high school. They had both been jocks at heart, but Sam had never had what the guidance counselors had referred to as Zach's "attitude problems." Zany, happy-go-lucky Sam had provided relief from Zach's brooding intensity. Sam brought out the kid inside Zach that he tried so hard to keep hidden, and in turn Zach kept Sam's wild side in check. No matter how much heartache had become twisted up with it in the end, the fact remained that some of the best times of Leah's life had been spent with Zach Blackmore and Sam Costello.

By rights, the three of them should never have ended up at the same school. Leah should have attended the decrepit high school in her district, Sam the more modern and well-equipped school on the other side of the city and Zach some fancy private boarding school that would further prepare him for a life of rubbing the right elbows. However in the late seventies, the city's ongoing efforts to improve public education through innovative means included opening an alternative high school that offered a variety of programs to the best and brightest from throughout the city. And so fate had lifted their separate paths and, for just a little while, let them run together.

Providence wasn't a small town, and there were many people from high school whom Leah hadn't seen in years. Sam Costello was one of them. The last time she had seen him was the summer after she'd gotten pregnant and Zach had walked out of her life. She and Sam had run into each other at the mall and stopped to talk for a few stilted moments.

By then Leah had lost the weight she'd put on while pregnant. On the outside, she supposed she'd looked the same as always and although Sam had to have known all that had happened, he didn't say a word about it. Or about Zach. Leah recalled standing there and smiling a brittle smile and telling herself that she'd be damned if she'd ask about him no matter how much she longed to.

Instead they'd talked awkwardly about summer jobs and the weather, of all things. They talked as if they were two strangers seated next to each other on a bus, in spite of the fact that at one time Sam had been as close as a brother to her and had habitually lent Zach his car so that he and Leah would have a place to make love. Remembering the hours spent on the wide back seat of that old Chevy made her cheeks catch fire, and Leah slowed her steps as she climbed to the third-floor landing so she had time to cool them with her gloved hands before knocking.

From inside the apartment, she heard the muffled sounds of a television and footsteps and then the door swung open and Sam was standing there, his faded jeans, plaid flannel shirt and sudden, wide grin peeling away the years.

"Lordy," he said, "will you look what the cat dragged in?"

Leah grinned back at him. It was impossible not to. Sam had the kindest eyes and the most infectious smile of anyone she'd ever known. "Hi, Sam."

"Hi nothing," he countered and reached for her. Suddenly the stiffness in the air between them gave way as he captured her in a hard, rocking hug. In the process he somehow maneuvered her inside, into a dimly lit living room, and shoved the door shut behind her.

"How the hell are you?" he asked when he finally let her go and leaned back to look her over. "Besides gorgeous, that much I can see for myself."

"I'm fine," Leah replied with a small laugh, automatically smoothing her hair and the collar of her coat. "I came to see Zach, if he's here."

"I'm here."

Zach moved from the shadows behind Sam, sliding into the flickering glow from the television screen. The only other light in the apartment came from the kitchen, but even in the near darkness the lean, masculine lines of Zach's face consumed Leah's full attention with a jolt.

She had expected to feel the same uneasiness facing him as she had last night. She hadn't expected to feel the same sensual shock of awareness, as if her skin was wired and he held the detonators. Suddenly she was filled with a very primitive understanding of why just thinking about Zach could make her sweat.

"Hello, Zach. I guess maybe I should have called, but..."

"Why? Turnabout's fair play."

She shrugged, and noticed Sam's brows lift with curiosity.

"Something going on that I should know about?" he asked, raking his fingers through his shaggy brown hair.

"Leah and I have some unfinished business," Zach explained before Leah had a chance to speak.

Sam grinned. "Ah, so that's how it is. Well, unfinished business is the best kind, I always say. Speaking of which, this movie is almost finished, and it has to be back to the video store tonight, so while I'll gladly offer you my home and everything in it to finish whatever business you've got hanging, it'll have to keep hanging until after the movie."

Leah jumped as an explosion occurred on screen, her reaction underscoring just how tense she was. She glanced from the screen to find Zach observing her closely.

"Give me your coat," he said, extending his hand.

"No, really, I only came to talk . . ."

"We can talk later." He angled his head toward Sam who was absorbed by the mayhem being enacted before him. "*The Terminator.* It's his favorite movie . . . and this is his place," he reminded her.

"Maybe we could go for a ride," suggested Leah.

"On a bike? In this weather?"

"We could take my car."

Zach shook his head. "I don't let women drive me around."

"Of all the stupid—"

"Shh," Sam hissed at them.

"Look," Zach said in an impatient whisper, "just once can you not insist on having things your way and just give me the damn coat?"

Leah shrugged it off and handed it to him and was instantly sorry. She'd forgotten how drafty old tenements could be, and besides, the heavy coat had been one more layer of armor. Zach's lingering gaze as he moved to hang it on one of the hooks by the door reminded her that her dark green knit dress was formfitting enough not to leave much to the imagination. Despite its long sleeves and high neck, she felt ridiculously exposed.

Wordlessly she crossed the small room and claimed a seat at the opposite end of the sofa from Sam and was relieved when Zach, rather than sitting between them, chose the overstuffed chair beside his old friend. The three of them stared at the small color television perched on top of a piece of wood stretched across two stacks of cinder blocks.

As her eyes became accustomed to the darkness, Leah glanced around. The room reminded her of countless old apartments she'd spent time in during college. None of the scant furnishings in the room matched and the wallpaper was peeling off the walls in places. All in all, not much of an attempt had been made at decorating the place. There were no pictures hung and no knickknacks anywhere. Aside from a pile of newspapers and a few ashtrays, the only thing in sight was a single framed photograph on the end table. Leah couldn't see it clearly from where she was seated, but it looked as if it was a picture of a child. The room, and the photograph, made her wonder how Sam had spent the past fourteen or so years.

It felt odd to be sitting there with them after so long, watching a movie while Sam and Zach chuckled and exchanged comments as if the three of them did this all the time. As if they had spent the afternoon in school and afterward piled into Sam's car for a stop at the International House of Pancakes on the way home and as if later Sam would find some excuse to leave them alone for a while so that...

Leah abruptly steered her thoughts from that dangerous path. Already she'd felt the heated magnet of Zach's occasional glance. She was afraid to turn her head and meet it directly. She suspected that his own thoughts had to be wandering in the same direction hers were, and she was afraid that if their eyes met and all those steamy memories collided, something horrible would happen. Some sort of

cosmic explosion would occur that would send her shooting entirely out of control. And so she kept her eyes riveted
to the television screen.

Actually *The Terminator* was one of her own favorite
movies, although she'd been amazed to discover how much
she enjoyed it when she accidentally caught it on cable one
night. Her favorite moment in the entire movie was coming
up now, with Kyle and Sarah hiding out, alone. She
watched, leaning forward unconsciously as Kyle explained
to Sarah the real reason he was there.

As it had the first and every time she heard that he had
come back for her, Leah's heart clutched in her chest, overwhelmed by the power and romance of his revelation. What
kind of man risks the future and braves the nightmares of
the past to rescue the woman he loves? Automatically her
gaze slid to Zach, drawn to him by a power stronger than her
own free will. He turned at the same time and their eyes met
and held. Now her heart was really going crazy, pounding
out a message she didn't want to hear.

No, she told herself emphatically, what was happening
on-screen bore no relation to their situation. Zach wasn't
some time-traveling warrior and he wasn't in love with her
and she sure as hell didn't need rescuing ... by him or anyone else.

She forced her attention back to the screen and kept it
there this time. At one point Sam left the room and she
continued to sit tensely, facing straight ahead, not wanting
to know if, as she suspected, Zach was watching her rather
than the movie. She heard the sound of the water running
in the bathroom and then the refrigerator door swinging
shut. When Sam returned he flipped open the can of diet
soda he was holding and handed it to her.

"I'd offer you something stronger," he said, his smile sheepishly apologetic, "but this is an alcohol-free zone these days."

"This is fine," Leah told him, taking a sip.

Finally the movie ended. Sam stood and hit the button to rewind the tape while he and Zach debated the merits of the ending and how it meshed with the sequel. Leah listened in silence. She felt odd, part of what was going on and yet not. Or maybe the real reason she was uncomfortable was simply because it felt *too* familiar to her to be with them at this reunion of old friends who really weren't anymore. Because it was so easy and so tempting to slide into the past.

She'd been anxiously waiting for Sam to leave so that she and Zach could talk, but when he finally excused himself to return the movie, she panicked. Had she really expected to feel more at ease with him gone? Had she expected to feel relaxed being here alone with Zach? What an idiot.

Zach went to the kitchen, returning with a can of soda for himself. He dragged a straight-back chair across the room, straddled it backward and looked straight at her. Waiting.

"So," said Leah, her small smile unsteady. She'd decided it would be best to ease into her reason for coming rather than confront him directly. "It sure was great to see Sam after all these years. He hasn't changed...flannel shirt, action movies, still the same old Sam."

It was just patter, mindless and generic, intended to break or at least chip away at the glacier between them. Judging from the disdainful look Zach shot her, however, you might think she'd just compared his old friend to the Midnight Strangler.

"He's changed all right," he told her. "More than you or I can ever know."

"I'm sorry. I only meant..."

He waved off her apology. "Forget it. I guess living here and seeing firsthand what's going on with him has made me a little overly sensitive where Sam is concerned. He's a good friend."

"I know that. It's nice that you two have kept in touch."

"We didn't. Not enough anyway. After you . . ." He hesitated, weighing his words. "After I left town, I cut myself off from everyone and everything back here. For a long time, I didn't even want to run into anyone from the past, anyone who might mention your name to me, or force me to put words to your memory."

She stared uneasily at the can in her hand. "I see."

"No, I don't think you do. You couldn't possibly. It was bad enough just having the memory with me constantly, waking up to it every damned morning, going to sleep with it every night, remembering your face, your body, the way you smelled, and never sure from moment to moment if I was remembering someone I loved, or hated."

"Zach, really . . ."

"You don't want to hear it, right? Why not, Leah? When did the truth start making you so uncomfortable?"

"Maybe when I realized I didn't have the power to change it," she snapped.

"And maybe you have more power to change things than you want to own up to." He paused, letting the words hang in the air between them, and then went on. "Anyway, Sam was a big part of the past I was running from, and we just sort of lost touch for a long time. We finally hooked up again around three years ago, when I came back here for his wife's funeral."

Leah's eyes widened in shock. "His wife's . . . Oh, Zach, how awful for him." She shook her head. "I can see why you gave me that look when I said he hadn't changed. Losing someone you love..." She pressed her eyes shut briefly. "It changes you. Forever."

Zach shrugged. "Yeah, well, you didn't know."

"No, I didn't. How did it happen? Was there an accident or was she sick or...?"

"She ODed," he said, his voice curt and matter-of-fact. A cop's voice, thought Leah. "Cocaine. She was hooked big-time, and either it was bad stuff or just a bad day and she took too much because she wanted to wink out, Sam will never know for sure."

Leah shook her head, feeling a great wave of sadness. "God, you were right... I guess neither of us can really understand all that poor Sam has been through."

"He knew that she was using. Mandy—that was her name—Mandy was younger than Sam. They met at a club he was managing. She had different friends, different hangouts, but they fell in love anyway and he figured that she would change once they were married. You know, outgrow all that." He shrugged. "She didn't. Then when she got pregnant..."

"They had children?" Leah interrupted, the private nightmare that never completely went away stirring to life inside her.

"Just one," replied Zach as he reached for the framed picture she'd noticed earlier. "Adam. He's four. A really super kid."

He handed her the picture of a little boy with sandy hair and Sam's single dimple in his left cheek, and suddenly Leah wasn't sure how much longer she could go on holding back the tears she wanted to cry for Sam, and for herself.

"He's adorable." She looked back to Zach, her expression confused. "But where is he?"

"He lives with Sam's folks," Zach told her. "After Mandy died, Sam sort of fell apart himself. A medium-size drinking problem became a major one. Nothing that I said, nothing anyone said, could get through to him. All I could do was stand by and watch while he drank himself in deeper and deeper, piling up a string of DUIs—driving under the influence," he explained.

Leah nodded.

"He wrecked his car, lost his job…lost everything in the end."

"Including Adam?"

Zach nodded grimly. "Yeah. He was leaving him with anybody handy so that he could get to the bar, even left the kid alone a time or two I understand. Finally his folks had had enough and his old man turned him in and went to court to get custody."

"Poor Sam," Leah murmured, rubbing her hands together, but there was no warming them. "And poor Adam. But Sam seemed fine tonight," she said, recalling his remark about this being an "alcohol-free zone." "How long ago was all this?"

"About a year. The good news is that losing custody of Adam finally shocked Sam to his senses. He checked himself into a clinic and he hasn't had a drink in nearly a year. That's the number one condition the judge set for him regaining custody… he has to stay sober and employed for a full year."

"And has he…been employed, I mean?"

Zach nodded. "As a matter of fact he's started his own landscaping business. Of course, he's still fighting to get it off the ground and this time of year is particularly rough. But he's on the highway department's emergency crew list and he's hoping to use his truck to do some plowing this winter. The important thing is that he loves it. And he's got a goal, getting Adam back. He's just living for that one-year anniversary. It's as if that milestone won't just prove to the judge that he's fit to raise Adam, it'll prove it to Sam himself.''

"I guess in the end that's what really counts," said Leah, her thoughts collapsing inward.

"I guess." For a moment, Zach watched her intently. When she didn't say anything more, he shrugged. "You know, every once in a while lately, I even think maybe Sam is happy in his own way."

"He seemed to be in a good mood tonight."

He grimaced impatiently. "Forget the movie and the jokes . . . that's all on the surface. Underneath, Sam is still reeling, wondering what the hell he did wrong."

Leah bit her lip. She sure knew how that felt.

"So now you know all about Sam," Zach said, taking another swig from his soda can. "Why don't you say what you came here to say, Leah?"

Leah took a deep breath. She hadn't expected him to seize control this way. But she should have.

"I suppose you already know what it is I came here to talk about," she began.

Zach's mouth twisted. "I guess you didn't come to chat about you and me and old times."

"No, I'd say we covered all that last night," she shot back.

"I'd say differently." His voice was soft, his gaze steady. "But we'll leave that alone for now."

"Fine."

"So?"

"I came here to tell you why you can't go ahead with this crazy idea of searching for . . ."

"Our son?" he suggested when she faltered. His dark eyes narrowed. "Can't you even say the word for God's sake?"

"Of course, I can say it. Our son, all right, now are you happy?"

"Not by a long shot."

Neither Sam nor Zach had bothered to turn on a lamp when the movie ended, so that the only light still came from the kitchen and suddenly instead of feeling hidden or shrouded by the shadows, Leah felt more vulnerable than she would have lying naked beneath a blazing sun.

"Anyway," she continued, straining to organize her thoughts into the well-rehearsed, logical presentation they had been when she arrived, "I'm not only thinking of myself here, there are reasons, good reasons, why you can't do this."

"I assume that by *this* you mean my intention to find my son?"

Leah nodded, wondering when those two words—*my son* —uttered in his deep, smooth voice, would cease to have the effect of a whip cracking across her soul. "Yes."

She jumped as Zach swung himself off the chair and sent it skidding along the scarred wooden floorboards to crash against the wall. "Thanks for stopping by."

"But..." Leah got to her feet, automatically tugging on the knit dress that had crept up as she sat. "Aren't you going to listen to hear what I have to say?"

"Why should I? It'll just be a waste of time."

"Because your mind's already made up, is that it?"

His dark brows lifted at her angry tone. "That's it all right, and I never suggested otherwise."

"Listen, Zach..."

"No, you listen," he snarled, stepping toward her so that the backs of her legs were up against the sofa and the space between their bodies didn't even hold enough air for her to draw a full breath. "I'm in no mood for more games. I spent all day breathing dust, bent over files in the basements of record departments in three counties. My head aches, my back aches, and you know what I found? Nothing."

His smile was quick and dangerous and if Leah could have backed up any further, she would have. Fast.

"But you already knew that, didn't you?" he went on. "You knew exactly what I'd find by looking for his birth certificate around here. You know where our baby was born, where the birth certificate was filed, and when you walked in here tonight I was crazy enough to think you were going to tell me all that."

"I can't, Zach."

"You mean you won't."

"All right, I won't. The baby I gave birth to isn't a baby anymore. He's a boy, a young man really..."

"Thirteen," Zach interjected, his eyes like lasers. "Thirteen years old."

"Right. Almost fourteen, with a home and friends and a life of his own. He deserves to live that life without our interference."

"Interference?" he echoed incredulously. "I'm his father."

"Biologically," Leah added, wounding herself with the clinical term along with him.

"Yeah, well, that's good enough for me."

"But it's not good enough for him," she persisted, growing increasingly desperate. "We made our choice... all right, all right," she quickly added when he looked ready to lash out at her. "*I* made a choice, but now we both owe it to him to live with it. He has a right to live in peace, and not to be burdened with the past and our mistakes, until he chooses otherwise."

"What about my right to know that my son is all right? To know that he's even still alive, for God's sake? That he didn't get hit by a car when he was four, or die of a burst appendix when he was eight, or get himself—"

He stopped abruptly, swallowing hard, as if forcing back something too horrible to even say aloud. But it was already too late for that. His words were echoes of hundreds of similar thoughts that Leah had been battling on her own for years.

"You don't know," she said softly. "Maybe we'll never know." She sighed, then threw him one of the scraps of hope she lived on. "But maybe someday, when he's older, he'll want to know who his birth parents were. Maybe he'll come looking for us. Maybe..."

"Maybe?" Zach squinted at her as if she were some rare, baffling life-form. "Is that really good enough for you? Knowing that *maybe* someday your son *might* want to know who you are?"

"Yes. It has to be good enough for me because that's all there is."

"Well, it's not good enough for me."

"You mean you still plan to keep looking for him?"

"Damn right, I do."

"And when—*if*—you find him, what then? What will it take to satisfy you? Will you walk up and ring his doorbell and announce to him who you are? Or will just knowing that he's all right be enough?"

"I don't know. I don't know what will be enough."

Leah supposed that subconsciously she'd been hoping for a compromise, a promise that even if he pursued this he wouldn't do anything final, anything that might send her world crashing around her. Frustration and fear bubbled inside her.

"Damn it, Zach, you can't do this. You have to hear me out...then you'll see that the only right thing to do is to drop this whole thing and—"

"No," he cut her off. "What you mean is I have to listen so that you can smooth-talk me into thinking your way is the right way."

"Facts are facts. And the fact is..."

"The fact is, I don't give a damn about facts, or about right and wrong. These days, I just go with my instincts, with what my gut is telling me to do."

"And right now your gut is telling you to go messing up the life of a boy who is probably happy and content and..."

Zach shook his head. "Wrong. Actually, right this minute my gut is telling me to do this."

He never should have touched her. Zach knew that for sure the instant his fingertips came into contact with the soft stuff her dress was made out of. After that it took less than an instant until he sensed the even softer and warmer skin underneath and of course, then it was too late to stop.

His mouth crashed against hers, taking her by surprise it seemed, although part of Zach was certain that part of Leah had to have known—as he had known ever since she opened the door to him last night—that sooner or later something like this had to happen. He kissed her with fourteen years of misdirected desire, kissed her with his lips and tongue and teeth until he felt her resistance split wide open and suddenly she was melting against him, just the way he dreamed of her doing, just the way he wanted. Just the way he had always wanted.

He couldn't possibly outtalk Leah, or outreason her, not now, not back then. He could never change her mind or bend her to his will. But he had this power over her; he always had.

It wasn't the first time he'd kissed Leah to shut her up, and it sure as hell wasn't the first time that a kiss had exploded into something more for them, drawing them with quicksandlike ferocity into something dark and sweet. This was a place he knew well, a place where he could lead and Leah was willing to follow. Maybe, deep down, this was why he'd touched her, because he knew this would happen and he wanted in whatever way he could to chip at the wall she had built around herself.

There were no walls between them at this moment. As if to prove that to himself, he slid his hand along her spine, to her waist and lower, pressing her deeply into the cradle of his spread thighs. His body rocked against hers with movements that were slow and incendiary. He was kissing her hard and thinking about how good it would feel to lie down on the sofa with her under him when Sam walked in.

"Hey, have you guys looked out the— Oh, sorry," he said looking both surprised and sheepish as Leah struggled to break free of Zach's embrace. "I had no idea ... Maybe I ought to take another walk or something."

"No," Leah exclaimed.

Zach made a soft sound that was somewhere between a laugh and a curse.

Sam glanced at him and shrugged. "I really am sorry, man."

"There's no need to be sorry," Leah told him, smoothing her hair. She could smooth it all she wanted, thought Zach, it wouldn't take away the whisker burns around her mouth or the soft, puffy redness of her lips. Just looking at them had his jeans feeling too tight. "Actually I was just leaving."

Zach laughed again. *Yeah, right,* he thought.

"I don't think so, Leah," said Sam. "Until I get out there with a shovel, you're not going anywhere."

"What are you talking about?"

"The weather. That's what I was saying when I walked in. Have you guys taken a look out the window?"

Leah shook her head as she hurried toward the window overlooking the street. She groaned when she saw how quickly the snow had accumulated. Worse, sometime since she arrived a plow had come by and plowed a foot high mound of snow around her car.

"Great," she muttered.

Zach joined her at the window. "Don't worry, I'll get you out."

"Maybe I can just drive over it," she said hopefully.

Zach shook his head. "I don't think so." He turned to Sam. "You said you've got a shovel handy?"

"Sure," Sam replied. "I've got a half dozen of them down in the truck, but this ought to do the job." He opened the closet door and pulled out a snow shovel. "I've also got this," he said, eyes sparkling as he produced a sled that was nearly as high as his shoulder. "What do you say we break it in for Adam?"

Leah shook her head automatically.

"Come on," Sam wheedled. "You used to love sledding, Leah. Take a look at that hill out there—hardly a car in sight, the snow mixed with just enough ice—and tell me you aren't itching to try it out."

Leah couldn't suppress her small smile as she followed his gaze out the window. The hill did look perfect for sledding, but the only thing she was itching to do was get away from there, and from Zach.

"Even if I wanted to," she said, "I'm hardly dressed for sledding."

"Is that the only thing stopping you?" Sam countered with a grin.

"No," Leah cried, "it's not..."

But he was already gone, disappearing into the other room and leaving Leah alone with Zach and the knowledge that she had just made a strategic mistake. Sam returned less than a minute later with a pair of jeans, a red sweater and one of his trademark plaid flannel shirts draped over his arm. "Here you go, problem solved."

He tossed the clothes to her and Leah realized her second mistake was catching them. Would a court of law interpret that as implied intent, she wondered. Her third mistake was meeting Sam's earnest, pleading gaze.

"Sam, really," she began.

He cut her off. "One ride," he said. "Please. Alone out there, I'd look crazy. Two guys on a sled will look weird. Just one ride. Come on, Leah, what do you say?"

Throughout this discussion, Zach had remained a silent observer, but Leah had hardly forgotten he was there, his brooding presence a reason both to stay and to run. She glanced at him now and although his expression was empty, she saw in his eyes a confirmation of what she was thinking. She wasn't sure what Sam needed, but she was sure he needed something, and if riding down a snow slick hill in a storm helped him, she guessed it wasn't too much to ask in return for all those nights he'd loaned them his car.

"All right," she said. "One ride."

Of course it wasn't only one ride. There might be a woman somewhere who could breathe that clear cold air and feel the snow shooting at her as she sped full throttle down an icy hill and settle for only one ride, but it wasn't Leah. Some things were so good you had to do them again and again even if the scent of danger was all around you.

She rode double first with Sam, then with Zach, his strong hard thighs gripping her much tighter than Sam's had. Or did it just feel that way because her senses were more alert whenever Zach was close to her? Leah wasn't sure and she never figured it out even though they took turns again and again, until she was breathless and the cold air made her lungs ache.

Pleading for a break, she flopped down in the snow, heedless of the cashmere coat she usually treated as if it were gold, and on impulse she made scissor motions with her arms and legs, the way she used to when she was a little girl. Scrambling to her feet the same way she had back then, she eagerly inspected the impression she had left in the soft snow.

"Look," she called to Zach and Sam who were busy shoveling her car out.

Zach nodded and laughed as he playfully tossed a shovelful of snow in her direction, but Sam stuck his shovel in a snow pile and walked the short distance to her side. He gazed down at the indented snow, his grin nowhere in sight. In fact he looked so forlorn suddenly that Leah regretted calling him over in the first place.

"You know," he said quietly, "I did that for Adam the other day, and when I called him over to see it, he took one look and said, 'Look, Daddy, a bat.' And I told him that it wasn't a bat, it was an angel. And you know what he said to me?" His voice cracked painfully. "He said, 'What's an angel?' What's an angel, can you imagine?" He shook his head. "I mean, what kind of kid his age doesn't even know what an angel is? What the hell kind of parents are too busy or whatever to even tell him about angels?"

Leah touched his arm. "Sam, please don't . . ."

"And then," he continued as if he hadn't heard her or felt her touch, "you begin to wonder what other things he doesn't know that he ought to? What else has he missed out on? And you begin to wonder if you'll ever be able to make it all up to him or if it's already too late."

"No." She hadn't heard Zach approach, but he was suddenly there, and his touch wasn't so easy for Sam to shrug off.

"I don't want to hear you say that," he told Sam. "It's not too late for you or Adam. It's never too late. It can't be."

No one had to tell Leah that he was talking about himself as well as Sam, and that somewhere inside he was a lot less sure of what he was saying than his harsh cop's tone would lead you to think.

After a minute, Sam shrugged and picked up his shovel again and after another few minutes of working silently, side by side, they had her car shoveled out. Leah stood and watched, fighting the urge to kick snow over the angel she'd created on Sam's front lawn.

Sam insisted she wear the borrowed clothes home, claiming he didn't need them back anytime soon.

"The roads are slippery. I ought to drive you," Zach said as she slid behind the wheel of her car. Sam had ambled down the driveway to put the shovels away, leaving them alone again. Intentionally, Leah was certain.

"No," she replied quickly, much more afraid of having Zach drive her home and maybe being forced to spend the night at her place than she was of braving the slippery roads. "I drive in the snow all the time."

In spite of the stubborn set of his mouth, he nodded reluctantly, as if accepting that he really had no right to tell her what to do. "Stay on the main roads at least. They've probably already been sanded."

Leah nodded and started the engine. Zach backed away with a short wave, but when she reached the corner he was still standing in front of Sam's house, his hands shoved in his jacket pockets, staring after her car. Leah wondered if he was thinking about what had happened upstairs and what might have happened if Sam had taken a little longer to return the movie. She couldn't run away from the fact that she had been out of control, on the verge of doing something she would never do in a more rational moment.

Or were Zach's thoughts moving in another direction entirely as he stood on the curb and watched her drive away? Was he wondering, as Leah was, how the three of them, who had started out with such high hopes and great promise, had ended up walking around with giant holes in their lives, and their hearts, and with no idea how to fix them?

Leah was still wondering about it when she returned home to a ringing telephone and lifted the receiver to hear Zach's gruff, anxious voice say that he was just checking to see if she had made it home safely. She was still wondering long after she slipped beneath the covers of her bed and prayed for sleep. She wondered how doing the right thing could leave you feeling so wrong, and she wondered if her son, wherever he was, had ever learned to make angels in the snow.

Chapter Four

Leah spent most of the weekend worrying about what Zach's next move might be. He'd admitted that he had no idea where their baby had been born and without a starting point it would be difficult to conduct any kind of search. Or so she told herself over and over again. It didn't help much. Zach was stubborn and he was a cop, and that combination left Leah feeling very uneasy about the future.

If he kept at it hard enough and long enough would he eventually succeed in tracing the steps she'd taken fourteen years ago? Would his cop's instincts and contacts help lead him to the rural Virginia town and the home for unwed mothers run by nuns who somehow managed to be both sympathetic and sternly disapproving of the predicament of the girls who went there? Would he find her records at the local hospital and see the birth certificate she had filled out? She could still remember how her tears had fallen and puckered the paper as she signed it.

Would the stains still be there for Zach to see? And if he got that far, how long would it be until he discovered the name of the attorney and the adoption agency who had handled matters for her? How long until he knew what she didn't . . . the name of the child who had once been part of her. And who, in ways she was afraid to put into words, still was?

It would have been nice if all her worrying over what Zach was going to do could keep her mind off what she herself had to do on Monday. No such luck. Thoughts of Zach's search and the daycare center were intertwined in her mind, both tapping into the same bottomless well of fears and painful memories. For years she had tiptoed around those memories in her mind, like a soldier picking his way across a live mine field. Now suddenly they had her surrounded and Leah feared that this time there was no safe way past them.

On Monday morning she woke early, unable to sleep, anxiety a tight knot in the pit of her stomach. She dressed with even more care than usual, deliberately choosing a white wool suit and a blouse of pale pink, dry-clean-only silk. It was ridiculously inappropriate for where she was going, but it suited Leah's purposes perfectly. No one in their right mind would ask a woman dressed as she was to hold a baby or hand out snack-time cookies to toddlers.

Leah had no reason to expect that she would be asked or even allowed to do those things by the daycare personnel, but she'd been in this business long enough to expect the unexpected. She wasn't taking any chances that someone there might mistake her for the kind of woman who would want to hold a baby and feel it snuggle against her, inhaling that unique scent that was a blend of powder and innocence. More than that, she didn't want to be that kind of woman.

What she wanted was to be the kind of woman she pretended to be, the woman everyone who knew her believed her to be: cool, ambitious, totally focused on and fulfilled by her work. She had long ago decided that was what she had wanted to be, what she *had* to be, and she had reaffirmed that decision at the time of her divorce. She didn't trust herself to be anything else. She certainly didn't trust herself to have more children. That was the main reason her marriage had ended. Only when it was too late had she realized that she never should have married at all.

Before accepting Gus Stanton's marriage proposal, she made sure he understood that and agreed with her that they could have a full and happy life without children. At least he had seemed to understand and agree. Then something changed. Gus changed. His biological clock had rung and it hadn't done so gently. It was as if she went to bed with the somewhat self-centered, but charming corporate barracuda she had married and woke up with Father Knows Best. Or rather, a would-be Father Knows Best. All of a sudden Gus wanted babies. As many as she would agree to, he had told her with utter sincerity, but he'd settle for just one.

Leah had been stricken. One baby would in fact be one more for her, and that was more than she could bare to contemplate. It would be bad enough reliving her first pregnancy, a lonely miserable time with a heartbreaking outcome. But that hadn't been her greatest fear. What if it turned out she was unfit to be a mother? What if she lacked the right instincts? Maybe that was why she had been able to simply hand her own son over to strangers. In spite of the pain and guilt she still carried around with her, there was no question in Leah's mind that that's what she had done. What sort of mother could she possibly be? And even if by some miracle she managed to be a decent enough mother to any children she and Gus might have, what if those children someday found out about the half brother she had given away? What would they think of her then?

Then, too, there had been that small part of her buried deep inside that had been thrilled when she'd first learned she was carrying Zach's baby—in spite of all the complications—and that had been unable to come to grips with sharing that experience with another man, not even the man she had married.

Leah had known all along that what she felt for Gus wasn't the same wild passion she had once felt for Zach; she had even told herself that these feelings were preferable, that they were more solid and mature. She had settled for that because it was safe, but when it came to having a baby, something in her resisted fiercely. Maybe it was because a child signified a level of intimacy and commitment she didn't feel with Gus. Maybe it was just because she was scared. Whatever the reason, where Gus saw a baby as a possibility, a bridge to eternity, Leah could see only risks that she wasn't willing to take.

They had debated the matter for months, until they were both battle weary, but in the end she had been just as desperate in her resolve as when they started. Gus had no choice but to accept the fact that Leah was not going to change her mind. Eventually he bowed to her insistence that the only logical solution was for them to divorce. Their marriage had ended the same way it had been conducted, with great practicality and friendly concern for each other...leading Leah to conclude that she hadn't been the love of Gus's life any more than he had been hers. Then and now, Leah sincerely hoped that Gus would find the woman who was...a woman able to give him the children and the life he deserved.

In the aftermath of the divorce, Leah had felt both sorrow and relief. Her relationship with Gus had forced her to confront truths about herself that she preferred not to think about. That's when she had decided that feeling as strongly as she did about not having children, it wouldn't be fair to marry again.

Now Leah checked her reflection in the bathroom mirror a final time and swept the whole subject of marriage and children from her mind as best she could, concentrating instead on applying her lipstick with a steady hand. Usually she was very good at dismissing unwelcome thoughts. But that was before Zach's return had turned everything inside her upside down. For now she'd be thankful if she could get through the next few hours without breaking down.

The Happy Days Daycare Center was located in a small building adjacent to the redbrick high school. The three large rooms that had once been used for storage had been completely renovated, the walls painted a soft yellow with giant murals of cartoon characters. The floors were sparkling clean white tile and a large bright colored rug warmed the play area.

Leah believed that buildings can have personalities, some might call it atmosphere, and when she entered a building for the first time, her reporter's instincts went into high gear trying to sense its unique personality. She knew as soon as she set foot in the Happy Days Daycare Center that it had been well named. This was a happy place, she thought with a quick glance around, the sort of place any mother would feel comfortable leaving her child.

Leah was greeted by Greta DiCarlo, the director of the center. Greta was a tall, sturdy woman with curly dark hair, friendly eyes and a calm, competent manner. Originally a home economics teacher at the high school, the center had been her brainstorm and it had taken six years of pleas and demands before she convinced the school department to fund it.

"Why?" Leah asked her once they were seated in her small cluttered office for a cup of coffee. They had agreed to do the interview first, while the children were being settled in and fed, and then she would give Leah a complete tour of the place. Leah wasn't in any hurry.

"Why did you think it was so important to have a place like this?"

Greta DiCarlo thought hard about her answer. "Because," she said at last, "when you're a teenager and unmarried, being pregnant is punishment enough. A girl who gets pregnant loses a part of her childhood. She doesn't need to lose everything else, too."

"What else does she stand to lose?" Leah asked, trying to maintain a reporter's detachment, and failing.

"For starters, before the center existed, most of them lost the chance to finish their education . . . and it's not easy to raise a family when you have only a ninth or tenth grade education. Lots of girls also lost control of their own lives, and their babies."

Leah wet her lips. "In what way?"

"Because without support from the school and from community programs, like the one that provides milk while they're pregnant and infant formula later on, they don't have as many options. Perhaps the girl will be shunted off somewhere until the baby is born, losing her home and family and everything that's familiar to her at a time when she's vulnerable and really needs them. And, after all that, more often than not she's convinced to give up her baby as well. Still others might decide on having an abortion they might not have thought through."

"Don't you think those are the most viable options for an unwed teenage mother?"

"I don't think there's anything viable about a pregnant fifteen-year-old," Greta retorted, giving Leah a glimpse of the no-nonsense force that had ultimately won over the school committee. "But it happens, and it happens for a variety of reasons. You might be surprised to know that a growing number of the girls I work with are not pregnant by accident, but by choice. Go ahead, shake your head, it's a fact. Sad but true. As to what's missing in their lives that they feel the need to create someone whom they can love and who will love them unconditionally in return, I can't say for sure. I just see the result. And what I see are girls who want to keep their babies, not abort them or give them away.

"Now," she continued, her dark eyes sparkling as if she knew she was usurping Leah's next question, "are these girls qualified to raise children? No way. That doesn't change reality."

"So you're really providing these girls with options in two ways," commented Leah. "First by making it feasible for them to have their babies and keep them, and then by providing them with child care so they're able to graduate from high school. That in itself gives them greater opportunities for jobs or college . . . a chance to provide for their baby."

Greta nodded, beaming. Her pride in the center was unmistakable. "Exactly. But we provide much more than daycare. We hold classes in everything from nutrition to dealing with the stress of raising a child. And we act as a contact point between the girls and the various community programs available to them, like the one I mentioned earlier. Last, but certainly not least, we also provide moral support."

"Yes," said Leah, jotting notes that were so jumbled she hoped she could decipher them later. Not that she was worried. Most of what Greta was saying was finding its way straight to her heart and would remain there. "I imagine a girl in this situation needs a great deal of moral support. She must need to hear that she's doing the right thing, whatever she decides to do.''

"You hit the nail right on the head. There is no right or wrong choice for a girl in this predicament . . . each girl is different and each situation is different. But they all need help learning to live with the decision they make, and with the new responsibilities that might come with it. That's what we try to do here. Before there was this safety net, a lot of young lives were ruined because of a single error in judgment."

Leah quickly dipped her head to hide the tears that swamped her eyes, taking more elaborate notes than she needed to as she struggled to regain her composure.

"Now these girls have a place they can come to when they need help," Greta continued, "and they have someone who will listen." As if on cue, one of those girls came charging into the office with a tall lanky teenage boy at her heels. He was dark, while she had fair skin and straight pale blond hair that hung halfway down her back, but they were both dressed in faded jeans and jackets in the school colors of blue and gold. Above the emblem on the front of hers was scrolled the word Cheerleading, and on his, Basketball. Except for the baby braced on her hip and the diaper bag he was toting along with his backpack, they looked like the all-American high school couple.

"Hi, Mrs. DiCarlo. You told me to stop by when I dropped Kyle off this morning so...oops." The girl stopped short as she noticed Leah sitting there. "I'm sorry, I didn't realize you had someone in here."

"That's all right, Nicole. I just wanted to give you the application for that summer job program we discussed." She pulled open her desk drawer and glanced inside as she spoke. "It must be in the other room." Turning to Leah, she said, "Will you excuse me for just a minute?"

Leah nodded. "Of course."

While Mrs. DiCarlo went in search of the application, the young couple waited just outside the office door, directly in Leah's line of vision. She pretended to review the notes before her, but couldn't help stealing glances at the baby in the girl's arms. Inside she was dying. Could this be what her son had looked like at nine months? Had he worn denim coveralls and a tiny red baseball cap? Had he been as happy as this baby was, breaking into a toothless smile when you did no more than make eye contact with him? Leah had no idea, only dozens of questions that she usually did her best not to think about. Not that it helped. The questions were always there just the same, layer upon layer of them, encasing her heart. Not knowing the answers to those questions was like a gaping wound at her core.

Finally Greta DiCarlo returned.

"Sorry about that," she said after the girl had left with the application. "The deadline for the application is tomorrow so I didn't want to put it off. She's a nice kid, and she can use the job."

"No problem," Leah assured her, adding as casually as she could manage, "was that her baby's father?"

"Yes. Ricky Martin."

"I see. Do they live together with their baby?"

"Oh no." Greta laughed. "Ricky's a bag boy at the Foodmart. That just about covers gas for his car and diapers for Kyle. They both live at home with their parents. That's typical of the girls we work with. What's atypical about Nicole and Ricky is that they're still together nine months after their baby was born. Lots of couples don't even make it through the delivery."

Leah swallowed hard. "I see. What do you think makes them different?"

She threw up her hands. "Who knows. True love maybe? They plan to be married as soon as Nicole graduates. For Kyle's sake, I hope they make it."

"But you don't think so?" asked Leah, picking up on the note of skepticism in the other woman's voice.

"What I think is that her graduation is still two years away, and for a sixteen-year-old, two years is an eternity. Now," she said, getting to her feet, "are you ready for the grand tour?"

No, thought Leah even as she nodded her head. She wasn't sure she would ever be ready, but she could hardly leave and write the story without at least looking at the center itself.

First Greta showed her the kitchen and other basic facilities, then they went to the room where the toddlers and older babies stayed. Some young mothers dropped out of school entirely for the first year or two after having their babies, Greta told her, which explained why they had children as old as four at the center.

"Is there a cutoff?" inquired Leah. "If, say, a woman who dropped out years ago and now has a young child, wants to come back to school and use the daycare facilities, would she be allowed to?"

Greta tilted her head and pursed her lips as she considered the possibility. "It hasn't happened yet," she replied, "but, yes, I would have no problem with that. I can't imagine turning away any woman who wanted to finish high school and needed help."

Greta moved easily among the children, admiring finger-paintings and tying shoelaces where necessary with a personal touch that further convinced Leah that she was perfect for her position here.

She couldn't help wondering what might have happened if there had been a Mrs. DiCarlo around when she needed someone to talk to. How might things be different for her today? And for Zach? Would they have been like Nicole and Ricky, bound and determined to beat the odds stacked against them?

One thing Leah had no doubt about. If—as Greta had suggested —the crucial element was true love, they would have made it. No matter how it had turned out, at one time she had loved Zach with her whole heart and she was certain he had loved her the same way. But it took more than love to survive. Didn't it? That's what she had told Zach when he demanded to know how she could change her mind about marrying him, how she could even think about giving their baby away. She had believed it then. And she believed it now, she told herself firmly. She had to.

Leah made it through the toddlers' room with her composure intact. She simply avoided focusing on any one particular child and refused to allow herself to contemplate the assortment of toys and security blankets all around, the relics of childhood.

Things weren't so easy in the softly lit room set aside for infants.

She had only known her son as an infant and so those were the sights and smells and sounds that held the power to pierce her most deeply. Leah felt herself begin to fill with emotion as soon as they entered the room and heard the plaintive crying coming from one of the cribs lined up against the far wall, each with it own brightly colored mobile suspended overhead.

She wanted to run. Instead she grit her teeth and followed Greta who moved quickly to the crib that held the crying baby.

"There, there, Brandon," she cooed as she lifted the infant from the crib. He couldn't have been more than a couple of months old and his head bobbed weakly against her shoulder, his tiny face puckered and red from crying so hard. Greta supported his head gently as she patted his back. "There, there, little fella, what's the trouble? A burp maybe?"

"May I try?"

Leah shook inside, unable to believe she had actually said those words.

"Sure," replied Greta, holding the baby out to her. "Careful with his head."

Leah felt sick as she reached to take him in her arms. What was she doing? She usually avoided babies like the plague, even her own nieces and nephews, and here she was asking if she could hold this one. The baby snuggled against her shoulder, still sobbing, and as Leah murmured to him, softly and instinctively, she burrowed her face against his small, downy head. The soft baby scent that clung to him was as intoxicating as a drug. A knifelike pain cut through her and her chest ached as if there wasn't enough room in there for all that she was feeling.

"Sweet baby," she whispered, gently rubbing his back. "Sweet, sweet baby."

The baby suddenly gave a loud burp and stopped crying.

"My goodness, you must have the magic touch," exclaimed Greta, then frowning she added, "Oh, no..."

Leah wasn't sure what was the matter until she saw Greta snatch a diaper off the end of the crib and began dabbing frantically at her shoulder with it. Glancing down she saw that the baby had spit up there when he burped.

"I should have thought to give you the diaper to cover your suit," moaned Greta. "Your beautiful jacket."

"Don't worry about it, it can be cleaned," Leah assured her, shifting the baby slightly so that she could study his face. His eyes fluttered open and met hers and she was lost.

"I hope so," said Greta. "I know from experience that formula can leave a stain, especially on white. I just hope it isn't ruined."

"Forget it," murmured Leah, smiling at the baby staring up at her so solemnly. "It doesn't matter."

And it didn't. After all, she thought sadly, a jacket can be replaced.

When Leah finally left the Happy Days Daycare Center and hurried back to her car she felt trapped inside a suffocating web of painful memories and longings. They closed in on her from all sides, so powerful and relentless that only one thought stood out, clear and strong enough for her to latch onto. *Zach.*

The past couple of hours had left her feeling sixteen again, confused and vulnerable and frightened. When she was sixteen Zach had been her best friend, her first lover, and the glue that held her world together whenever it threatened to crash around her. It was natural that she should think of him now.

Without giving herself time to think logically, she drove straight to Sam's house, for no reason other than that she needed to see Zach. Not until she pulled up out front did she calm down enough for it to occur to her that she probably ought to offer some excuse other than that for coming. Sam's clothes, washed and neatly folded in a bag on the back seat, provided her with just that.

She gripped the bag tightly as she climbed the steps and knocked on Sam's door. While she waited for someone to answer, she unconsciously stuck her hand in her coat pocket and squeezed the tiger pendant, which, for reasons she couldn't name, she had begun carrying with her everywhere.

Sam opened the door and as he had the other night, he broke into a grin at the sight of her. "Hi, Leah, come on in."

"I brought back your clothes," she explained, stepping inside, her heart pounding anxiously as she casually glanced around for Zach.

Not casually enough apparently.

Sam's grin softened with understanding. "He's not here, Leah."

"Oh." She swallowed hard, trying to bank down on her disappointment.

"Is everything all right?" Sam asked, peering at her closely. "You look upset."

Leah shook her head, placing the bag with the clothes on a chair. "No... No, I'm fine. Everything is fine. I have to go."

She turned quickly, escaping through the door she had left open even as Sam called after her.

"Hey, don't rush off. I've got Adam here and I want you to meet him."

"No, really..." She only half turned, shaking her head as she began moving sideways down the stairs. "I can't."

"Come on," Sam wheedled. "Stay for five minutes... let me show off my kid."

"I can't, Sam, not today... Some other time, I promise."

Sam looked uncertain, as if not sure whether he should follow her or let her go.

"Daddy?" a child called out from the other room. "Will you come help me?"

Sam glanced back toward his open apartment door, hesitating for no more than a second. "Sure, Adam. I'll be right there."

"Go ahead, Sam," Leah urged, moving more quickly now. "I'll talk to you soon."

"Right. I'll be sure to tell Zach you stopped by," he promised as he headed back inside.

Leah wasn't at all sure that once she had regained her emotional equilibrium she would want Zach knowing how she had come running over here to see him. She hurried down the stairs, the clatter of her boot heels on the wood floor preventing her from hearing the outside door open and as she rounded the corner to the bottom landing she collided with the person coming in.

Zach.

"Whoa, slow down," he warned, looking as startled as she was by the impact. His arms moved around her at first to steady her. Then came recognition and a change in the way he was holding her. His touch became less instinctive and more deliberate.

"Leah?" His eyes narrowed curiously. "What are you doing here?"

"Nothing. I mean, I just stopped by to drop off the clothes I borrowed from Sam."

"And?" He was still holding her, making it hard for her to breathe.

"And? Did I say there was an and?"

"You didn't have to. This is me you're talking to, remember? What's the matter, Leah?"

"Why does everyone think there's something the matter? I just wanted to return Sam's clothes. Period."

He shook his head. Concern had replaced the curiosity in his dark blue eyes. "I don't know about what everybody thinks, but I think there's got to be a good reason you're sweating and panting and running out of here like you just stole the silverware from the second-floor apartment."

"Is that your professional opinion, Officer Blackmore?"

His smile was a tight, thin slice of sarcasm. "It's Detective Blackmore, ma'am, and that happens to be both my professional and my personal opinion. Cops know about people in general. I know about you... Up close and personal."

"You may have, once. Not now."

He responded with a slow, sure nod. "Yeah, I do. Some things never change."

Their eyes met and Zach watched hers slowly fill with tears. When she didn't say anything, he shook her as hard as he dared. She felt all tense, wired. He was afraid she'd bolt if he pressed her to know what was going on, and afraid she'd bolt if he didn't.

"Come on, Leah," he said, "I know you didn't come here just to bring back Sam's clothes. Tell me what happened."

She hung her head, staring down into the five-inch-wide tunnel of shadows between them. "Nothing. It's stupid. I'm being stupid." She thrust her head back to look up at him. "This isn't like me at all."

"I know. That's what worries me. Tell me, Leah."

"I..." She stopped, shook her head, bit her lip and searched for a safe spot over his shoulder to talk to. "I had to do an interview at a daycare center today... a daycare center operated by a local high school for students who get pregnant and want to finish school. I didn't want to go there in the first place. I never do stories like this one, never. But this time I couldn't get out of it and... And while I was there, I held a baby."

She brought her gaze back to his, her tears now overflowing her bottom lip in a silent flood. Her soft mouth trembled and Zach could actually feel the shock waves of anguish that shook her from the inside out. "I held a baby, Zach."

Zach pulled her against him without saying a word. What the hell could he say? He was thunderstruck by her announcement. Not that she had held a baby. Hell, she was thirty years old. Even if she hadn't had other children of her own, she certainly must have had friends or relatives who had them. She had sisters and brothers, for Pete's sake, surely one of them must have had a baby somewhere along the line. What stunned him was that she was this shaken by the mere act of holding a baby in her arms.

I held a baby.

She had said it with the sort of numb intensity another woman might announce that she had wrecked the car or lost her job or was getting a divorce. Obviously, for Leah, this ranked right up there on the emotional devastation scale. The way she laid her head on his chest, her fingers gripping the front of his jacket, threw into question everything that he had been telling himself about her for days now. That she was cold and self-centered and that she had given away his son without a qualm.

He wrapped his arms more tightly around her, running one hand over her back, wishing that she would cry or scream or that he would miraculously think of the right thing to say.

Before that happened, she straightened and pulled away from him, running a hand through her hair. Zach watched as her expression smoothed out. It was as if she was donning a mask. As if by magic she was once more becoming Leah the cool, calm and collected. Leah the invincible. Something inside him wanted to reach out and do whatever it took to stop that mask from slipping back into place...shake her or shout at her or carry her down to the floor right there in Sam's front hallway and make love to her until she remembered what he had never been able to forget, the way it used to be for them.

"I'm sorry," she said, a soft self-deprecating laugh in her voice. "I can't imagine what got into me."

"A heart maybe," he muttered.

"What did you say?"

"Forget it."

"I really am sorry for acting that way. Must be stress. I've been under a lot of pressure at work lately, deadlines and rewrites and..."

"Will you shut up?" he said, grabbing her by the shoulders and backing her into the wall beside the front door. He put his face inches from hers in a way he knew was intimidating as hell. "Will you just shut up and stop pretending everything is fine when it's not?"

"But it is," she insisted. "Everything *is* fine. I'm fine. I told you, I'm just a little overtired and overworked, but all in all—"

"All in all," he said roughly, "you're lying through you're teeth."

"I am not."

Zach found her guilty flush immensely satisfying, sort of like hitting the bull's-eye on a dart board.

"You have no right..." she began.

"I have lots of rights that you keep trying to convince me I don't have. At the moment the only one of those rights that concerns me is the right to know exactly what got to you so badly at that daycare center today, and why."

"What makes you think you have the right to know anything about me?"

"Because of the things we have in common, Leah, things that just don't go away because you wish they would, things that keep us bound together whether you like it or not."

"You're right, I don't like it," she snapped, her eyes bright with anger. "I don't like anything that's happened since you came back. I don't like having to feel this way. I don't like having you manhandle me. I don't like having the past stirred up again when there's nothing I can do to change anything."

In deference to her manhandling charge, Zach loosened his hold on her, leaning slightly forward so that the weight of his body held her captive. "Tell me why you didn't want to go to that daycare center today?"

She shrugged and avoided his gaze. "I just didn't. I don't like doing stories like that."

"Like what?"

She shrugged again. "Like that. Stories that..."

"Involve children?" he offered when she hesitated.

"Yes, that's it." She met his eyes with a stubborn, defensive look. "Is that a crime, Detective?"

"No, it's not a crime. It does, however, prove that you were lying when you said things were fine."

"They are. I just don't like writing about children."

"Uh-uh. You more than just don't like writing about them. You're scared to be around them. You said yourself you didn't want to go to that daycare center, and that's the reason why, because you don't want to have to be with children. You call that being fine? To go through your life avoiding kids? You think that's normal?"

"I think it's understandable, considering."

"How about not being able to hold a baby without breaking down afterward? You think that's fine, too?"

Leah flinched. "Don't. I don't want to hear this."

"How about this, then... You think it's fine that when you do have the ground ripped out from under you the way you did today, that you come running to see a man you haven't seen in fourteen years?"

"I didn't come running here to see you," she said half-heartedly. "I came to return..."

"Bull. Why, Leah? Why me?"

She shook her head, her fierceness draining from her. She looked lost. "I don't know. I needed to talk to someone and I didn't stop to think. I thought maybe... Oh, I don't know."

"I do, but I'm not sure you're ready to hear that, either."

Zach wasn't sure how long they stood there staring into each other's eyes. When he couldn't stand it any longer, he bent his head to kiss her. As usual, his impulsiveness ruined everything. Leah flinched and shoved him away.

"No," she cried. "I didn't come here for this."

Whirling toward the door, she reached to open it, but Zach was quicker. He slapped his palm against the solid slab of wood, forcing it shut.

"Don't go," he said, a note of pleading in his voice that he wasn't familiar with. "I promise I won't try to touch you if you stay. You said you came here because you wanted to talk and... and I want that, too, Leah. Come on upstairs. Please."

"I don't know, Zach," she said reluctantly. At least she'd stopped struggling with the door however. "Sam has his son with him and I'm not in the greatest mood. I don't want to spoil things for them."

"You won't. They have plans for the afternoon. At least come up for a cup of coffee. I don't want to let you go driving off while you're still upset."

She thought about it, then nodded. "Okay."

Zach felt a rush of pleasure just knowing he would have her with him a while longer. Which was stupid, he reminded himself, very, very stupid.

"I should warn you," she added, "I haven't changed my mind about anything. I mean, you know, about helping you with your search."

"I didn't think you had," he told her. He held out his hand and to his surprise she took it. "Come on."

When they reached Sam's apartment, he was zipping Adam into a red plaid snowsuit and pulling on his mittens.

"Hey there," he said when they walked in. "I see you two ran into each other."

"Literally," Zach murmured. He pulled Leah into the room, aware of her tension and the reason for it. There was no question that Leah was uncomfortable around children. "How ya doing, Adam?"

"We're going to see Santa Claus," Adam announced without preamble. "Can you come, Uncle Zach?"

Zach smiled, reaching out to tousle the boy's sandy hair with the hand not holding firmly onto Leah's. "I'd love to, pal, but I can't today. You want to give him a message for me?"

The little boy nodded vigorously. "Yup."

"Tell him I'll be hanging my stocking here at your dad's house this year. Think you can handle that?"

He nodded again. "Yup."

"Good boy. What else are you going to tell him?"

"I'm going to tell him I want the G. I. Joe Landrover and a bike with two wheels."

"How about a two-wheeler with training wheels?" Sam asked his son. "Would that do?"

"All right," agreed Adam. "But just two big wheels. Like Steven's."

"Of course." Sam glanced at Leah to explain. "Steven is the big kid who lives next door to my folks. He's nine and he's Adam's hero."

"I see." Leah's smile was tight around the corners. Zach doubted that Sam or Adam would notice, but he noticed.

"Hey, you two haven't met, have you?" Sam said suddenly. "Leah, this is Adam. Adam, say hi to Ms. Devane."

"Hi," said Adam mangling her name when he attempted it.

"Hi, Adam," replied Leah. "You can call me Leah if you like."

"Okay," he said agreeably, then turned to Sam. "Can we go now, Daddy? I'm all hot in here."

The three adults laughed, understanding why he would be hot inside the layers of jacket, scarf and hat into which Sam had so lovingly sealed him.

"You bet, partner. Just let me grab my—" He broke off as the telephone rang in the kitchen. "Be right back."

Zach saw Leah's alarm at being left there alone with Adam and him, and in an attempt to ease the moment for her he crouched down and talked to Adam about Christmas and the big Christmas tree he and his Grandpa were planning to chop down at the tree farm.

In a way, Zach could understand why being around kids made Leah uneasy and how it could bring up things she probably didn't want to think about. Spending time with Sam and Adam always made him think of the son he didn't even know, and of all the things he'd never had a chance to do with him, things such as taking him to see Santa Claus or teaching him to play checkers. Knowing that he probably never would have the chance to do those things, or a lot of others, hurt like hell. But while those thoughts only made him more determined to find his son, he suspected that Leah dealt with her pain in a very different way, by sealing herself off from it.

Sam returned after a few minutes, looking glum.

"Problem?" Zach asked him.

"Yeah. That was a guy calling to offer me a plowing job, a funeral home that didn't get cleared out when the snow was fresh so they need a truck like mine to do the job, one with a lot of horsepower and an ice cutter."

"That's great," said Zach, knowing how anxious Sam was to earn whatever he could in these last days before Christmas. "So what's the problem?"

"They want it done right away, this afternoon."

Zach frowned and glanced at Adam who was hopping from one foot to another, oblivious to the cloud that had just drifted into his life.

He looked up at his father in the silence that followed. "Can we go now, Daddy?"

Sam leaned down to talk to him. "Listen, Adam, Daddy's got a big problem. You remember what I told you about using my truck to plow the snow off the roads?"

"Yup," Adam replied, nodding.

"Well, here's the problem."

Zach and Leah looked on as Sam struggled to explain to a four-year-old how plowing a parking lot could possibly be more important than a long-awaited trip to see Santa Claus. It wasn't easy. When Sam finished, promising they would definitely make the visit to Santa before Christmas, Adam nodded agreement, but the spark had gone out of him.

Somehow the image of Adam's crestfallen face got mixed up with Zach's memory of how Leah had looked up at him just a few minutes ago and the thought of how tragedy is measured in such purely personal terms, and he knew there was only one thing he could do.

"Adam, how about if I take you to see Santa this afternoon and then maybe you and your dad can visit him again before Christmas? Would that be okay?"

Adam nodded, his eyes growing as bright as fireworks. "Real okay. Can we, Daddy? Can me and Zach go see Santa?"

"Sure, if Zach's sure he has the time." Sam glanced at Zach quizzically. "I thought you wanted to check out that new lead?"

Zach shrugged. "It can wait."

A friend on the force had given him a tip about a national organization willing to stretch the rules to help both birth parents and adoptees with their searches. He'd intended to get in touch with the woman in charge today, but that was before he'd seen Adam's disappointment. It would have been worth the change in plans just to see the kid's face light up, and the look of gratitude Sam had flashed him. But he would have done it a thousand times over for the sweet look Leah had sent his way.

"That was a really nice thing you did, Detective," Leah said to him when they were alone. Sam had hurried off after making sure Zach knew to return Adam to his grandparents' house after the visit to Santa.

"Yeah, well," Zach replied, hoping he didn't look as idiotically pleased by her praise as he felt, "chalk it up to Christmas spirit."

"Right," she retorted, her smile telling him she wasn't buying his line at all. She reached for the doorknob. "Have fun, you guys. Say hi to Santa for me."

Once again Zach reached over her to push the door shut as she tried to open it.

"Where do you think you're going?" he demanded.

"Home. You have a date with Santa, remember? I'll take a rain check on the coffee."

"Forget it. We're in this together."

"We?" she echoed, already shaking her head. She darted a glance at Adam who was standing by looking bewildered and overheated. She flashed him a quick smile, then turned back to glare at Zach once more. "How can you even think of asking me to do a thing like this after what we talked about downstairs?"

"It's not a question of asking. It comes down to this—I *need* you, Leah."

Chapter Five

"What did you say?" Leah asked, feeling everything, including her heart, go still in anticipation of his response.

"I said *I need you, Leah.* But I guess what I should have said is that I need your car."

"My car?"

"Right." His expression grew smug. "Even I know better than to strap a four-year-old on the back of my bike."

It took her a few seconds to digest that he wasn't announcing anything earth-shattering about his feelings toward her, but simply that he needed her as a means of transportation. That shouldn't disappoint her in the least, but it did and Leah wasn't sure why. "Of course you can't take him on the bike," she told him. "You should have thought of that before you volunteered."

Zach met her annoyed gaze calmly and smiled. "I did."

"You mean you just assumed that I would drive you?"

"Yep."

"What if I say no?" she demanded, tossing her short hair back.

"You won't." Zach leaned closer, dropping his voice so only she could hear. "I think you're scared as hell of kids, but I don't think you hate them. And I don't think you'll say no to Adam."

He was right, of course, and that made her even angrier. Standing by while a parade of small children took turns whispering in Santa Claus's ear, reminding her of one more childhood ritual she had surrendered her rights to, was just about the last thing Leah wanted to do this afternoon. The very last however, was to see that crushed look reappear on Adam's little face.

"You win," she said to Zach. "Let's go."

Downstairs, Zach held the driver's door for her while she slipped behind the wheel of the black BMW that was her pride and joy. After belting Adam into the back seat, he climbed in beside her.

"Whatever happened to your macho opposition to having a woman drive you around?" she asked him.

"I got some sensitivity training. I'm hurt that you didn't notice."

"I don't know how I could have missed it," Leah remarked in a dry tone. "There was something so blatantly sensitive about the way you shoved me up against that hallway wall."

Zach's wide mouth sloped into a smile. "I aim to please."

"And bruise," she muttered.

"No way. I'll have you know that manhandling is an exact science, one I have perfected. I'll bet anything I didn't leave a bruise on you anywhere."

"Bet all you like," Leah shot back. "You'll never know."

"If you say so," Zach murmured, and settled against the seat with a look that was entirely too self-assured for Leah's peace of mind.

The trip to the mall was every bit as difficult for Leah as she had expected it to be, but it was also enlightening in a way she never anticipated. Usually she retreated at the first hint of anything that had to do with kids, anything that would focus her attention on her own loss. She had trained herself to turn her head, walk away, close her mind to it as quickly as she could.

That was impossible this time. She had no choice but to stand in line with Zach and Adam. She had to watch and listen to the little boy's mounting excitement as his turn with Santa approached. And when he finally climbed up onto Santa's knee, she couldn't look away from the innocence and awe in his expression, his small head bobbing up and down in utter agreement as Santa spoke to him gently.

And as she watched, something inside Leah broke free of the heavy locks and chains she had tied around her heart through the years. It was, she discovered, impossible to watch a four-year-old with Santa Claus and not feel something good. There was an instinctive, gut-level human warmth that came from seeing a child so happy. Sort of like the feeling a new kitten or puppy incites, but magnified a thousand times.

Not that it really changed anything for Leah. She still didn't want to have to think about all the visits to Santa that she had missed out on and she was still opposed to Zach finding their son and interfering in his life. But at least when Adam came running to show them the coloring book Santa's elf had given him, she didn't have to feign a smile and that alone was a relief.

Afterward they took Adam for pizza and then drove him to Sam's parents' house in a nearby town. Leah parked in the driveway of the modest white ranch house and turned to Zach.

"I'll wait here," she said.

"Better not," advised Zach. "Sam's dad is a talker and I haven't seen him in a while. No telling when I'll get out of there."

Adam had already unfastened his seat belt and was charging up the driveway to meet his grandfather who had come to the back door when they pulled into the driveway and was waiting for his grandson with open arms. Zach and Leah followed, standing by as Adam filled the older man in on the important details of the afternoon. Sam's father reminded Leah of an older, softer version of Sam. His hair was gray, his face wrinkled, but his eyes held the same friendly gleam.

"And he said for me to be good," Adam concluded with endearing somberness. "I am good, aren't I, Grandpa?"

"The best," his grandfather told him, catching him up in a huge bear hug.

After a minute Adam squirmed free. "I'm gonna show Grams my new book," he said, taking off inside at a trot.

Mr. Costello shook his head with a chuckle. "What I wouldn't give for some of that energy." He stuck his hand out to Zach. "Hello, Zach."

Zach greeted him warmly. "Did Sam call and tell you we'd be dropping Adam off?"

"He sure did," Mr. Costello replied. "It was real decent of you to fill in for Sam this way. I'd have done it myself, but it's not easy for me to get away on the spur of the moment. I never know..." He trailed off, pressing his lips together as he gestured broadly toward the inside of the house.

"I understand," Zach told him. "No problem. I was glad to do it."

Mr. Costello's gaze drifted in the direction where Adam had disappeared. "I hate to think of that little fella losing out on anything else. What with all he's been through already."

"He won't," Zach assured him, his tone strong and solid. "He has Sam, and he has you. I'd say that makes him luckier than most."

The older man shot Zach a grateful smile. "Luckier than a lot of kids anyway. Now who have you got here with you?" he asked, turning his attention to Leah.

Zach quickly made the introductions and to Leah's amazement Sam's father remembered her from high school. He invited them inside for tea, explaining that he had just made a fresh pot and ignoring their protests. Hanging their coats on the hooks in that back hall, he offered them seats at the kitchen table. While they talked about high school and Sam's new business, he moved easily around the kitchen, setting the table with four cups and saucers and pouring a glass of milk for Adam. From the breadbox he took a tray of cookies and placed it in the center of the table, then poured the tea.

"Let's see," he said, rubbing his hands together as he surveyed the scene. "There's sugar and milk and lemon. I guess that about covers it. The cookies are store-bought, I'm afraid. I'm not much of a baker."

"They look great," Zach replied, helping himself to one. "No such thing as a bad cookie."

"Good. Dig in. I'll just go and see what Adam and his grandmother are up to."

"It's funny," Leah remarked after he disappeared into the other room. "I barely remember Sam's father from high school, but I do recall him being sterner, all business, not the type to be such a homebody," she finished, waving her hand at the snack he had prepared for them.

"Yeah, well, he's had to adapt," Zach told her, stirring a spoonful of sugar into his tea.

"Because of Adam coming to live here?"

"That and other things. Look, Leah, I probably should warn you that about a year ago Sam's mother—"

He broke off as Mr. Costello returned leading his wife by the arm, leaving Leah curious about what he'd been about to tell her about Sam's mother. She was a petite woman with a pretty smile, dressed in a pale pink sweatsuit and fuzzy pink slippers.

"Here we go, honey," Mr. Costello said as he led her to her place and held the chair for her. "The seat of honor."

The older woman smiled and nodded pleasantly as her husband introduced Leah.

"And of course you remember Zach," he said.

Mrs. Costello swung her gaze to Zach without even a flicker of recognition. "Are you a student here, too?" she asked, an odd thread of excitement in her voice.

"No, Mrs. Costello, I'm a friend of Sam's remember? From high school."

"I remember Sam," she said, nodding earnestly. "He lived here once. He's gone now."

"That's right," her husband agreed, his expression relaxed and patient. "Grown and gone. He has a place of his own over on Garrison Street."

"I don't know where that is," she said, quickly folding her hands in her lap. She looked worried, frantic almost, as if she had forgotten something very important. "I really don't. I can't remember where that is."

"That's all right. Maybe we can take a drive later and I'll show you where he lives. I think that will help you to remember." As he spoke in the same tone, as unhurried as a caress, he poured milk into her tea and stirred it for her.

"There, just the way you like it. Now have a cookie, Gracie, they're your favorites."

His wife smiled, her panic of a moment ago forgotten as smoothly and quickly as if someone had switched channels on a television set. Leah glanced across the table at Zach, who indicated with his expression that they would talk later. Leah felt a rush of sympathy for both Sam's parents, suspecting what was going on even without knowing any of the details.

The conversation over tea returned to Sam and his landscaping business. Both Zach and Mr. Costello seemed convinced he was going to make a success of it. Sam's mother remained silent throughout, concentrating on her tea and cookies as single-mindedly as Adam did his snack. Adam climbed down from his chair as soon as he was finished, rushing off to watch "Sesame Street," and a few minutes later his grandmother pushed back her chair as well.

"I have to go now," she said politely.

Her husband stopped talking midsentence. His expression remained relaxed, but something told Leah that inside he was always on guard. "Where do you have to go, Gracie?"

"Home," she replied. "I have to go home now."

"You are home, sweetheart."

She shook her head, her chin taking on a stubborn set. "No. This isn't my home. I have to get home before dark or my father will be angry with me. He always wants me home when the streetlights come on." She shuffled over to the window and peered out. "They're on now. You see?"

Mr. Costello was already on his feet as she moved toward the back door. He stopped her easily, pulling her back into the kitchen as she began to struggle and cry out that she had to leave if she wanted to get home on time.

Zach caught Leah's eye and tilted his head toward the door. "I think we should get going now."

"Right," agreed Leah. "I still have a story to write."

They quickly got their coats and said goodbye, leaving a still calm Mr. Costello doing his best to convince his wife that she was already home. Leah marveled at his patience.

They walked to her car in silence. Just as they drew near it, Sam's father caught up with them.

"I just wanted to say thanks again," he told them. "For taking Adam, I mean." He looked from Zach to Leah and for the first time she saw a hint of awkwardness in his expression. "I guess you can tell that Sam's mother isn't exactly right. Alzheimer's the doctors say."

Leah nodded. "That can be very hard on a family."

"You said it," Mr. Costello agreed. "It wouldn't be so bad if I could think just of her, but with Adam here, too, well, it's rough."

"I'm sure it is. Have you thought of daycare, Mr. Costello? Either for Adam or your wife or both. It would give you a little time to yourself. I'm sure you could use it."

He nodded, his eyes shifting back toward the house where a light had just been turned on in the basement. "That's for sure. Adam does go to nursery school a couple of mornings a week. I don't think Grace would like having to go to one of those centers for the elderly, though."

"Maybe she'd surprise you. Some centers are wonderful. I've been doing some research in this area lately. If you want, I could get together some material on centers that specialize in Alzheimer's patients and drop it off for you."

"That would be very kind of you," he said. "And who knows? Maybe she'd like it after all. Now I have to go. I don't like to leave her and Adam alone for too long."

"That poor man," Leah said, watching him hurry back up the driveway. "These retirement years should be the best years of his life and instead he's spending all his time taking care of a grandson and a sick wife."

"He doesn't complain," Zach countered.

"He doesn't seem the type to complain. Did he know about his wife's illness when he took custody of Adam?"

"Yes, although she's gotten progressively worse since then."

"Even if he did know," mused Leah, "I suppose he really had no choice. She needs him and so does Adam."

"Wrong, Leah," Zach said quietly. "You always have a choice." He swung open the passenger side door before she could reply. "Get in. I'll drive."

"So much for your sensitivity training," Leah muttered, but she didn't argue. The truth is she was exhausted and knowing they would be hitting the commuter traffic around the city, she was glad to have him take the wheel.

His words lingered in her head as he drove through the side roads that led back to the highway. *You always have a choice.* That was true, she supposed, but some choices weren't nearly as simple and straightforward as Zach's comment seemed to imply. There were all sorts of contingencies and considerations to be taken into account. And consequences.

Sam's parents had moved out of the city sometime during the past fourteen years and settled in Fairfield, a small town about twenty miles south of Providence. At the town center stood the town hall, a redbrick building with tall white columns, and across the street was the green, lined with birch trees and park benches. If a movie producer wanted a quintessential New England setting, he couldn't do better than Fairfield.

As they approached the center of town, traffic slowed almost to a crawl. Eventually they inched their way close enough to see a crowd of people gathered before the town hall. On the steps was arranged a choir clad in red robes. Zach lowered his window and the familiar sounds of "Silver Bells" drifted into the car.

"What do you know, a rush-hour concert." He turned to her with an amused grin. "Only in Fairfield, huh?"

Leah frowned out the window. "Do you suppose they're almost finished?"

"Nope," replied Zach after studying the scene for a moment. "People are still piling up out there and there are still parking spots left. They must be just getting started," he concluded, signaling the driver behind him and then deftly backing her car into one of those parking spaces he mentioned.

"What are you doing?" asked Leah.

"Parking." He turned off the engine. "I know a bottleneck when I see one and this traffic's not going anywhere in a hurry. I figure if we can't beat 'em, we might as well join 'em. Come on."

"I'd rather not."

He paused with his hand on the door handle and stared at her in disbelief. "You'd rather not listen to Christmas carols? Since when?"

"Since now, okay? I'm tired and cold and I don't feel like standing out there listening to a concert."

"Okay, we can listen from right here. Hey, don't blame me," he said, raising his hands defensively in response to her scowl. "I didn't plan the concert or the traffic jam."

"No, obviously someone with no common sense planned it," muttered Leah.

"Either that or someone with an excess of Christmas spirit, which I might add doesn't seem to be your problem."

"Just because I don't want to freeze my butt off listening to *Jingle Bells* doesn't make me Ebenezer Scrooge."

"You're right. It doesn't. So how do you plan to celebrate Christmas?"

Leah's eyes narrowed. "What do you mean?"

"Nothing bad enough to deserve that look, I can tell you that. I just wondered how you're going to spend Christmas."

"I haven't decided. My sisters invited me to have dinner with them and their families. I might do that."

"Sounds good. Got your tree yet?"

"Why?"

His brows shot up. "Just asking, making conversation. I thought as long as we're stuck here for the duration we might as well talk."

"No, I don't have a tree yet. Truthfully it seems like a lot of trouble to go lugging one home and setting it up and decorating it when I'm all alone there."

"Maybe. Me, I always figured that because I live alone I need a tree more than most folks."

Leah shrugged and turned to look out her window at the choir. She lowered her window halfway, hoping that if she pretended to be concentrating on the music he would stop talking about Christmas. It seemed to work and gradually the lump lodged in her throat began to melt. The choir performed an enthusiastic rendition of "Frosty the Snowman" and then "The Twelve Days of Christmas." How many more songs could they possibly sing, Leah wondered. A short pause led her to believe that might be it, then they launched into "Away In A Manger" and without warning the ache that had been building inside her surged, erupting in a rush of tears.

It was too much to hope that Zach wouldn't notice. He noticed everything, she thought, his eyes seeming to find their way to her no matter where they were.

"Ah, Leah," she heard him whisper. She felt his fingers close over her shoulder and sensed him leaning closer.

"Come here," he urged softly.

Leah stiffened in response to his touch and covered her face with her hands. "I told you," she rasped between soft muffled sobs. "I told you I didn't want to stay and hear this."

"Leah, baby, you have to stop running sometime. Don't...don't turn away. You don't have to be ashamed of crying. You know, when I was at the academy, we really did have sensitivity training, and one thing I learned is that grief can be strongest at this time of year. That's what you're feeling, grief, and it's normal."

"That's just part of what I'm feeling, believe me," she retorted, her voice cracking with emotion.

"Then tell me about it. I know you don't have anyone else to tell. I know that because if you did, you wouldn't have come running to me today. And I know how it feels not to have anyone to talk to, to have to hold something this big inside you all the time. Come on, Leah...."

He reached for her, trying to turn her toward him and suddenly Leah was filled with the image of another night when they had sat next to each other in a car, arguing, Zach pleading as she cried and cried. God, when would it ever end?

"Stop shutting me out," he pleaded roughly.

Leah jerked away from him. "Then stop closing in on me. I want to go home, Zach. I mean it, I want to go home right now."

Zach pulled back so that he was on his own side of the small car. He hung his hands over the steering wheel and stared at her, his expression grim. "Fine, you want to go home, and I'll take you. There's just one more thing I want to say first—you're not alone in this, Leah, so don't ever think you are. You're not the only one with doubts and questions and second thoughts...."

"I don't..."

"Bull. You're not the only one who remembers, and you're sure as hell not the only one who hurts."

Somehow Zach managed to do a U-turn and find an alternate route to the highway. The traffic was heavy, but at least it kept moving. They drove in silence until Leah noticed he had passed the exit for Sam's house and was headed straight for hers.

"I have to drop you off," she reminded him.

"Forget it. I'll walk or catch a bus back to Sam's. I meant it when I said I don't want you driving home alone from his place at night, especially not just so you can give me a ride."

Leah didn't argue. She knew it wouldn't have done any good. Zach was relentless when he made up his mind about something. Such as finding their son for instance. For the first time that thought brought Leah something besides instantaneous panic. Oh, she still felt panic to be sure, but somewhere inside something indefinable had softened toward Zach.

You're not the only one who remembers, he'd told her. *You're not the only one who hurts.*

He had been speaking from the gut. It wasn't so much what he said as it was the look on his face and the rough edge to his voice when he said it that convinced Leah of that. She wrapped her arms around herself as they turned onto her street, but it didn't help to halt the scary sensation that she was crumbling from the inside out. It was hard to keep building the walls higher, she thought, when what was on the other side no longer looked like the enemy.

Zach parked the car in her driveway and handed her the keys.

"Thanks for letting me use the car," he said in a polite stranger's voice. "And for coming along. It meant a lot to Adam."

"I'm glad you talked me into going. It wasn't as bad as I thought it might be."

Zach looked hard at her. "Did you ever think that maybe... Ah, forget it. Come on, I'll walk you to the door."

Walking beside him to her front door brought back memories of a thousand other times they had done this same thing. A different car, a different front door, but maybe that didn't matter as much as it seemed to on the surface. Maybe the things on the inside that really did matter were still the same. Thinking about that and remembering what they had once shared didn't help Leah's objectivity any.

Neither did the awareness of him that permeated every part of her when they were together. That hadn't changed, either. It was as strong and overwhelming as it had always been. Leah wasn't sure how it was possible to want someone to go away and to just plain want him at the same time, but that's the way it was. She was poised on a carefully balanced seesaw of conflicting desires, and she was afraid that all it would take was one touch for that careful balance to disappear.

She fished her key from her purse and unlocked the door.

"You're sure I can't give you a ride home?" she asked.

"I'm sure."

His face looked lean in the pale glow from the overhead light, with no visible hints of the heightened sensitivity he'd laid claim to earlier. He looked hard and unyielding, a tough customer, Leah would think if she didn't know him. And she would probably be instantly on guard.

But she did know him, and she knew that a tough exterior sometimes hid a lot of things you wouldn't expect to find in a man like Zach. That had been one of the first things she discovered when she and Zach had been thrown together on the high school paper and he had gradually let her see beyond his cool, tough-as-nails attitude. The emptiness she sensed inside him had touched something in her then, and it touched her the same way now.

"Good night, Leah," he said, and started back down the walk.

From her open door, Leah watched him move away. His hands were jammed into the pockets of his battered leather jacket, his shoulders hunched against the cold and without stopping to think she called his name.

"Zach."

He turned and looked at her without saying anything.

"The baby. . . he was born on Christmas Eve," she said. "I just thought maybe you'd like to know."

Zach settled himself in a chair in an out-of-the-way corner of the Costello's living room and stretched his long legs out in front of him. This was the first Christmas Eve in a long time that he hadn't spent at home. Home, in the very loosest sense of the word being the two-story brick colonial surrounded by an acre of professionally tended lawn where he had grown up. In the past few years, as his father grew older, he'd made a special effort to grit his teeth and be there for the holidays.

He hadn't bothered to pay even a cursory visit tonight, knowing his presence wouldn't be expected or particularly welcome. Even without being there, however, he could have told anyone who asked that there would be a ten-foot-tall white tree in the living room, decorated with white tinsel and white satin balls. Beneath it would be stacked dozens of presents, most of them wrapped by strangers at the posh stores his stepmother favored. Zach didn't miss any of it a bit.

What had come as a shock to him was how much he did miss his father. He'd thought about the old man a lot in the days leading up to this, his first Christmas without him. This afternoon he finally decided that much of his gloom came from the realization that there was no longer any possibility of ever making things right between them. For years his father had volleyed between ignoring and disapproving of him. Zach in turn had gone out of his way at times to give him plenty to disapprove of.

The man had still been his father.

In spite of all the indifference and the disparaging remarks and the fact that after Zach's mother died he had remarried a woman who regarded Zach as a burden rather than a stepson and had never let him forget it, part of Zach had never stopped wishing things could be different between him and his father, and hoping that maybe someday, somehow, it would happen. He could never quite envision how that miracle might come about, but he'd hoped anyway. That's just the way it was with a father and son.

Now that hope was gone forever, he thought, taking a sip of his cider, which out of consideration for Sam was the strongest thing being served at the Costello's this Christmas Eve. He was grateful to Sam's parents for inviting him to spend the holidays with them. Although on a certain level he felt alone even here; at least he was with people he cared about. He'd spent his share of Christmases alone or with virtual strangers, but he sure hadn't wanted to spend this one that way. This year was different. *He* was different.

Being alone had suited him just fine once. Now it only made the empty places inside him feel more empty. It was ironic that it had taken until he lost whatever real family he had before he understood just how important family was. And before he understood the real importance of this season. At its heart, Christmas wasn't about shopping and parties and presents, it was about family. It was a day of celebration for all the hard, tough days throughout the year when you were there for those who needed you, and they were there for you.

The Costellos understood that with a vengeance, thought Zach. And though they weren't his family, he was damn happy to be here tonight. He was even happier because they had a real tree that filled the house with the scent of pine. It was decorated with candy canes and a hodgepodge of ornaments, most of which had their own tale to tell according to Sam. There weren't a whole lot of presents under the tree, and none of them had that slick professionally wrapped look that Zach deplored. If that mattered to Adam you'd never know it from his eager expression as he poked and shook them before being tucked into bed a while ago.

Even Sam's mom was having a good night. Two of Sam's aunts and several cousins had stopped by and the mood was a mixture of excitement and relaxation. Just what holidays ought to be, mused Zach. It reminded him of the one Christmas years ago when he had spent Christmas Eve with Leah and her family.

Like tonight, the contrast between Christmas in the Devane household and the holiday extravaganza he was accustomed to had been striking. There had been no champagne punch or trays of hors d'oeuvres and the highlight of the night had been when her youngest sister placed the statue of the infant Jesus in the manger her father had built. Not exactly what the crowd gathered at his house would have considered festive, but Zach hadn't wanted the night to end and he'd woken the next morning wishing he could spend Christmas day with Leah's family as well.

He recalled that Christmas morning clearly, sitting there at home, unwrapping a new suede jacket he hadn't wanted and listening to his stepmother tell him how lucky he was that she had been able to get the last one in his size and thinking that Leah was really the lucky one.

Sam's aunt had moved to the piano and was playing "White Christmas." It sounded good. Taking another drink of his cider, Zach thought again of the manger Leah's father had built, how he'd even put in a loft and had cut a hole in the back where one of the tree lights fit and lit up the scene inside. He wondered what had happened to it, whether Mr. and Mrs Devane had taken it with them when they moved to Florida or if one of Leah's married sisters had it now.

If that was the case, it was possible that right this minute Leah was watching a young niece or nephew perform the family tradition of placing the baby into the rough-hewn cradle inside. She had told him she would be spending Christmas with her sisters and their families. A sudden chill ran down Zach's spine, almost as if a cold breeze had blown through an open window behind him. Except there was no window behind him and if anything the Costellos had a tendency to keep the heat turned up about five degrees too high for his comfort.

The chill accompanied his sudden recollection that Leah had never actually said she would be spending Christmas with her sisters. She'd told him simply that they had invited her to have dinner with them and that she might go. *Might.* Ever since then he'd been so busy wrestling with some of the other things she'd said that he hadn't thought much about this. Now that he did think about it, however, he realized that she'd been pretty damn vague and that she hadn't mentioned anything at all about Christmas Eve...other than that on this night, fourteen years ago, their son had been born.

The cider he'd been sipping might have turned to acid, his chest suddenly burned that much. Carrying his half-full cup to the kitchen, he dumped the remainder into the sink, then motioned Sam aside and told him what he had to do.

"I understand," Sam replied, clapping him reassuringly on the back. "I just hope your guess is wrong."

"Me, too," countered Zach. "If I am wrong, I'll be back in a while. Otherwise..."

Sam nodded. "If you're not back, I'll know where you are. Merry Christmas, buddy."

"Yeah, you, too."

For a little while there it had been a merry Christmas, thought Zach as he zipped his jacket against the cold and straddled his bike. At least as merry a one as he had any right to expect. He carefully turned from the driveway onto the street, taking pains to stay on the dry surface near the center. This was suicide weather for a biker. Which, suggested a dark corner of his mind, just might be why he so steadfastly refused to drive anything else.

He'd ridden for about ten minutes when a light icy rain began to fall, making the trip even more dangerous and more miserable. It didn't take long, hurtling face first into the wet, frigid night air, for whatever was left of his Christmas cheer to be whipped away. What was left was familiar: the same fears and questions that seemed to be everywhere he turned lately, forming the solid new borders of his life.

If there was a way out of this darkness he'd tumbled into, he wasn't having much luck finding it. At the moment, however, it wasn't his mood or the dark edges of his own life that he was worried about. It was Leah.

Chapter Six

Leah had built a fire earlier in the evening, adding a log every half hour or so to keep it burning strong. No matter how much wood she tossed on, however, or how conscientiously she stirred the embers with the poker, she still couldn't get warm enough. She didn't really expect to. This was Christmas Eve.

Up and down her street, candles glowed in the windows of each house and inside most, families had gathered to celebrate the holiday together. But there was no celebration at Leah's, no candles in her windows. Here the only light came from the fireplace and the small crystal lamp by her chair.

She did hang a small wreath on her front door each December, mostly so that the neighbors wouldn't think she was a pitiful creature with no holiday spirit. Other than that, and the gifts she bought and had sent to family members a week ahead of time, there was no evidence anywhere that this wasn't simply any other day of the year. Leah earnestly wished that it was. For her, Christmas Eve and Christmas Day were obstacles to be endured by taking as few direct hits to the heart as possible.

Christmas Eve was also the only time during the year when she permitted herself to indulge for just a little while in memories she usually struggled to submerge beneath an intentionally hectic schedule. That was the reason she'd turned on the lamp beside her. Now, after two snifters of brandy, she was ready.

Dragging the ottoman across the room, she climbed up and felt around on the top of the bookcase for the box she kept tucked away there, out of sight. Inside the box were the only tangible reminders she had of the baby she had given away.

Holding the box as carefully as if it contained priceless family heirlooms, she returned to her chair. She settled back and took a deep breath before removing the elastic that secured the box and lifting the cover. There was a ritual to the way she looked through the contents, her own private ceremony to commemorate her son's birthday. Always as she did this she hoped and prayed that wherever he was tonight, he was having a real celebration, and that none of the questions and doubts that plagued her ever touched him.

Leah removed items from the box slowly, wanting the process to last as long as possible. There were so few things there. Each year she repacked them methodically, in order of importance, so that what mattered most and had the power to make her shake with a yearning so intense she sometimes thought she might explode from it, lay waiting on the very bottom of the box.

On top were the plastic bracelets that she and the baby had worn at the hospital. She had snipped his from him on the final morning she was there, feigning innocence when the nurse asked what on earth had happened to it. Taking the baby's bracelet, taking *anything* that might remind her of her baby, had been against the express orders of the nuns at the home. They had also strongly advised "their girls" not to ask to see their babies, insisting that would make it easier to forget afterwards.

For weeks before she went into labor Leah had anguished over whether or not to follow their advice. She didn't actually make up her mind for sure until she heard her baby cry, and then there was no decision to be made. Maybe it had been hormonal or pure elemental instinct, but when she heard him cry she knew that she had to hold her baby or die. For the next two days she had begged the nurses for as many extra visits with him as they would permit. And she had never regretted it. The nuns had been wrong, she knew that in her heart. It didn't matter whether you saw your baby and held him or sacrificed that right along with all the others. You never forgot.

Beneath the bracelets was the index card that had been taped to the tiny Plexiglas crib when they wheeled him into her room. It was trimmed in blue, once bright but growing more faded with each passing year. The message It's A Boy! was emblazoned on the top, as if his arrival was something to brag about instead of the private tragedy it had been for Leah. On the space for his name someone had written Baby Devane. That was because she hadn't been allowed to name him of course. But seeing those words there, Baby Devane, had been one of her few reasons to smile during that whole horrible time.

He was a Devane baby. *Her* baby, her own sweet baby, and somewhere deep inside she had drawn strength from the thought that no amount of paperwork and lawyer's talk would ever change that, no matter what happened afterward. Just as in a way he would never be hers, in a different, very special way he would always be. Holding the card in her hand now Leah was every bit as fiercely certain of that as she had been fourteen years ago.

Next she withdrew from the box one of the soft flannel receiving blankets that he had been swaddled in the first time they brought him to her. Leah closed her eyes and ran her fingertips over the soft fabric, remembering the first time she'd touched it, how she had eagerly peeled it away as soon as the nurses left the two of them alone so that she could do what every mother since the beginning of time has done, check to see that all his fingers and toes were in place and that he was, as she already knew in her heart, the most beautiful, perfect baby that had ever existed.

Sitting there now, she lifted the blanket to her face and inhaled deeply. Any lingering scent had long ago faded into oblivion. It didn't matter. Leah remembered. She carried the memory of his scent along with the memory of the way he yawned and pursed his lips when he was hungry and the unmatched softness of his skin with her always, in a place where they would never fade or change or age. In her heart.

After a long time, she put the blanket aside and with trembling hands reached for the envelope that lay at the very bottom of the box. It was imprinted with tiny teddy bears and the name of the photography studio that the hospital permitted to visit the nursery to take photographs of the newborns.

It had been an accident that the photographer's assistant had come to her room to ask if she wanted to order copies of the picture of her baby that had just been snapped. Leah had known from talking to girls at the home that the order form for the pictures routinely went with the baby to the adoptive parents. Overjoyed at her luck, she had seized the opportunity, paying cash for a single eight-by-ten photo and giving the woman her home address.

When the photograph arrived several weeks later her mother had handed the sealed envelope to her without saying a word. Leah had understood that she didn't know what to say. And she had wondered if then, when it was too late, her mother was sorry for all the pressure she had put on Leah not to make the same mistake she had. Even back then Leah had wanted to wrap her arms around her mother and tell her not to worry, that she didn't blame her for anything. If anything, she had blamed herself for not having the guts to take a chance.

Instead she had rushed to her room with the envelope and jammed a chair under the doorknob so no one could barge in without warning. Then she had sat on the edge of her bed and cried for nearly an hour before she even summoned the courage to open it and look.

She looked at the photograph dozens of times in the days right after it arrived, and now only on this one night of the year. It had ceased to amaze her that each time her reaction was exactly the same, a deep visceral wrenching that made her want to find her baby and gather him against her and run as fast and as far as she could. Tonight was no different. The rational knowledge that he was most likely by now far too big for anyone to pick up and carry off didn't change her longing to do so one bit. For Leah he would forever be the beautiful, placid, round-faced infant in the photo before her. And in spite of the careful reasoning she used to rationalize her decision so she could remain sane, she would forever be sorry that she had to let him go.

Leah finally slipped the photograph back into the envelope and wiped her eyes with the back of her hands. She wouldn't repack the box just yet, she decided. Seeing as she only permitted this self-indulgence once a year, she was going to make the most of it. Shivering in spite of the warmth in the room, she moved to stoke the fire once again. She was placing the poker back into the brass holder when the doorbell rang.

Leah froze.

She couldn't imagine who would be at her door tonight. The excuse she'd given her sisters had been flawless. She was certain neither of them had any reason to suspect she was lying or to come checking up on her. Maybe a neighbor? she wondered as the bell sounded a second time. Someone who had run out of ice for their party and had come to ask if she had some she could spare?

She turned toward the door, smoothing her hand over her hair and giving the belt of her robe a tug. Halfway there it occurred to her that it might not be a neighbor after all and as a precaution she hurriedly backtracked to pile everything into the box and shove it back on top of the bookcase, before moving to the door.

Of course, she thought, the instant she had swung it open. She watched Zach stop in the act of reaching for the doorbell a third time and let his arm drop to his side. She should have known it would be Zach.

He looked wet and cold and the urge to throw herself into his arms was so strong it scared her.

When their eyes met, Leah saw in his a sorrow to equal her own. She breathed deeply, feeling the night air quiver and tremble all the way to the pit of her stomach. For his sake, she hoped he wasn't here looking for holiday cheer.

"You shouldn't have come, Zach" she said bluntly. "I really don't want to be with anyone tonight."

"I know that."

She dragged her fingers through her hair uneasily. "Then why are you here?"

He stepped inside, bringing with him the scent of danger and night. All Leah's instincts were to back away, but something stronger than instinct held her where she was.

"Because this is where I want to be tonight," he said, his gaze intimate and searching, as if she held the answers to all his questions. "I came because I didn't want you to be alone. And because I didn't want to be alone tonight, either."

He touched her then, putting his gloved hands on either side of her head and leaning into her. His breath fanned her face; it was the only thing about him that was warm. The cold clung to his jacket and his hair and his face. She could feel it surround her as he bent his head and moved closer.

"And," he said softly, "I came for this."

His mouth quickly covered hers in a kiss that was hard and hot and hungry. As it drove relentlessly onward, it filled a need within that Leah hadn't known existed. For a long time now desire had been a forgotten part of her life, one more thing she'd either lost or surrendered. Or so she'd thought. The other night in Sam's apartment had suggested differently. And tonight the feelings unleashed inside her were more than a suggestion.

The way Zach's kiss was affecting her and the instant abandon with which she was kissing him back made Leah realize that desire had simply been on hold somewhere inside her all this time, waiting, growing slowly but surely, the way interest accumulates on a forgotten bank account. With one kiss Zach had released all that pent-up longing.

When he lifted his head he was breathing harshly and his eyes glittered with desire.

"Oh, baby," he murmured against her face, his rough tone held surprise and entreaty. "Do you know... Do you have any idea what it feels like to want someone the way I want you?"

"Yes," she said, turning her head so that their eyes met. "Right this minute I know exactly how it feels."

Understanding brought his jaw up sharply. He looked at her hard, as if convincing himself that what he heard was really what she meant. Then without saying a word he kicked the door shut behind him, bent and lifted her into his arms.

The brandy she'd sipped earlier had clouded her thinking, but Leah knew that what she was about to do was not the result of cloudy thinking. It had nothing to do with thinking at all. This was beyond thought, beyond reason. And as much as she wanted it, that made it uncharted territory for Leah.

It took him less than a minute to find his way to her bedroom, but that was plenty of time for second thoughts to intrude if she had any. She didn't. All night, no, longer than that, for days now really, she'd felt as if she were falling deeper and deeper into the darkness inside, with no way to stop the descent, nothing to grab on to. No way to save herself. Now, in Zach's arms, she had found the safe refuge she needed. Leah had no idea if it would last longer than the next few hours, but it was still more than she'd had going for her a few minutes ago.

On another night she might have come to her senses and called a halt, but this wasn't another night, and the need to be with someone . . . to be with Zach, transcended everything else. In spite of the cold, wet leather jacket that covered his chest, she pressed her cheek to him there and felt his dampness spreading to her throat and hair as he slid her to her feet beside the bed. It didn't matter. As crazy as it seemed, for the first time tonight she was warm.

Staring at her as if afraid she might disappear if he looked away, he worked the glove off one hand, then the other. He dropped them to the floor at her feet. Then he reached for her again. He tugged on the belt at her waist, loosening it so that her robe hung open. Sliding his hands inside, he pushed it off her shoulders and tossed it away, leaving Leah with only her white silk panties.

His gaze roamed over her, moving lazily from her breasts to her tummy and lower, sweeping hungrily along her legs. Leah watched the passion in his expression flare as he looked at her and whatever concern she had about how her thirty-year-old body would measure up to his memory of her at sixteen disappeared. The darkening of his eyes and the slow rise and fall of his chest convinced her that Zach wanted her tonight as much as he ever had back then.

Maybe more. There was a desperation in the way his arms dragged her against him now that was all new to her. His hands on her back, sliding down to caress the back of her thighs and between, were warm, but the rest of him was cold and wet against her heated skin. Leah found the contrast wildly erotic, driving her desire still higher. It made even the slightest contact more vivid and potent and tonight she needed that. She needed as much human contact as she could get.

Winding her arms tightly around his neck, she rubbed sinuously against him. When Zach groaned and slid one damp, denim-clad thigh between hers, Leah let him. She squeezed her legs around his and Zach pressed higher in response, sending a shaft of pleasure shooting through her.

His lips sought hers once again as his hand followed the curve of her hip around to the soft swell of her tummy and the angled hollows at the top of her thighs. His fingers lightly raked the soft nest of curls where they met, sliding deeper until he touched the hot, soft core of her growing desire.

Leah arched against his hand, tilting her head back to receive the hard, deep thrusts of his tongue. His mouth was hot and tasted faintly of apples and Leah couldn't get enough of him, of the way he felt and tasted and the dizzy, trembling way he made her feel.

On the few dates she'd had since her divorce, she had been studiously conscious of how much physical contact was proper. No man had made it beyond a few kisses on the sofa and most never made it that far. If she ever did make love with a man again, Leah had thought it would happen in measured increments, over a period of time. But that wasn't the way it was happening at all. There was no hesitancy in Zach's approach and no feigned coyness in her response.

Their bodies were both on fire and ready, his hard and aroused, hers melting and open to him, and neither one of them was making any secret of their desire, or their intent. There was no reason to. Just as there was no reason for Leah to waste time pondering whether this was right or wrong. Some things were so right you didn't have to stop and think.

When at last Zach nudged her down to the bed, she went eagerly. He shrugged off his jacket and stood before her, caressing her shoulders and sliding his fingers down her arms to grasp her hands. Then he lifted them to rest near the snap at the waist of his jeans.

Excitement licked at Leah's insides as she eagerly flicked it open and lowered his zipper over his straining erection. Looking up into his eyes, she hooked her fingers inside his jeans and shorts and tugged them down, freeing him. The last time she had touched him this way she had been a kid, still uncertain of the power of her own sensuality. Now she was a woman, surer and more confident, a woman who had seen and felt enough pain to treasure whatever joy came her way.

Caressing him and wrapping her fingers lightly around him she bent her head and took him in a way she wouldn't have dreamed of doing fourteen years ago. It was a first for Leah, an impulse, and the way Zach jerked in response made her very happy she had given in to it. His unmistakable pleasure filled Leah with a heady sense of her own passion. He groaned, his hands gripping her head for as long as he could take it until he pulled away with a sound of pleasure-pain and pushed her onto her back.

He joined her on the bed and they moved in a tangle of arms and legs and straining bodies as he attempted to strip his clothes off and make impatient love to her at the same time. The battle ended with Zach naked and inside of her, harder and hotter and more powerful even than he was in her memories or in the fantasies she'd been weaving with alarming frequency lately.

He held himself still, poised above her on firmly planted hands, then began thrusting slowly, letting her adjust to the full impact of his possession. With fierce control that showed on his rigid face and in his tortuously measured movements, he filled her and then withdrew, over and over again, stretching her, exciting her, driving her—and himself—to the edge of sanity.

Leah's head tossed on the pillow as her hips strained to quicken his pace.

Zach stilled, forcing her to look at him in bewilderment. "It never happened for you back then," he said.

"I... It was good," Leah protested, her voice husky with thwarted desire. "It was always good, Zach."

"It was good," he agreed in a strained tone, "but I was eighteen and my idea of good sex wasn't very enlightened. You never came back then...."

He pushed inside her once again, deeper and harder than before, and held himself there as he slipped his hand between their bodies, seeking the place where they were one. "But you will tonight."

He was true to his word. Under his patient touch Leah was carried closer and closer to the edge, finally exploding in waves that were electric and involuntary as Zach kissed her breasts and used his sure, deft fingers to propel her on that final leap into a storm of sensations so white-hot Leah felt as if she might never recover. The last satisfying wave hadn't yet receded when she felt Zach tremble against her, a slow hiss of pure sensual agony escaping him as he reached his own climax and then fell lax on top of her for just a few seconds before rolling his weight to the side.

In the sweet, lazy aftermath, Leah turned to look at him, needing to reassure herself that this was really happening to her. She ran her hand over his chest slowly, delighting in his hair-roughened skin and the wonderful, uniquely male arrangement of bone and muscle beneath. Their lovemaking had been fierce, but fast and in places his skin still felt cold to her touch. Reaching for the extra blanket she kept folded on a chair by the bed, she drew it over both of them.

"Better?" she asked.

He slid closer so that their bodies were touching from chest to thigh before replying. "Much."

Leah smiled. "Thank you."

"It was my pleasure," countered Zach.

"Actually I think it was both our pleasure," she corrected with a wry smile, "but I was really thanking you for coming here tonight. I hated being alone."

"Then why were you?" he asked, his voice as soft and easy as the fingertips he trailed lightly over her skin. "You said yourself your family wanted you to spend the holidays with them."

Leah shook her head impatiently. "Because as much as I hated the thought of being alone, I've learned that it's worse being with other people and having to pretend to be merry and full of Christmas spirit when inside you're falling apart."

His hand curved around the back of her neck. "You know what I want?" he asked.

"For Christmas?" teased Leah.

"Forever. I want to put everything inside you back together so that you never have to dread Christmas Eve or spend it alone ever again."

Zach felt her stiffen against him and he half wished he hadn't said it. Even more, he wished there was no need to.

"And just how do you propose to do that?" she asked.

Zach hesitated, painfully aware that her light tone had become forced, the easy humor of a moment ago gone.

"No," she said just as he was about to speak, "let me guess. You're going to help me by finding our son and arranging for one great big happy family reunion. Right? That's your plan, isn't it, Zach?"

"Not exactly," he replied, being careful with his words. Suddenly she was like a tightly coiled spring and the last thing he wanted was to say something that would send her shooting out of bed, tossing his clothes at him and telling him to get the hell out.

"Then what is it, *exactly,* that you do plan to do?"

"I do think that finding our son is the first step."

"Wrong," she snapped. "Finding him would be the wrong step. What's done is done, Zach, let it go."

"The way you have?" he asked, taking great pains to keep his tone gentle when he knew his words might not be. "Should I let it go by allowing bad memories and a guilty conscience to dictate my life...to limit where I go and whom I see? Should I let it go by locking myself away with my pain because I'm so convinced that no one else can possibly understand...or maybe because I'm ashamed to even talk about it with anyone? Is that it?"

"No, that's not it. And I am not ashamed of allowing my baby to be adopted by a family that could love him and give him what I couldn't. I did what I had to do, what was best for everyone involved.''

"Nice spiel. You sound like the spokesman for an adoption agency.''

"And you sound like you're about fourteen years too late. You have no right to tell me I should have a guilty conscience when you—''

"When I what?'' he urged when she broke off, leaving a violent silence between them.

Leah yanked the blanket to her chest, knocking his hand aside as she struggled to sit up. "When you never even gave a damn about what happened to me or the baby.''

The accusation made Zach feel sucker punched. "Is that what you think? Is that what you've thought all these years? That I didn't care?''

"What should I have thought? You just walked away and...''

"Because that's the way you wanted it,'' he shouted. He couldn't help shouting, he was that incensed. He sat up, too, but with less care to see that the blanket remained in place. He'd always found it a lot easier to bare his body than his soul. "You made it clear that you didn't want any part of me.''

"I did no such thing,'' exclaimed Leah, her shock genuine. "I only said that I wasn't ready to get married and raise a child....''

"Seemed like the same thing to me. Especially since it was my child you were talking about.''

"Well, it wasn't the same thing...not at all. Think about it, Zach,'' she pleaded, curling her fingers over his forearm in a way he found very reassuring in spite of his anger. "I made a mistake, *we* made a mistake, but I still needed you. Maybe I should have thought about the consequences before we made love, before I got pregnant.'' She gave a bitter laugh. "No maybe about it. I should have been more careful. I wish to God I had been, but what happened, happened, and I handled it in the way I thought was right at the time. I tried to make you understand that. You were the one who said that unless I went against my own better judgment and gave in to what you wanted, that it was over for us."

"I didn't mean it that way. I was hurt and mad...and desperate. I saw everything I ever wanted slipping away and I just wanted to make you change your mind." He leaned his head back against the wall behind him, closing his eyes briefly as all that old pain washed over him. "It didn't work...and I didn't know what the hell to do next."

"You could have at least called me," she said.

The words, uttered in a soft, injured tone, brought back to Zach memories of all the times he'd picked up a phone to call her in the months and years afterward, and all the times he'd chickened out. The acrid taste of self-loathing filled his mouth. He was such a hotshot cop, not afraid to chase an armed gunman down a dark alley, not afraid of anything. But he had been afraid to hear Leah say outright that she no longer wanted him, that he wasn't worth wanting. And in a way, he still was.

That was the real reason he'd issued that ridiculous ultimatum, insisting to her that it was either marriage and the baby or nothing. It had been a preemptive strike. Deep down he'd been scared to death that Leah blamed him for everything and had either stopped loving him already or soon would.

"...never even called to ask about the baby," she was saying, "or to ask if I was all right."

"I knew you were all right. I did ask...I just didn't ask you." He took a deep breath. He was thirty-two years old for God's sake. Plenty old enough to stop hedging all his bets. "The truth is, Leah, that I was afraid to talk to you, afraid to hear you come right out and say that you didn't want any part of me."

"How could you even think that?" she demanded, with a slow shake of her head that made her hair flutter in the moonlight and made Zach think of how soft it had felt against his face and how it had smelled like lavender and wood smoke...like Leah. "We were so close back then," she reminded him.

"Yeah, well, back then I was real used to people close to me not wanting to be bothered."

"You're talking about your father."

"No, actually I don't want to talk about him. I've worked it out as much as I'm ever going to. I've accepted that his work was more important to him than anything else, certainly more important to him than I ever was, and that he let himself be hoodwinked by my stepmother into thinking everything on the home front was just hunky-dory no matter how much I tried to let him know otherwise."

"You never said much about your stepmother...about how things were with her at home."

Zach shrugged, his mouth settling into a grim smile. "Yeah, well, by the time I met you I was old enough to be out of the house most of the time and there wasn't much to tell. It was different when I was younger, right after my mother died."

He felt her hand sliding over his back in a slow circular caress and he sensed himself relaxing in spite of himself.

"It's not too late to talk about it now," she said.

"Yes, it is. It is absolutely too late. That's one thing I've learned. Besides," he said, "it was stupid stuff. Kid stuff. Nothing that would sound like any big deal now. She just always managed to make me feel like the outsider in my own house."

Leah nodded. "I always sensed that she somehow favored her own kids in subtle ways."

"And in not-so-subtle ones," he added, the raw memory of that time much closer to the surface than he had realized, too close to shut off now that he'd started. "Except when my father was around, of course. And even then he was too preoccupied with his own thoughts to much notice what was going on with me."

"Once," he said, reluctantly sliding back into memories he hadn't probed in a long time, memories of the days when all the enemies in his life—his stepmother and her son and daughter who were both close to him in age—had lived under the same roof with him, "when I was in the sixth grade we all had to do science projects. I remember how she made sure that their backboards were done just right, with all the letters even and perfectly cut out. She didn't offer to help with mine, though," he continued, aware of the hard edge that crept into his voice. "Which suited me just fine, because I didn't want her help. I didn't want anything from her."

"I did the project all on my own. It was on magnetism and it took me weeks, but in the end it was worth it. Mine was the best of the three of them. I knew it and they all knew it, too."

"That doesn't surprise me. I can't imagine anything you couldn't be the best at if you put your mind to it."

Zach flashed a quick smile in response to the affectionate humor in her remark before sinking back into the past. "I knew my project would win first place and I couldn't wait, because my father would have to acknowledge that."

"And did you win?"

"Nope. It was raining the day we had to bring our projects in and she couldn't fit everything in the car. Of course there was no time to make two trips because she had a hairdresser's appointment or something. So she shoved my backboard in, handed me the box with my report and samples and said she was sure I wouldn't mind walking."

"In the rain?"

"Only a little sprinkle according to her. I was still soaked through to the skin when I got there, along with my report and the stuff in the box. I didn't even want to set it up alongside everyone else's."

"How awful for you. I can imagine how you felt after all your hard work."

"What I felt was mad as hell, at her and at my old man for letting it happen to me."

"What did he say when you told him what happened?"

"I didn't tell him."

"But, Zach, why?"

"Because it wouldn't have done any good. He never wanted to hear it from me."

"Are you sure about that?" she asked, her touch growing even more gentle. "The way I remember it, you might have tried getting through to your father in your own way, but you never tried talking to him directly about anything that was bothering you."

"I did try talking to him," he protested, then looked away with a weary shake of his head. "I just couldn't do it."

"Like you couldn't call and talk to me?"

Zach forced himself to turn and meet her intent gaze. "Yeah. Just like that."

Her soft laugh of dismay drifted over him.

"Boy," she said, "when it comes to handling our emotions, we're quite a pair, aren't we?"

"With one big difference. I learned from the mistakes in the past. For instance, I learned from my old man exactly the kind of father not to be."

Instantly he sensed a change in Leah. Her wariness was silent, but unmistakable.

"Zach, I know your relationship with your father wasn't all that you wanted it to be..."

Zach snorted, aware of the beat of caution in her every word.

"But," she continued, "if you're trying to draw some comparison between that and the situation between you and our son, you just can't do it."

"Why the hell not? It occurred to me recently that the comparisons between my father and me are way too close for comfort. I'm a lot like him, you know. I've lived for my job, letting it be the center of my life, using it to avoid anything I didn't want to think about or deal with."

"But we did deal with..."

Zach shook his head. He wasn't in the mood to listen. "I finally realized that maybe the reason my old man shut himself off after my mother died was because he couldn't handle that much pain, and maybe I was a part of that pain, so it was easier to simply ignore me, too. And as much as I hated him for it, damned if that isn't exactly what I ended up doing to my own son."

"No, it's different...."

"The hell it is. A father has a responsibility to know what's going on with his kid. More than that, he has a God-given right to know. You can talk till you're blue in the face about the papers you signed and you won't convince me any differently."

"All right, I won't talk about signing papers," conceded Leah. "But I will tell you that I'm sure our son is fine. I'm sure he went to a good home and..."

He looked at her in disbelief and in the split second of hesitation his hard stare caused her, Zach saw that somewhere in her gut, where it counted, she didn't believe what she was saying any more than he did.

"Are you really sure of that, Leah?" he asked, his tone deceptively calm. "Have you got proof that he's fine? That he went to a good home? Because if you do, you just drag it out here for me to see and I promise you I'll go away a happy man. But if you don't," he finished, unable to stop his tone from turning hard, "then just back off."

"What sort of proof could I possibly have?" she countered, shifting to face him so that she was twisted tightly into the blanket. "I went to a reputable agency and . . ."

"And I'm sure their record and their intentions were the best. But I've spent the past ten years on the streets, learning firsthand that even the scum of the earth have what they consider good intentions from time to time."

Leah had leaned forward in her attempt to reason with him. Zach saw the desperate panic in her beautiful eyes. He saw how much she wanted him to leave this alone and for Leah's sake he wished he could, he wished there were some way he could walk away from it. But there wasn't, and she needed to understand that once and for all.

"I have to know my kid is all right, Leah," he said, reaching for his jeans and stepping into them. It suddenly felt as if there wasn't enough air to breath in her bedroom. Not bothering with the snap at the waist, he turned back to face her. "I have to know because six weeks ago I pulled my gun on a thirteen-year-old boy and blew his head off."

Chapter Seven

Zach strode from the room, leaving Leah on the bed, paralyzed with shock. His words seemed to linger in the air, like the echoes of a huge explosion.

Six weeks ago I pulled my gun on a thirteen-year-old boy and blew his head off.

Shock gave way to a dull nauseous feeling. It wasn't possible that Zach had killed a child. It had to be a mistake, a misunderstanding. Even as the desperate thoughts whipped through her brain, Leah knew this wasn't the sort of thing anyone could make a mistake about. And she hadn't misheard or misunderstood him, either. His words had been too brutally blunt for that.

She breathed so deeply it hurt. Zach had meant to be brutal. He had meant to force her to understand why he was so vehement about finding their son. He'd succeeded. She hadn't wanted to encourage Zach by admitting it, but she lived each day of her life with a similar need to know...just to know if her child was all right, if he was happy. How much more frantic that need would be if she were in Zach's position.

I pulled my gun on a thirteen-year-old boy and...

Leah's stomach muscles suddenly clenched so tightly she shook. Bolting from the bed she managed to make it to the bathroom in time to be sick. Afterward she stood gripping the sink, automatically splashing cold water on her face and rinsing her mouth with mouthwash, all the while feeling the razor's touch of the thought that had sent her running in there in the first place. Zach had shot and killed a thirteen-year-old boy.

She grabbed her robe, dragging it on and knotting the belt haphazardly in her hurry to reach him. He was sitting on the sofa in the living room, the lights off, his bent head in his hands.

He looked up when she flicked a lamp on, meeting her gaze with tortured, red-rimmed eyes.

"Made you sick, huh?" he asked. "Don't worry, it made me sick, too."

"Who?" Leah asked, her throat so dry the word was barely audible. "Who was the boy you shot? Zach, you don't think that maybe...?"

She couldn't even say the words.

She didn't have to, because Zach was already shaking his head, his jaw clenched so tightly a muscle at the edge ticked violently.

"No, it wasn't him. I thought of that afterward and I couldn't help myself... I dug through that poor kid's family history until I knew beyond a shadow of a doubt that there was no chance he'd been adopted." He dragged both hands through his long hair and stared up at the ceiling. "I don't know if you can understand this, but even though knowing for sure that it wasn't him was a relief, it didn't make things one damn bit better."

"Of course I can understand," she said, feeling her own version of that contradiction of feelings at that very moment, relief that her son wasn't the one who'd been shot and aching for the child who had been.

"What happened?" she asked. "Can you even stand to talk about it?"

Zach exhaled slowly, pushing the air out as if even breathing hurt. "For weeks afterward I did nothing but talk about it...to the force shrinks and to the guys from IA...Internal Affairs," he explained. "I talked about it all day and I dreamed about it all night, over and over, and even after I was sure I hadn't shot my own kid, I still woke up sweating, thinking I had. Sometimes I still do."

"Oh, Zach..."

"Forget it," he said, shrugging off her touch. "I don't want your pity. I sure as hell don't deserve it."

"It's not pity...it's compassion, and we all need that sometimes."

"The kid's family are the ones who deserve compassion."

Leah sat close beside him, refusing to be discouraged by his sudden stiffening. "I'm sure they do, but my listening to you isn't going to take anything away from them. Talk to me, Zach, tell me what happened."

He didn't reply, but Leah could tell from the way his hands were tightly fisted and the way the cords in his throat rippled, that he was fighting hard for control. She didn't push.

"You want to know what happened?" he said at last. "What happened is that a million bits and pieces of fate all came together in exactly the wrong way."

"I . . ." She wet her lips, searching for the right words, if there even were any right words in a case like this. "You said something about an internal investigation?"

Zach nodded.

"Did they say you were at fault?"

"Not yet. The investigation is still going on, which is why I have so much time on my hands these days. I have been officially relieved from duty pending the decision of the board."

"What do you think they'll decide?"

"I don't know, and I don't much care. I know what I did. I'll have to live with that for the rest of my life regardless of what they decide. If they find it was a justified shoot, they'll reinstate me." He paused, swallowing hard. "I guess in a selfish way, that's what matters most to me . . . the force is my life and I wouldn't know what else to do." He shook his head as if to clear it. "That matters and finding my son matters."

"I think maybe I understand that better now, too . . . really I do," she added at his sideways glance of skepticism. "But what happens if the board decides it wasn't a . . . What did you call it? A justified shoot?"

"Right. If that happens they'll hand the whole matter over to the state's attorney and he'll probably charge me with manslaughter."

"Oh, Zach, no . . . I can't believe you could ever, ever hurt anybody intentionally, especially not a child. I know, I know, you're a cop and cops are supposed to be tough and all, but I know in my heart that you're not guilty of anything besides what you called it a minute ago . . . an act of fate."

His bleak expression grew wry. "That's not what you said that first night when I told you the years we've been apart didn't change the fact that I know you inside out."

"Well," Leah said, shrugging, "I was wrong. I guess some things don't change after all."

Zach nodded and reached for her hand, gripping it tightly. "You'll probably never know what it means to me to hear you say that right now."

"I mean it . . . everything I said. As awful as this is, you can't blame yourself for it."

"I can't *not* blame myself," he countered. "I was the one who fired the gun. But in a strictly rational sense—if it's possible to be rational about a thing like this—I know that I did what I had to do at the time. If I didn't know that, if I didn't believe it in my gut, I couldn't live with myself."

Leah nodded. "If you'd rather not talk about this, I understand. But if you want to tell me about what happened that night, I want to hear it."

Staring down at their joined hands, Zach nodded. It was several minutes before he spoke.

"When I said that about fate," he began, "I was referring to all the coincidences that came together that night . . . like the fact that my partner and I weren't supposed to be on duty, that we weren't supposed to be in the place we were when that call came in, that even then we didn't have to answer it and probably wouldn't have except for the fact that it was in the same direction as my partner's place and he wanted an excuse to swing by and apologize to his wife for a fight they never should have had." He paused and shook his head. "Dozens of things that shouldn't have happened did."

"You had no control of that," Leah pointed out.

"No, but I should have had better control over the situation." He shook his head again, and Leah had the impression that no matter how many times he relived this night, it still held an aura of unreality for him, like a horror movie too preposterous to be real.

"Anyway," he said after a minute, "this kid—his name was Ricky—was mixed up with a gang, older guys, some not even juveniles, and all of them real trouble, characters that we dealt with all the time…on drug busts, shootings, armed robberies, you name it. They'd stolen a car earlier that night and held up a convenience store. Par for the course with this bunch, except this time when they were making their getaway, they mowed down an old lady who was crossing the street."

"Was she hurt?"

"Not too badly from the accident itself, but she had a heart attack in the emergency room. She died later."

"My God," Leah said, shuddering, "what a tragedy all the way around."

"Yeah, well, most tragedies are like that. We heard the radio call on it and like I told you, we decided to take it. It didn't take long for us to spot their vehicle, but as soon as they made us, they ditched the car and bailed out. My partner and I took off after two of them, then lost one when he disappeared into an abandoned building. We stayed with his pal, Ricky, and eventually chased him into an alley. He fired at us from the shadows and that was the first we knew he was armed."

"So you fired back?"

Zach shook his head. "Not then. We radioed in our position and requested backup. Jack—that's my partner—wanted to wait for them to get there, but I wanted to go in, take him before he got lucky and slipped away up a fire escape or out through one of the buildings. And since I have—or had—a reputation for having great instincts, he agreed to do it my way. We went after him."

Leah noticed that his words had grown clipped and tense. She reached out and touched his shoulder lightly, silently telling him that she would wait or listen or hold him or do whatever he needed her to do.

"About a third of the way down the alley, Jack tripped over a trash can...a trash can that didn't even belong there," he added with grim sarcasm. "The crash spooked the kid and he fired again. I saw his shadow moving... Hell, it looked immense on the wall in that dark alley. I didn't know he was just a scared kid, I only knew he had a gun pointed at my partner's head and I fired before he had another chance to."

He trembled as Leah instinctively moved closer.

"I fired once," he said, "and he was dead before he hit the ground."

"You had no choice, Zach," Leah said softly. "It was either him or your partner."

"Yeah, right, except that the kid had never even held a gun before that night. He probably couldn't have hit the side of a barn."

"But you couldn't have known that at the time," she protested.

"I didn't," Zach agreed, but sounding as if he believed he should have known. "God help me, I didn't. If I had known it was a kid...if I could only go back to that night and do it over."

He hunched forward. "Afterward, when we finally managed to find out who the kid was, and that was tough to do since he wasn't even old enough to be carrying any ID, we went to his house. I insisted on being there when they broke the news...I had to be there. His old man answered the door, stinking drunk, and told us he didn't even know the kid was still out, thought he'd gone to bed hours ago."

Leah felt the tension that gripped him.

"I looked at that wheezing old son of a bitch and I had nothing but contempt for him...and it wasn't until much later, one night when I was staring into my own bleary eyes in the bathroom mirror, that I understood that as rotten a father as that guy was, I was a hundred times worse."

"Please, Zach...it's not the same. Surely you can see—"

He turned to her, his look silencing her instantly. "Save your breath, Leah. I know what I am, and I know what I have to do."

She looked into his eyes and nodded. Without saying anything more she stood and crossed to the bookcase, climbing up on the ottoman that was still there. She took the box down and reached inside, then stopped at her desk and hurriedly wrote something on a piece of notepaper.

She walked back to Zach and handed it to him.

"Here. This is the name of the place I stayed when I was pregnant and the name of the attorney who actually handled things for me. It's in Virginia. I don't know the street address...they didn't exactly encourage us to keep in touch. I have no idea if the place is still there. I understand that a lot of these homes have been closed since then. I guess attitudes have changed and..." She stopped long enough to quell the ache in her throat. "I hope it helps you do what you have to do," she continued when she felt she could. "Maybe this will help, too."

She slipped the photograph of their son from the envelope and handed it to Zach, who took it with trembling fingers and a look of almost reverent amazement that Leah knew she would cherish forever.

"It's the only picture I have of him, so if you could take care of it..."

"I will," he said, his tone filled with awe. "I won't let anything happen to it, I promise you, Leah."

He looked up at her and Leah believed him with every-thing that was in her. Part of her wished she had been able to believe in him that way fourteen years ago.

"Isn't he beautiful?" she whispered as Zach's gaze returned to the portrait in his hand.

He moved his head, beyond words for what he was feeling. Leah knew how that felt. After a long time he placed the picture carefully on the table beside him, stood and reached for her.

"I mean it," he said, "I promise you that I won't let anything bad happen to him. Or to you."

Leah nodded, her eyes stinging with unshed tears as she allowed him to pull her close. He held her for a long time, neither of them needing words to understand exactly what the other was feeling at that moment. Eventually he kissed her cheeks, where tears had left silent tracks, and then her closed eyelids and finally her mouth, and slowly, slowly comfort turned to desire. This time, as he gently pulled her down to the sofa, their lovemaking was less rushed. Their caresses were lush and lingering, their kisses seeming to wind on forever.

As if, thought Leah before she ceased thinking entirely, as if they had only this one night to make up for all those lost years.

To Leah's surprise, this turned out to be her best Christmas in a long, long time. Not merry exactly, but satisfying and not marred by the loneliness of so many in the past. On Christmas morning they made love and ate a breakfast of cinnamon coffee and hastily defrosted cranberry muffins and made love again. They curled up together to watch *It's a Wonderful Life* on television and Zach took her totally by surprise again later, when he pulled from his jacket pocket a small package wrapped in silver paper and tied with a wide red bow and handed it to her.

"A present?" she asked, feeling both excited and awkward. "But, Zach, I don't..."

"If you dare to say you don't have anything for me, after everything you've given me in past twenty-four hours, I'll..."

"Yes?" she prodded teasingly.

"I'll think of a very creative way to punish you."

Leah's mouth quirked thoughtfully. "That sounds almost too tempting to resist."

"Witch," he growled, kissing her quickly. "Open your present."

Leah carefully peeled away the ribbon and paper to find a box from a local department store. Inside was a Christmas tree ornament, a crystal angel so delicate it appeared to be made of spun glass.

"Zach, it's beautiful," she said, holding it up so that the sunlight streaming through the window created a prism effect.

"Yeah, well, I was shopping for presents for Adam and Sam's folks and I just happened to come across it. It reminded me of the other night when you lay down in the snow."

He shoved his hands into his pockets, ill at ease in a way Leah found amazing...and incredibly sexy. But then, lately everything about Zach seemed to have that effect on her.

"I'll always think of that night when I look at it."

"I sort of hoped that if I gave it to you, you might break down and get a tree next year so you would have someplace to hang it."

Leah dropped her gaze to the angel in her hands.

"Leah, I meant it when I said I wanted to fix everything so that you can make a fresh start...so that every Christmas for the rest of your life is as good as you deserve for it to be."

"Maybe," she said softly, "they already are as good as I deserve."

Zach shook her lightly. "That's bull. Maybe some things that happened in the past were mistakes, maybe not. Either way I believe we can make things better if we're willing to. I have to believe that."

Leah heard the desperation in his voice and for his sake, she forced a smile as she looked up at him.

"So tell me, Blackmore, what did you get the Costellos for Christmas?"

"A new toaster oven."

"And Adam?"

"A service station for his matchbox cars."

"I see, and where did you just happen to come across this angel? In toys or housewares?"

He grinned unabashedly. "So maybe I didn't just happen to see it. As an officer of the law, I can tell you unequivocally that it's no crime to turn the city inside out looking for the right present for the woman you love."

Leah's eyes widened. It was the first time since he'd arrived, cold and rain-soaked, at her door last night that either of them had said anything that might remotely conjure up thoughts of their future or what might happen between them when the holiday ended and real life resumed. She fiddled nervously with the gold chain around her throat, not knowing whether to be thrilled or alarmed by his statement.

"Don't worry," he said dryly, before she had come up with a response. "It was just a figure of speech." He bent to kiss her lightly, almost clinically, thought Leah. "Merry Christmas, Leah. Now where's your phone book?"

Puzzled, Leah fetched it for him. "There's a phone in the den if you want to make a private call."

"I do want to make a call," he told her, flipping to the yellow pages. "But it's not private. What's your favorite restaurant?"

"Why?"

"Because if I have to drink one more cup of coffee with cinnamon or raspberry or maple syrup or—"

"I never served you coffee with maple syrup," she interjected indignantly.

"No? Hard to tell . . . they all become a sticky sweet blur after the first couple of cups. Anyway, I figure there has to be a restaurant in this city open on Christmas where we can have dinner and get a decent cup of coffee."

There was, although it wasn't one she was familiar with and Zach had to do some expensive bargaining to get them a table at the last minute on a holiday. Dinner was wonderful and relaxing. Neither of them dwelt on the sadness that touched their lives so deeply, but for once Leah didn't feel as if she had to keep it all locked away inside her, either. She was free to say to Zach whatever she was thinking. Even more of a blessing was the fact that some things she didn't even have to say to know that he understood. They meshed that perfectly.

That's probably why the next morning was so jarring for each of them. Zach woke before Leah, showering first so that he was waiting, sipping a cup of the instant coffee he'd driven to a nearby convenience store to pick up, when she finally joined him in the kitchen.

He was dressed in jeans and the dark cotton shirt she'd washed and ironed for him. He whistled at the sight of her.

"I was going to complain about how long it took you to get dressed in the morning, but I've changed my mind."

Leah shot him a look as she poured her juice. "Figure it was worth the wait, huh, Blackmore?"

"And then some. But are you going to be comfortable driving in that getup?"

She glanced down at the getup in question, a forest green wool suit with a short tapered skirt and a jacket nipped at the waist. "I think I'll manage. After all, my office is only about ten minutes away."

"Your office?" His mug hit the table with a thud. "What are you talking about?"

"I'm talking about going to work," replied Leah, a different sort of thud taking place in her belly. "What are you talking about?"

"I'm not sure . . . wishful thinking it looks like."

"What exactly were you thinking?"

"I thought that after all that happened the past couple of days, and after you gave me the name of the home and attorney and the picture . . . I assumed that . . ."

"You assumed what?" Leah prompted, aware of the defensiveness in her tone.

"I assumed that you'd be coming with me today when I went to check this place out. I *assumed* we were in this together."

"I never said that," she countered more harshly than she intended.

"That's right. You didn't. Silly me." He stood and carried his mug to the sink and rinsed it.

"I'm sorry if you misunderstood," she said to his broad back. "I never meant to suggest that I . . . God, Zach, please listen to me. I understand now why you feel you have to do this, please try to understand why I can't."

"You mean," he said, turning to her with an unreadable expression, "that you're willing to give me the information I need to find our son, but you don't want any part of it."

"Not exactly," she replied, crossing her arms tightly in front of her.

"Then what exactly do you want? Do you want me to let you know if I find him?"

"I... Yes, I think I'd want to know that much at least."

"How about where I find him? Do you want to know that, too? What about his name? Do you want to see pictures of him?" He went on, firing questions too fast for her to respond. "Do you want to meet him?"

"No." At last there was a question she didn't have to think about before answering. "That wouldn't be fair to him now and...and to meet him and have to give him up again... I think it would just make everything harder for me."

"Yeah, I guess maybe it might at that." He levered away from the counter where he'd been leaning, his careless pose not fooling her a bit. He was about as carefree as a ticking bomb. "Thanks," he said as he moved past her at a safe distance. "For...everything."

Leah hurried out of the kitchen after him, her heart hammering wildly as she watched him pull on his jacket and head for the front door.

"Zach, wait," she cried.

He stopped and turned slowly. "For what?"

"I don't want you to leave this way."

"Why not? Leaving this way makes me feel right at home...not to mention stupid. What's that saying? Fool me twice, shame on me. So long, Leah."

For the next week or so, Zach dedicated himself to the search for his son as if there was nothing else in his life worth a damn. Which pretty much summed up matters, he thought glumly as he sat and waited his turn at the Department of Catholic Services in Charlotte, North Carolina. He had a job that he loved and would probably never be able to do again, and a woman he loved who had burned him twice.

Great track record, Blackmore, what do you plan to do for an encore?

Charge in and mess up the life of another innocent kid.

The thought came out of nowhere, unbidden and unwanted. Years of practice made him an expert at not thinking about things he'd rather not and he would definitely rather not think about all the things that could go wrong with his plan even if his search was successful. Especially if his search was successful.

He pushed aside the impending second thoughts and concentrated instead on the route his search had followed thus far and where he hoped to be after his meeting with Elaine Baker, director of services here in Charlotte.

His thoughts focused on where that route began. Even without a street address it hadn't been difficult for him to locate the Good Shepherd Home For Unwed Mothers. It was located in Virginia, as Leah had told him, in a small town outside of Williamsburg. And it had been closed for over five years.

He'd parked his rental car in the driveway overgrown with weeds and spent a long time walking around the building, speculating about which of the windows in the rambling three-story structure might have been Leah's room when she was here, trying to imagine what it had been like for her to spend all those months here, pregnant and alone, knowing that when it was all over she would be leaving without her baby. *Their* baby.

For a long time he'd allowed himself to believe that Leah was ambitious and self-centered enough not to care about giving away her baby. He'd *needed* to believe that. Deep down, however, that nice safe explanation for why she'd made the choice she had never really squared with his knowledge of Leah and the kind of person she was. Now, after spending time with her again, he couldn't ignore how wrong he'd been all these years.

No matter what he'd said to her or tried to tell himself after storming out of her house the other day, he knew that deep down Leah was running scared. It wasn't that she didn't care about their son or want to know all about him. She wanted to know so badly that whenever the subject came up he could feel the craving coming off her like the heat waves that shimmer in the air on a steamy summer day. But no matter how much she longed to know, her fear was even stronger. She was afraid to find out that she had made a mistake by giving him up. And Zach was at the exact opposite end of the spectrum, afraid of what might happen if he didn't find out.

The Good Shepherd Home might have been a more appealing place when it was open. As he stood there staring up at the vacant windows, Zach had sure hoped so, for Leah's sake and the sake of all the girls who had wound up there. Now, deserted and ill kept, it had an aura of sadness. How many tears were shed in those empty rooms, Zach couldn't help wondering. How many hearts broken? How many lives ruined by a single good intention?

As he drove away he passed a group of young girls walking a few blocks away. They were laughing, their long hair blowing in the breeze, all of them wearing brightly colored jackets and mittens and hats. Most likely Christmas presents, Zach thought. The girls reminded him of Leah at their age, and at the risk of being taken for a pervert, he slowed and watched them in his rearview mirror with a sorrow that grew steadily stronger.

They looked so young, he thought. As if there was nothing more important in their lives than homework and parties, nothing more potentially disastrous than a pimple on prom night. Had Leah really been that young when she was

forced to make a choice that they would both have to live
with for the rest of their lives? Realizing that she had been
had put things in a new perspective for Zach.

With each step of his search since then, his understanding of the ordeal she had endured became clearer, his compassion for her deeper, the need to reach out and comfort
her more overwhelming. He wanted to call her and tell her
that everything was going to be all right and a dozen times
he'd stopped himself in the act of doing just that. The trouble was, that for a lot of reasons, he had no right to tell Leah
any such thing. He certainly had no right to go making her
any more promises.

Acting on a hunch, he had gone from the now defunct
Home to the rectory of the local Catholic church. The pas-
tor, Father Halloran, had told him more about the Home's
history than he really wanted to know. He'd also told Zach
that he recalled that the Home's records had been moved to
another location, he just couldn't quite think where that
was. After a lengthy visit, he ended up referring Zach to the
bishop's office, where a much less talkative assistant had
informed him that the records were now kept at the
Diocese's Department of Children and Families. *Children
and Families.* It struck Zach as highly ironic, but then, he
supposed it all depended on your definition of *family*.

The woman he spoke to there was pleasant and helpful,
although she did take pains to point out that Zach's search
was illicit. He smiled his most winning smile and clamped
down on the urge to tell her that "illicit" was often a matter of opinion.

She told him there was very little in the files maintained
by the home, other than a record of the mother's health,
weight gain during pregnancy, things like that. Was Zach
still interested? she asked. He was, the sudden urge to share
in what he hadn't been allowed to share in at the time made

him want to push her aside and go plowing through the boxes of old records himself. Only the patience acquired from years of wading through departmental red tape held him in his seat, chatting politely with the woman.

She took Leah's name and telephone number and promised to call and speak with her about signing a release that would enable her to send Zach a copy of the file. She also gave him the name of the agency in Charlotte, North Carolina, that had handled the actual adoptions.

Zach had driven straight through, checking into a motel in that city and killing time until his appointment here late this afternoon. Along the way it had occurred to him that he should have thought to get a letter of release from Leah before leaving Rhode Island. At the time, however, he hadn't been thinking of anything so logical. He also hadn't been in any mood to ask her for another favor and give her another chance to shoot him down....

"Mr. Blackmore?" The voice intruded into his thoughts.

Zach tossed aside the magazine he'd been flipping through and glanced up at the tall slender woman standing before him.

"That's right. Ms. Baker?" he countered, getting quickly to his feet.

"Yes, I'm Elaine Baker. Won't you come in?" She turned, indicating the open office door at the end of a short hallway and Zach followed. Elaine Baker looked to be in her late forties. She was a soft kind of pretty, with short gray hair and a nice smile. For no good reason other than a cop's gift for hunches, he had the sensation he was about to get a break.

Once they were seated in her pleasantly cluttered office, she smiled that nice smile across the desk at him and said, "So, Mr. Blackmore, what can I do for you?"

She listened attentively, asking only a few questions and jotting down his replies, as Zach told her his reason for being there and as much as he knew about Leah's stay at the Home and the adoption . . . which, he realized in the telling, was depressingly little.

"I have to tell you, Mr. Blackmore," she said when he was finished, "it is rare indeed to have a birth father come here in search of his child."

Birth father. Zach turned the words over in his mind, cognizant for the first time that there was a name for what he was. For her to utter the term so easily must also mean that there were other birth fathers in existence. He wasn't the only one who had ever felt the way he was feeling. Others—few, she had said, but others nonetheless—had traveled this path before him. Needing to know the same things he needed to know, asking the same questions. Somehow just knowing that Zach felt reassured that there would be answers.

"I guess it's mostly mothers who come looking?" he asked.

"That's right. I find it very commendable that you feel a strong enough connection to your child to want to find him or her."

"Him. It was . . . *is* . . . a boy. A son."

Her smile was gentle. "I see. I'm afraid, however, that whether it's a mother or father who is searching for information, there is really very little I can tell them. You see North Carolina law prohibits disclosure."

Zach sensed the hopefulness he'd felt walking here begin to slip away. "Just my luck."

"I'm afraid so. There are states where adoption records are easier to obtain. Unfortunately, this isn't one of them. You're sure your son was placed through this agency?"

"Truthfully, Ms. Baker, I'm not sure of anything any-more...except that I need to find out for myself what happened to my kid."

She pressed her lips together as she studied him, then pushed her chair back from her desk. Zach was afraid she was about to end their meeting when instead she said, "Let me go check the files and see what I can find. I don't break rules," she informed him in a warning tone. "Not ever. But there are easy ways and hard ways to go about what you're doing. Perhaps I can... Well, first let's see what I find, shall we?"

She excused herself and was gone for about twenty minutes. Zach paced the small office while he waited, unable to shake the feeling that something big was about to happen. Ms. Baker looked like a rule follower all right, but she also looked kind. Zach had the feeling she understood how desperate he was and wanted to help. How far could she be nudged? he wondered.

When she returned she was holding a manila folder in her hand. It was slim and crisp, as if it hadn't been touched very often in the past fourteen years. Zach knew that the condition of the folder was no reflection on what his son's life had been like all those years, but as happened so often lately, the sight filled him with a heavy, inexplicable sense of loss.

Ms. Baker reclaimed her seat behind the desk and waited expectantly until Zach forced himself to also sit. Again he fought the urge to lean across the desk and take matters into his own hands.

"The information is encoded," Ms. Baker said, eyeing him assessingly.

Zach shot her a questioning look.

"The information on your son and the adoption is all encoded in this file...so that even if someone were to snatch it off my desk, it wouldn't be of any use to them."

"The thought did cross my mind," Zach admitted with a shrug. "But I wouldn't do it."

"Good," she countered in that soft drawl that made everything she said sound like a flowery compliment. "Then we can work together. What you're endeavoring to do isn't impossible, Mr. Blackmore, it simply isn't easy. A search can be very roundabout and time-consuming."

"How time-consuming?" he asked, thinking how little he may have before the board wrapped up its investigation.

"It depends . . . It could take many years or as little as a few weeks. I've seen it work both ways."

"Weeks I've got."

"I'd say that to do it in that short a time span you need to be very lucky and you need to be ready." She held his gaze as if that had been a question.

"I am ready," replied Zach.

"Good."

She carefully opened the folder before her. Zach held his breath, feeling as if she somehow held his whole life in her hands.

"As I told you already," she said, "I can't reveal a great deal. I can tell you that there was no contact with this agency after the first year . . . which is normal," she explained, glancing up briefly.

"A year? Does that mean that if anything had happened to him after that, you wouldn't have anything in your records about it?"

"Exactly. The adoption itself was finalized in the normal amount of time, and after that there was no need for us to make further inquiries or request reports from social workers. At the time of last contact he was reported to be a happy, well-adjusted baby boy."

Happy and well adjusted. A small piece of the fear Zach had been carrying around with him was chipped away by those words. So at least as a one-year-old he had been happy and well adjusted, whatever the hell that meant for a one-year-old. One down and thirteen to go, thought Zach.

"What else does it say?" he asked her.

She furrowed her brow as she read the typewritten lines of code. "He had a hernia repair done at a little under a year."

Zach's heart wrenched. Poor kid. Who had held him afterward? Who had rocked him and told him everything was going to be all right? Had anyone? And what was he doing thirteen years ago at the moment his own son was being operated on? He had no idea, of course. At the time it had just been one more unremarkable day in his unremarkable life. And somehow that made him feel even worse.

"I can also tell you that he went to a warm and loving family," she continued, her voice growing even gentler it seemed to Zach, as if she sensed his pain. "The parents were described as outgoing, intelligent and well educated."

Great, thought Zach. But how about kind and wise and dedicated enough to know where their son—his son—was at night? He immediately felt like a heel for even thinking it. Whoever these intelligent and well-educated people were, they had done what he hadn't, given his son a home. He owed them for that and he would never forget it.

"The adoptive mother is reported to have said that she felt 'so very blessed' to have him. At one year he had dark brown hair and deep blue eyes and a small cleft in his chin." She glanced up quickly, as if realizing she had just given a thumbnail sketch of the man seated across from her. "And I'm afraid that's as much as I am permitted to tell you."

"As much as you're permitted to tell me," Zach echoed grimly. "Meaning you know more. Do you have his name there? The name of the family he went to? Where they live?"

She nodded, her expression somber.

Zach blew out through his clenched teeth and got up, not to leave, just to burn off some of the tension inside.

"I am sorry, Mr. Blackmore," she said quietly. "I do have some understanding of how frustrating this is for you . . . believe me, it is frustrating for me, as well. Adoption is often a blessing, but even in the best situations it has far-reaching repercussions. I deal with those repercussions on a daily basis."

"I'm a cop," Zach told her, his head tipped back so that he was studying the ceiling. "I understand the value of laws." He turned back to her. "But this just doesn't make sense to me."

"Or to me sometimes," she confessed.

"What if my son wants to know about me and about his real mother as much as we want to know about him?"

Her smile was a gentle rebuff. "From my experience with adoptees I can tell you that in all likelihood your son feels he already does know his 'real' mother. She is the mother who raised him."

Zach nodded, accepting the body blow her words delivered. "You're right, of course. I guess I should have referred to her as his birth mother."

"The fact is that even if you and your son's birth mother were in one room and he and his adoptive mother were in another, all wanting to be reunited, I still couldn't do anything to help you all. State law forbids it."

"Tell me what state law doesn't forbid," demanded Zach impatiently, slamming his hands on her desk and bracing himself on them. "You must be able to tell me something, do something, that will make this a little less like searching for a needle in a haystack."

"Off the record I can give you the name and number of an organization, a 'mutual consent' registry that tries to match searchers, whether they be birth parents, adoptees, or adoptive parents. Officially, the best I can do is to include a letter from you in the file, in case your son ever does contact us. You can't include any name or address or anything too specific. I know it's not much," she said when he made a sound of disgust. "But it's something that might someday encourage him to keep searching."

"Thanks. I don't mean to sound ungrateful."

"You don't. You might want to take some time to think about what you want to say to him in the letter. You can send it to my attention whenever you like."

Zach nodded, thinking instantly of Leah. Maybe she, too, would want to say something to their son.

"... which means your letter will remain in the file permanently," she was continuing to explain. "The only exception to the rule would be if there were a medical reason. Then I would be obligated to contact your son's adoptive parents. Is there a medical reason, Mr. Blackmore?"

Zach had been lost in thoughts of Leah's reaction to all this and only half listening. Her last words snared his complete attention however.

"A medical reason?"

She nodded. "A potential problem, something hereditary perhaps, something it would be helpful for his family to know. At the same time I contact them to relay that information, I could possibly mention your desire for news about your son. Of course it would be up to them what they choose to—"

"A melanoma?" Zach interrupted, unable to curb his excitement. "My father died recently, but in the last year he had several bouts with skin cancer... all diagnosed as melanoma. Does that sort of thing count?"

"I'm sure that counts," Ms. Baker told him. She reached for a notepad. "Now you tell me everything you can about your father's condition. I'll need to know his doctor's name and where he can be reached for verification, everything you can think of.''

Zach's heart soared. It counted. At last something he could provide counted for something. That didn't guarantee anything, of course, but it was another step in the right direction. Slowly he told her everything he could recall about his father's illness, promising to forward her the doctor's name and any other specifics as soon as possible. How ironic that it should be because of his father that he was allowed to make even this roundabout gesture to his son.

For a long time after he'd thanked Ms. Baker and left her office Zach stood outside, leaning against the rented car and staring up at the darkening sky overhead. No matter how long he stood there or how hard he thought, however, he still couldn't think of the right words to say. Maybe he never would. Just the same, as he drove back to his motel room Zach felt closer to his father than he had in a long, long time.

Chapter Eight

"There," said Leah, depositing the finished version of the daycare piece on Bud Hirsch's desk. "Signed, sealed and absolutely wonderful—if I do say so myself—and in spite of all the last-minute interference. I hope you're happy."

"That would make one of us," Bud called after her as she made a hasty retreat.

Leah stopped at the door of his office and whirled to face him. "What's that supposed to mean?"

"Nothing," Bud countered, all ruddy-cheeked innocence. "Just that you haven't exactly been the epitome of Christmas cheer around here lately."

"Ho ho ho," she snapped. "Is that better? Besides, Christmas is over."

Along with a lot of other things, thought Leah.

"Says who?" Bud clasped his hand to his heart with exaggerated indignation. "Christmas never has to be over in your heart."

"Maybe," she conceded, again turning to leave. "But only if it's there in the first place."

"Come back here," Bud bellowed after her.

Leah stopped, keeping her back to him.

"Please," he bellowed just as loudly.

She stepped back inside his office reluctantly, leaning on the open door. "What is it?"

"You tell me." He leaned back in his chair with a sigh. "Ah, hell, Leah, in my own inept, but well-meaning way I'm trying to help. Obviously something is bothering you. I'm not such a complete clod that I haven't noticed in the past that this isn't your favorite time of year, but this year seems to be different, worse somehow. Am I right?"

Leah shrugged, idly tracing a ridge in the door molding with her fingertip to avoid meeting his searching gaze. Bud was a good friend and the concern in his voice had been too genuine for Leah to do what she felt like doing, walking out and ignoring his inquiry the same way she'd been desperately trying to ignore her own feelings.

"I guess this year has been worse," she admitted finally, "and better." She managed a droll smile. "Does that make sense?"

"No. Want to talk about it?"

She shook her head. "I can't, Bud. This is something very... close to me. It's only recently I've even been able to let myself think about it. I'm not ready to talk yet, not to anyone."

"In that case, you want a drink?"

This time Leah's smile came more easily. He looked so lovably ill at ease in this role of would-be confidant, his big hand poised on the handle of the drawer where he kept a bottle of twenty-four-year-old Scotch, as if he sincerely hoped that Leah would opt for the brand of comfort he was best at dispensing.

Again she shook her head. "I don't think so, but watch out, some night when I am ready to talk I'll probably drain whatever's left of that good stuff you keep hidden."

"It'd be worth it," Bud replied, "if it meant seeing you smile around here again."

She smiled then, just for him. "Thanks, Bud...and don't worry, I'll work it out just fine."

"Just as long as you know I'm here if... You know, if you ever do need an ear."

"Gotcha," she said. "By the way, would you mind if I cut out a little early this afternoon? I promised the father of a friend that I would drop off some information I have on daycare centers specializing in caring for Alzheimer's patients. I think it might eventually work into a nice follow-up on the current piece."

"Sounds good," agreed Bud, clearly relieved to be back on more familiar conversational terrain. "Take whatever time you need."

Leah hurriedly cleared her desk and grabbed the folder with the information she'd put together to bring to Sam's father. It was getting late and she didn't want to arrive at the Costellos' at dinner time. A phone call and detouring to give some last-minute instructions to one of the interns working on the magazine put her even further behind schedule so that she was almost running when she at last headed for the elevator.

"Please hold it," she called out as she saw the elevator doors begin to slide shut. Just as she was about to mutter a curse about her bad timing, the doors stopped and then slid back open.

"Thanks a lot," Leah said, rushing inside.

"Anytime," replied the woman who had held the elevator for her, the only other passenger.

They exchanged smiles and then, bowing to elevator etiquette, faced the door in silence as they made their slow descent. Leah didn't recall seeing the other woman before, although with all the doctors and lawyers with offices in the building it wasn't unusual to ride the elevator with total strangers.

She was a lot older than Leah, probably in her sixties. That was obvious from the lines and creases on her face and neck. There wasn't a gray hair on her head, however. Her hair was so dark in fact, that it was the first thing you noticed about her. Almost blue-black, it harshly called attention to her face and somehow made the signs of age there more pronounced.

Which Leah was certain was the exact opposite of what the woman intended. She couldn't help thinking how much more flattering a soft shade of brown—or even the gray that was probably her natural shade at this age—would be. It was so obvious, she wondered how such an otherwise stylish woman couldn't see that for herself, and she vowed that as she grew older she would accept the signs of aging gracefully and not take extreme measures to hide them.

Leaving the elevator, Leah hurried to her car and managed to make it to the Costellos' in record time.

Mr. Costello greeted her at the door. "I didn't want you to have to ring the bell," he explained in a hushed tone. "Adam and his grandmother are both taking naps."

"Then I won't bother you," Leah countered, preparing to hand him the folder and leave. "I know you probably don't get much time to yourself."

"Bother me?" He looked incredulous. "A visit from a beautiful young woman is never a bother. The fact is," he added, his smile sheepish, "I could use the company. Will you have a cup of tea with me?"

"I'd love it," said Leah.

She had called earlier to make sure that today was a good day for her to stop by and she was touched to see that he was all ready for her visit. The table was set with what looked like their best china and a doily-lined plate of cupcakes. The water for the tea was keeping warm on the stove.

"Mr. Costello, you are truly amazing. I'm not sure my father could make himself a cup of tea, never mind set such a lovely table for a guest."

"Oh, he might just surprise you if he ever had the chance. Of course I did have an advantage in learning from the best. In her day, my Grace was quite a hostess. Why, when folks stopped by unexpected, she could throw together a meal from whatever was on the shelf and make them feel they were eating like royalty. And give her a few weeks' notice and she'd put on a spread that would knock your eye out...and do every bit of it herself, too. Gracie was never one to call a caterer. She even crocheted her own table-cloths and doilies, like that one right there." He nodded at the plate in the center of the table. "She was something, all right."

"I'm sure she was," said Leah, deeply moved not only by the love with which he spoke of his wife, but by the absolute lack of bitterness. She couldn't imagine how she would handle herself in his situation, but she prayed she would have just a fraction of his grace and generosity.

"Will you listen to me?" he said, shaking his head. "Rambling on about the past. No one's interested in hearing about an old man's memories." He glanced at her quickly as he poured the tea. "Except maybe Adam."

"You're wrong, Mr. Costello, I love hearing you talk about your memories."

"You're a nice girl, Leah. Have a cupcake."

She smiled and took one. "How is Adam?"

"Fine. Better than fine. He's hell on wheels, if you want the truth, and giving his old Gramps more of a run for his money every day."

"I imagine it will make life easier when he can go back to living with Sam."

He nodded, his smile fading. "Easier, and harder, if you know what I mean."

Leah nodded, thinking how similar his remark was to the one she had made to Bud just a while ago. "Yes, I think I know exactly what you mean. You'll miss him."

"Like I would my right hand. But a boy belongs with his father, especially now that Sam's got himself straightened out. 'Course we'll still see plenty of the little fella, and it will give me more time for Grace. That's the most important thing."

"Of course." Leah slid the file across the table to him. "Mr. Costello, this is the information I promised you. You don't have to read it now, there are all sorts of brochures and clippings in there for you to look over when you have some quiet time. I also included names and telephone numbers in case you want to get in touch with one of the centers that I would rate top-notch."

While she was talking, he leafed through the file contents, looking up with a grateful smile. "You went to such a lot of trouble for me. I thank you. And I will take time to go through all of this." His smile wilted. "With every day that passes I know I'm that much closer to the time when I'll have to find some sort of help, but God knows I hate to think that I can't do for my Grace what she needs to have done. The way she would do for me if things were turned around."

Leah impulsively covered his weathered hand with her own. "Don't think that way, Mr. Costello. You are doing everything you can for her. I'm sure that Mrs. Costello would understand that there are limits to what you can handle alone. That's why there are places and professionals out there to help you. It's not wrong to admit you need help.''

''No, not wrong, but it's still plenty hard.''

Leah felt the shudder that ran through him and she understood how hard it was for such a proud man, a man who was used to doing whatever needed to be done to hold his family together, to admit that he couldn't handle it alone any longer.

''But I do know that something has to give somewhere,'' he admitted to her. ''It's getting so I can't leave her alone long enough to do the grocery shopping or pick up her medicine. Something has to give.''

''Maybe if Mrs. Costello was to spend a few mornings a week at one of these centers you would have enough time to do all those things.''

''Maybe.'' He looked up suddenly and the fierce determination in his eyes was also palpable in the tensing of the muscles beneath her fingertips. ''But I'll tell you one thing for sure, I'll never send Grace away to one of those places for good. This here's her home for as long as she lives.''

''Of course,'' Leah murmured, trying not to think about how in the course of looking into this on his behalf, she had heard over and over how frequently a move to a nursing home becomes necessary.

''There are some friends, some *supposed* friends of ours,'' he added, his mouth puckering as if he'd tasted something bitter, ''who've been telling me to do just that, you know, telling me I'm cheating myself out of the best years of my life.''

Leah felt a stab of guilt, thinking how her own thoughts had followed a similar path on her first visit here.

"What those folks don't understand," he went on, "is that Grace is my life. For better or worse, in sickness and health, I said those words nearly fifty years ago and by God I meant every one of them."

"That's a very rare sentiment these days," Leah told him, "and very noble."

"That's just it, I'm not being noble. This is what I want to do with the time I have left. Those doomsday folks will say to me, 'But she's such a burden' and 'She doesn't even know you half the time.' And I suppose that's true enough. There are days when she doesn't know me from the paper boy. But that doesn't matter," he said, his voice losing its angry quiver, growing stronger and more content as he met her eyes with a calm smile. "It doesn't matter a whit, because you see, Leah, I still know her."

Leah blinked back tears as she finished her tea and cupcake. She left a while later, driving away through the gathering darkness as if she was running for her life, as if something big and powerful enough to swallow her whole was right on her tail and closing fast. That something caught up with her at a stoplight a mile away. Leah barely managed to pull through the light and steer her car to the side of the road before her hands began shaking and her eyes filled with tears she couldn't blink away, making it impossible to drive any farther.

Sam's father was a remarkable man, even more remarkable than she had realized before this afternoon. In just one short visit he had handed her the most important piece of a puzzle she had been struggling with for almost half her life. And he didn't even know it. She had listened to him talk about his wife, watched his face as he smiled and said, *"You see, I still know her,"* and she had understood a fundamental truth about life, about people, about herself.

She could see now that it was something so basic that she had carried it around inside her all these years, suppressing it, ignoring it, blind to it in the same way the woman on the elevator was blind to her own appearance. But haunted by it always. By exposing her to this truth in his own life, Mr. Costello had made Leah see how it affected hers. She understood now that there are certain bonds between people that can't be surrendered or forgotten.

For Sam's father, his marriage vows constituted that kind of bond. For better or worse, in sickness and health. His commitment to his wife was total. In his eyes it was irrevocable, something unchanged by the passing of time or the capricious twists of fate. His dedication was all the more admirable because it was a matter of choice. A blood bond couldn't have made his commitment to "his Gracie" any stronger or more real.

For Leah, circumstances were a little different, but the truth was the same. Her bond with her son, a bond she'd tried to convince herself had ended when she signed the adoption papers, was a blood bond and she could see now that choice didn't enter into it at all. The brain might be able to accept the legal severing of the bond between a mother and child, but the heart never would. Certainly hers never had.

All these years of hiding the true depth of her loss, first from Zach, then from her family and friends, and always from herself, hadn't made it go away. She kept waiting for that to happen, desperately hoping that if she just didn't think about it, gradually the memory would hurt less and less and eventually it would fade completely and her heart would finally be free...that she would finally be free to live again.

That wasn't going to happen. Not if she went on forever wearing these blinders except for that single night of the year when she permitted herself to act and feel and ache like a mother. She saw that so clearly now, and as soul wrenching as the realization was, she already felt lighter inside. She was a mother, she thought with awe. Fourteen years ago she had given birth to a beautiful baby boy and that simple act made her a mother forever.

She was a mother who had made the decision to allow her child to be raised by others, but she was a mother just the same. And whoever, wherever, that little boy was today, he was her son. That bond she had felt when she first held him in her arms existed still and it always would. It might be different in nature than it might have been if she had been able to keep him with her, but it was still real.

He might not know enough to wonder about her; he might not have even been told he was adopted, he may not even know she existed, she realized with a small lurch of her heart. It didn't matter. She could never be his parent, the one he learned about life from, the one he turned to in times of need, the one he thought of first in times of joy, but in a special way, she would always be his mother.

A feeling of peace washed over her as she sat in her car, staring at the blur of passing traffic and accepting the truth at last. The warm feeling lingered, spreading outward, and Leah almost held her breath as she waited to see what thoughts would follow, where this newfound insight would lead her.

It was a slight surprise that it didn't make her instantly change her mind about not interfering in her son's life. No doubt it would take more time for her to find her way through all the memories she had kept so carefully buried for so long and fully come to grips with the past. Already, though, she felt more, not less, at peace with her decision to give up her child for adoption, more, not less, able to let go.

It was as if knowing that she hadn't surrendered everything, that this bond between them was real, she was now able to accept what she had surrendered, and why. Now that she was free to allow herself to think about it, she could recall how it had felt to be so young and unmarried and pregnant.

Recollections of that time came rushing at her from all sides. She recalled the horror with which she had felt her jeans getting snug, the fear that her secret sin would be exposed. She recalled morning sickness and being sick in the girls' lav at school and being worried the whole time that she would be late for math class and not allowed to take the test scheduled for that day. It was almost comical now, she thought sadly, that she had been so worried about a math test when her whole future was hanging by a thread.

But then, it was easy to look back as a successful, well-educated thirty-year-old woman and rationalize or trivialize the fears and emotions she had felt back then. At the time, her fear and shame had been very real. She might not bow to them today the way she had then, but unfortunately the decision wasn't hers to make over again.

She had to accept that. She had to let go of the past, for better or worse, before she could begin to really live again. She had to face what she had done, give herself credit for the good that may have come from it and forgive herself for any mistakes she might have made in spite of her best intentions, and even rectify them if she could. The catch was that to do all that, she had to know for sure how all those good intentions of hers had turned out, not only for her and for Zach, but for their son as well.

For the first time she acknowledged that she had a need, even a right, a mother's right to know their son was alive and well and happy.

Their son. Leah actually smiled as she thought it.

Zach was right, those words were nothing to run away from. Zach was right about a lot of things, she thought sheepishly. All along he had been trying to make her see what she had finally discovered on her own. Maybe she just hadn't been ready then. Leah wasn't entirely sure she was ready now, but it was time to take the chance.

Trembling slightly, she turned the key to start the engine. She was suddenly eager to get home. It was also time that she got that box down from the top of the bookcase once and for all and stopped parceling out what little joy she allowed herself.

Driving along, she felt the same mixture of apprehension and absolute certainty that what she was about to do was right that she had felt fourteen years ago, when she had finally told her mother to go ahead and make arrangements for her to stay at the home for unwed mothers her parish priest had referred them to. She also had the same potent sense that her life was about to change forever. The only thing that was different was that this time she no longer felt she had to go through whatever lay ahead alone. The last time she had been afraid to trust Zach. She wouldn't make that mistake again.

Later that night she tried calling Zach at Sam's. Her heart sank when Sam told her he wasn't there. Worse, Sam didn't know how to reach him or when he would be back. He did offer to give Zach the message that she wanted to talk to him whenever he heard from him. Leah detected from his tone that Sam was feeling divided loyalties and she had to grin thinking that was actually a positive sign since, when they were younger, Sam had always been squarely in Zach's corner whenever they had an argument.

Back then he'd probably been acting on that fierce adolescent instinct for male bonding. But attitudes change with age, she mused, emotional boundaries broaden and blur

Coalitions and compromises that once seemed impossible can overnight seem so very possible that just thinking about it can make your heart skip madly.

Leah discovered that for herself whenever she dared to let her mind wander toward thinking about what might lay ahead for her and Zach. Although she still opposed the possibility that he might force a meeting with their son, she very much wanted to be part of his search. She wanted to know as much about the boy and his life as possible. Just knowing would be enough, she told herself. And after that . . . anything was possible.

A week passed without her hearing anything from Zach, and while in some ways she was more at peace with herself than she could ever remember being, in another sense she was also a raw bundle of exposed nerves . . . Waiting, wondering what Zach might have already found out, wondering when—and if—he would call her.

In retrospect she could see why he'd reacted so angrily that last morning. Now that she had made the decision to find out whatever she could about her son, the longing to know and to know right this very minute was nearly overwhelming. She imagined that must be how Zach had been feeling ever since he came back, maybe even more frantic, she thought, remembering the added pressure he was under from the investigation. Zach had a very real reason to want this settled quickly.

He'd probably wanted her to be part of his search as much as she now wanted to be, and her flat, panicky refusal to do so must have been more than merely disappointing. It must have cast doubts on what had happened between them over the course of Christmas Eve and Christmas Day. Had Zach been hoping even then, when she was still afraid to scrutinize her feelings too closely, that the closeness and passion they had rediscovered might last this time? Was he still hoping that? she wondered. Or had he decided that two strikes hurt too much for any sane man to set himself up for a third?

Another week passed before she finally heard some news. Rhode Island was caught firmly in the grasp of one of the coldest Januarys on record and Leah had just fought her way home through an ice storm and shoved the front door closed against a roaring wind when the phone rang. As always these days, she lunged for it.

"Hello?"

"Leah?"

It was Sam, which was better than nothing, thought Leah, with an unavoidable twinge of disappointment that it wasn't Zach.

"Hi, Sam," she responded. "What's up?"

"You sound out of breath."

"I am... I just ran into the house." Where's Zach...where's Zach...where's Zach? she wanted to scream. "It's horrible out there."

"Tell me about it. I'm on my way out now to do some preemptive plowing."

"I didn't know there was such a thing."

"Sure." She could hear the grin in his voice. "It's for those who want to avoid the after-storm rush and be the first on their block with a snowless driveway. If you like I can swing by on the way home and do yours."

"I don't want you to go to any trouble, Sam."

"No trouble at all. I never did thank you for the help you gave my old man."

"Hmm? Oh, you mean the daycare information," she said, her thoughts still riveted on his reason for calling and her hope that it had something to do with Zach. "Did it help?"

"Help? You may have saved my dad's sanity. He called one of the places you recommended and my mom started this week. It's just two mornings, but it gives him a breather . . . and he needs it, believe me."

"I know he does, Sam. I'm so glad it worked out."

"It did. Mom even liked the place, spent the whole time there working on a puzzle. It's going to be good for both of them, I think."

"Great." Pause. "So . . ."

"Oh, right, my reason for calling. Zach finally checked in with me and I told him you had called and that you wanted to talk with him."

Wanted to talk with him, as in wild, desperate, crazed to talk with him, thought Leah.

"Oh, good," she said. "What did he say?"

"He said he's going to be at his place in Boston for the next couple of days, after that he's not sure. And he said if you want to talk to him you can call him there."

His voice dropped at the end in a way that led Leah to suspect Zach might not have said it quite that politely. It sounded as if there was at least a fifty-fifty chance that he was still angry, she thought.

"I see," she said to Sam.

"I have his number," he added. "If you want it."

Leah reached for a pen. "I want it."

After saying goodbye to Sam, she took her coat off, turned up the heat and went to the kitchen for a glass of water. Then she called him before she could lose her nerve, or worse, think of all the sane, pragmatic reasons it would be safer to simply wait and let him make the next move.

He answered on the third ring.

"Hello?" Even with a bad connection that made him sound very far away, his smooth, deep tone had the power to make her spine tingle.

"Hi, Zach. It's me."

"Me who?" he countered.

"If you really can't tell, then maybe I'm wasting my time."

"Now I get it. Leah, right? The tone was fuzzy, but the attitude came through loud and clear."

"Very funny."

"Maybe on that end."

"Look, Zach, I didn't call you because I needed a sparring partner."

"Good, because I'm too damned tired to partner anybody in anything." There was a brief, static-filled pause before he added, "Why did you call me, Leah?"

Right to the point, she thought, gulping a deep breath. Good old Zach.

"I called," she said, "because I changed my mind."

"About what?"

"About, you know, everything."

"Everything, hmm?" More static. "That covers a lot of territory. Did you change your mind about liking me to kiss that spot at the side of your throat? Is that part of the everything you called to tell me about, Leah?"

"No, of course not."

"Then you're probably going to have to be more specific about this 'everything.'"

"I meant everything we've been talking about lately."

"Mmm." Static. "That's still pretty vague."

"It is not," she snapped. "You know exactly what we've been talking about and what I'm talking about now.... I'm talking about finding out what happened to our son."

"What's that?" he asked through another burst of static. "I lost you at the end there."

"It's this damn connection," she said. "Must be the storm. Maybe I should try calling you right back."

"Better not," advised Zach. "My line is quirky in bad weather. You might not get through again. Must be fate that you reached me at all. In fact, we could be cut off any second. Better say what you have to say, Leah."

Leah couldn't be sure because of the static, but he almost sounded amused.

"All right," she said, "I'll make this quick. I'm trying to tell you that you were right about facing up to the past and about needing to know for sure that everything is all right. Oh, for heaven's sake, Zach, what I'm trying to say is that I want to help you find our son."

"Find who?"

"Our son," she shouted over the static. "Our son... can you hear me now, damn it?"

"Loud and clear, baby," he said. In spite of the static his words carried the warmth of a caress. "I figure if you can shout it, you must mean it. Now the question is, what are you going to do about it?"

"What would you like me to do?"

"Come here," he replied, and the huskiness that had crept into his voice gave the invitation a wealth of meaning. "At the stage of the search I'm at it's easier for me to stay on top of things from here."

"What stage are you at?" Leah asked him excitedly.

"I'll tell you everything when I pick you up at the train station tomorrow."

He was so sure she'd come, thought Leah, thrilled in spite of herself.

"Will you come?"

Were nickels round?

"I guess I could get away for a few days. I have some vacation time saved and maybe..."

"Good. Call and let me know what train you'll be on."

"Okay. But, Zach..."

"Yeah?"

"There is something I should tell you. I may have changed my mind about finding him, but not about intruding in his life, especially not against the wishes of his adoptive parents. Will you give me your word on that?"

"No," he replied without hesitation. "Will you come anyway?"

Leah sighed and gripped the receiver tightly, aware of what a loaded question he was asking. "Yes," she said, "I'll come anyway."

Chapter Nine

Leah arrived in Boston around noon the following day. Zach met her at South Station, shouldering her dark paisley tote as he led the way for them to catch the T, Boston's public transportation system, to his place.

She had crammed everything she thought she might need into that single, soft-sided bag and she was impressed that he could carry it so effortlessly. If she'd let herself go, she could have filled three more just like it without any trouble. She hadn't wanted to appear presumptuous, however. She had no idea what sort of clothes she would be needing or how long she would even be here. For that matter, although she had eagerly accepted Zach's suggestion that she come and had made open-ended arrangements to be away from the office, she really had no idea exactly why she was there.

If she expected Zach to shed instant light on that question by welcoming her with the news that he'd made a major breakthrough in his search, she was disappointed. Disappointment seemed to be more or less the order of the day. Although he seemed happy enough to see her, his greeting had been noticeably restrained, no touching and only minimal direct eye contact.

He might have been one of those hired drivers that hotels sent to airports and train stations as a courtesy to their guests, conjectured Leah as she hurried along to keep pace. Except that they were walking, not driving, and she wasn't going to be staying at a hotel. The thought of spending the night in his apartment seemed a whole lot more intimidating with Zach by her side, big and silent and tempting as hell. Leah found herself slanting hungry glances his way, wishing their arms would bump or their hands brush, wishing something would happen that would cause him to react. Then she might see in his reaction that, appearances aside, he wanted to touch her as much as she wanted him to.

During the short subway ride to Cambridge, where his apartment was located, he continued to be mostly silent, speaking only to point out stops along the way that he thought might interest her. A progression from driver to tour guide. For her part, Leah avoided asking what was uppermost on her mind, namely what he had managed to find out about their son.

She could afford to be patient, knowing he'd get around to it in his own way. Perhaps there was some reason he was holding back. It was, after all, too important a matter to be discussed on a crowded subway. She would just have to wait and see. In the meantime, the unpleasant memory of the way they had last parted seemed to hang like a lead curtain in the air between them.

"It's only a few blocks from here," Zach told her after they had gotten off the T in the middle of busy Kenmore

Square. Cars and people alike streamed steadily in all directions. "Are you cold?" he asked.

She shook her head. "No, I'm fine."

Actually she was cold, but not in the way she knew he meant it. She was cold on the inside, filled with an icy nervousness, wondering if coming here had been a big mistake. It had seemed like a wise move last night, when she'd lain awake for hours, carefully reviewing all the sound, logical reasons she had for coming. At least, she had made it seem like a wise move, she recalled a bit sheepishly. It was rare for Leah to slant an argument with herself in order to get the resolution she wanted. But then, it was rare that she wanted anything as much as she wanted this.

Wanted what? nagged a small inner voice. News of her son? Or this time alone with Zach? Or both?

"Here we are," Zach announced, stopping before a well-maintained brownstone. It was located on a corner, across the street from a small park. Two large maple trees, which would provide welcome shade in the summer, overhung the front sidewalk and a wreath of evergreens adorned the glossy black front door. Knowing how dismal and impersonal apartments in a city can be, Leah was very impressed.

She was even more impressed when she followed him up to the second floor and into his apartment. The miniblinds on the windows were tilted open so that sunlight filled the spacious living room, which opened on to a kitchen that was nearly as large. Leah's first impression was of a home decorated for comfort and peace of mind. The overstuffed chairs covered in a nubby cream fabric looked like the perfect place to curl up and watch an old movie and she could imagine spreading out the Sunday newspaper on the oversize oak table by the window and settling in with a cup of coffee.

There was no clutter in sight, and none of the sloppy giveaways that are associated with bachelor life. No dirty dishes were piled in the kitchen sink, no balled-up sweat socks peeked from under the sofa, no trail of magazines and sports pages lined the room. Leah might have thought he'd spent days cleaning in anticipation of her arrival except for the fact that he hadn't known she was coming until last night, and also because, in spite of its orderliness, the place didn't have that "just been spit-shined" aura. Leah would wager you could knock on Zach's door almost anytime and his apartment would look pretty much the same.

More surprises awaited as he gave her a quick tour. There were copper-bottomed pans hanging in the kitchen and co-ordinated towels hanging in the bath room. Not to mention the existence of a bona fide guest room.

Behind her staunch smile, Leah's throat tightened with disappointment as he plopped her bag on the bed in there. She had half expected—and half hoped—that he would put her on the spot by carrying her things straight to his own bedroom. At least that would have forced everything out into the open between them and cleared the air one way or the other. Was assigning her this room his way of saying that if a move were to be made, she was going to have to make it herself?

"It's not fancy," he said, "but I think you'll find every-thing you need without too much trouble. If not, just give a shout."

"I'm sure I'll be all set," Leah replied.

"How about if I give you a few minutes to change or freshen up or whatever, and then we can go out for lunch? Are you hungry?"

"Starved." A lie. Leah was so tense she was surprised she could swallow air, never mind solid food. However going out for lunch seemed preferable to remaining there alone with just Zach and the tension between them.

"Good. There's a great pizza place just a few blocks away. We could go there, if you like."

"Sounds perfect. I think I will change first, though," she told him, deciding that the miniskirted taupe plaid suit that had seemed so casually appropriate just hours ago felt neither casual nor appropriate when faced with Zach's well-worn black jeans and white T-shirt. How was it possible that so little could make him look so good?

The answer was obvious. It was the same reason her heart stalled, then kick-started again when he moved closer to show her the closet where she could hang her things. Sex appeal. He had it in abundance and it radiated from him in the exact same measure whether he was wearing jeans or a tux. That's just the way it was.

When he'd left her alone, pulling the door shut behind him, Leah quickly changed into a pair of black stirrup pants and a pale yellow lamb's-wool tunic. It wasn't quite jeans, but it was a step in the right direction. Besides, the yellow sweater brought out the gold in her eyes and it looked and felt so alluringly soft that if Zach could resist touching her with this on, she'd better resign herself to sleeping in the guest room for the duration.

Zach's favorite pizza joint turned out to be a popular hangout for local high school kids as well as students from Boston University and other nearby colleges. It was loud and friendly and served the very best pizza Leah had ever tasted. The aroma alone was enough to make you hungry and in spite of her fear that she wouldn't be able to swallow, she was stuffed by the time they left.

It had been much too noisy in there to do more than eat and exchange comments on the oldies that blared from the jukebox. Some of them brought back memories that Leah hadn't dared think about in a long time. Happy memories that she had buried along with the rest. It was a relief to let herself think about people and places and good times that had meant so much to her once. Zach was a big part of those memories and being able to share her thoughts with him and have him there to jog her memory in places, added to her pleasure.

Walking back to his apartment, Leah decided it was best that they hadn't been able to talk over lunch about anything deeper than what color dress she had worn to his senior prom. Their reminiscing had succeeded in cracking the tension and although Zach still hadn't come within three inches of her physically, she felt much closer to him than she had when she climbed off the train a few hours ago.

He put on a pot of coffee when they got back to his place, and slid a CD of slow, bluesy music into the CD player, keeping the volume low.

"It's not oldies," he said, "but it's still damn good listening."

Leah nodded agreement, kicking her shoes off and resting her head back on the sofa while he went to pour their coffee. By the time he returned, carrying two steaming mugs, she felt more relaxed than she had all day, relaxed and ready to hear whatever he had to tell her about what his search had revealed so far.

Handing her one of the mugs, Zach settled at the opposite end of the sofa. More progress, thought Leah. He could have sat clear across the room. She took one sip of her coffee and placed it on the table beside her.

"I can't wait any longer," she said. "Please tell me what you've found out."

"Not as much as I wanted to." Reading the disappointment in her eyes, he quickly added. "But I can tell you this much for sure, I know now that I will find him, Leah, and soon."

She nodded, trying to draw encouragement from his determined tone. She had been hoping for a miracle, she supposed. "What have you learned?"

"So many little bits and pieces about the adoption game that it's hard to know where to start." He paused to think for a few seconds. "I don't want to keep you hanging, so why don't I just tell you where we are now and then backtrack to answer any questions you have, okay?"

Leah leaned toward him in anticipation. "Fine."

He reached into his back pocket for his wallet and pulled from it a folded sheet of paper. Unfolding it, he handed it to Leah. It was a list of ten names. Ten boys' names, she noted with a small rush of excitement.

"The odds are overwhelming that our son's name is one of the names on that list," he said.

Leah's hands trembled as her eyes skated down the list. Daniel Steven Robertson. Jason Lee Rydell. John Robert Soares. Her son. One of these names belonged to her son. She quickly and silently read them all, then looked at Zach, amazed and bewildered.

"But how . . . where . . ."

"That list was put together for me by a woman at what's known as an adoption information exchange in North Carolina. I was referred to them by a national adoption registry called the Soundex Reunion Agency in Nevada. Basically, anyone who is searching, birth parents, adoptees, even adoptive parents, can register with them and if whoever they happen to be searching for has also registered and wants to be found, the people at Soundex can put them in touch with each other."

Leah's grip on the list tightened. "Zach, do you mean that our son wants to get in touch with us?"

"Not quite."

"But what about the list? How did his name . . . ?"

His wide mouth quirked into a pensive smile. "That list is something that exists outside the official framework of these agencies. You see, the fact is that some of them are more aggressive about helping than others. I better back up a bit more."

Leah nodded impatiently.

"I was told about the Soundex Registry by a woman at the Department of Catholic Social Services in Charlotte. Ring a bell?"

"No. Should it?"

"Maybe not. You probably never had any direct contact with them. That's the agency that actually handled the adoption."

A puzzled frown wrinkled Leah's brow. "But I was never even in North Carolina."

"Doesn't matter evidently," Zach replied with a shrug. "Maybe all church related adoptions within a certain area were funneled through there or maybe it was handled that way because North Carolina has some of the strictest secrecy rules in the country."

"You mean this agency won't tell you anything about who adopted him?"

"Won't or can't, the result's the same."

"Then how—"

"What the woman there did," he interrupted, "is put me on to the Soundex folks. They were the ones who advised me to also find an adoption information service as close to the actual place of adoption as possible."

"That would be the adoption information exchange you mentioned earlier, the one in North Carolina," she said, the pieces beginning to fall into place.

"That's right. I lucked out there when I met a woman who is very sympathetic to our situation. She's a birth mother herself. She searched for her daughter for nearly twenty years and—'' He stopped abruptly, as if catching himself on the brink of a faux pas.

"And?" Leah prodded. "Please, Zach... I want to know everything."

"All right. It really doesn't have anything to do with us anyway. When she was finally successful in locating her daughter's adoptive family, she found out that she had been dead for eight years."

A chill ran up Leah's spine. "How awful for her."

"Yeah." Zach took a drink of coffee. "Anyway, since then she's dedicated her life to helping others with their searches."

"I see," Leah responded, folding her arms against a sudden chill. "I know you're right, her story doesn't have anything to do with us, except that maybe..."

"No." He leaned forward and grasped her chin to silence her. "I refuse to think that and I don't want you thinking it, either."

Their eyes met and as if suddenly realizing that he had touched her and wasn't supposed to, Zach quickly dropped his hand.

"This woman," he continued, "her name is Karen, and she really went all out on this when I told her about how... when I told her how little time I might have to take care of this. She's the one who came up with that list of names."

With a nod he indicated the list Leah was holding onto as tightly as if it were a winning lottery ticket.

"But where did she get the names on this list?"

"I didn't ask. That was part of the deal. She told me up front that she could help narrow the field, but she couldn't tell me where or how she got her information. If she did, state officials would close off access to whatever sources she has."

"Is it legal?" asked Leah, not really caring. At that moment all she cared about was the joy of knowing that a few minutes ago her son was one of millions of nameless strangers, but now—thanks to a woman named Karen whom she'd never met—he was one of the ten on this list. He was within reach, she could feel it.

"It's not illegal," Zach replied vaguely. "What it is, is some sort of underground network designed to get around a very rigid system."

"Where do we go from here?"

"We know our son was born in Virginia, so we find out which of the names on that list have birth certificates on record in that state, then we request copies of them. I'm already working on that part of it. If we're lucky, one of them—and only one—will have been born on Christmas Eve."

Leah lowered her eyes to the list again, reading each name slowly to herself. One of these names, she thought, one of these names belongs to the child I gave birth to. She ran her finger down the list, stopping at the very last name on it, Ryan Patrick Wayland. A strange fluttery sensation occurred in the pit of her stomach as she stared at the name. Leah shook her head. It was crazy to think that she could somehow sense which of these was the right name... and still... with the flutters still going strong, she glanced at Zach.

"How long do you think it will be until we hear from Virginia?"

"The records clerk I spoke with promised I'd hear something by tomorrow. I'm keeping my fingers crossed that's true, but most people I've dealt with so far have been happy to help in any way they can."

"I guess your biggest stumbling block so far has been me," Leah commented with wry sheepishness.

Zach simply shrugged as he lifted his mug to finish his coffee. "Anyway, as soon as we have the right birth certificate, we'll also have the name of his parents, then we can begin tracking them down."

"But my name was on the birth certificate?"

Zach shook his head. "Only on the original application form. The official birth certificate will show only the adoptive parents' names."

A sharp pain flickered near Leah's heart. This process was a mixture of joy and pain. All these years she'd believed her name was on that certificate and that if the day ever came when her son wanted to know who had given birth to him, all he'd have to do was look at it and come find her. That didn't even make sense, she realized that now, but she'd believed it just the same. It was one more fuzzy bit of reasoning that allowed her to go on with a normal semblance of life.

"Once we know these people's names," she said, hesitating before forcing herself to add, "his parents, I mean . . . Once we know his parents' names, will it be hard to find them?"

"That's the million-dollar question, but don't worry, I have a guy ready to get right on it as soon as I have a name to give him. He used to be a cop, now he's in business for himself, and he's better at tracking people than a whole pack of bloodhounds."

Leah nodded, nervously running her fingers through her hair to brush it back from her forehead as she summoned all her courage to ask, "What about us? What do we do with ourselves in the meantime?"

Zach met her questioning gaze and felt a major crack rip through that rock-solid self-control he prided himself on. He knew exactly, precisely, in full-color and minute detail what he wanted to do with Leah in the meantime. He wanted to do the one thing he had promised himself he wouldn't do... make love to her.

He couldn't. The last thing he needed in his current frame of mind was another reminder that no matter how perfect everything between Leah and him seemed and felt, no matter how good he was stupid enough to believe it was, it was never good enough. For Leah, there was always something just a little more important, college and a career or her fear of facing up to whatever he might find out about the past.

Oh sure, she was here now—although for the life of him he couldn't figure out why he'd suggested she come in the first place and he'd been on edge all day hoping she wouldn't pin him down about it. He understood that she was here because she had decided she wanted to be part of finding their son. Because she had changed her mind, no doubt after making one of her precious lists of pros and cons. Not because of anything he had said or done. She'd never trusted him enough for that.

Even knowing that, he was enough of a sap to take another chance on her if it weren't for one important fact he'd conveniently forgotten the last time he took her to bed. Leah had thought he was a bad risk fourteen years ago and that he didn't have enough to offer her in the way of a safe secure future then; he had a hell of a lot less to offer her today.

None of which made him feel any better or want her any less. It also didn't provide any answer to the question that still echoed in the expectant, vaguely speculative look she was giving him.

"We wait," he told her. "I thought that having you here would make it that much faster when it came to having you verify the date and time on the birth certificate and answer any other questions that might come up in the process."

Yeah, right, Blackmore, much faster than making the fifty-minute drive from here to her place.

"Like I said," he continued, "I don't have any time to waste. There's one more thing you might want to consider while we're waiting for word. The lady I spoke with at the agency that handled his adoption said that we can write a letter to him if we want to—"

"They'll actually send it to him?" Leah interjected, her eyes widening with excitement.

"Not just like that," he said, snapping his fingers to illustrate how quickly the system did not work. "They will keep it on file as part of his record, and if he ever contacts them, they will tell him the letter is there if he wants to see it."

"All right," she said thoughtfully. "That's better than nothing."

"Not much better actually. The catch is that the letter can't include any specific names or places or descriptions, what she called 'identifying factors.' Evidently that would also violate the secrecy rules."

"Why do they have to make it so hard?" Leah demanded, an almost forlorn edge to her voice.

Zach fought the urge to reach over and pull her into his arms. "It doesn't matter how hard they make it, we're going to do it. No matter how many tough little baby steps we have to take." He paused, then added, "I've already started my letter to him. If you want to add anything, you're welcome to."

"Thanks, if it's all right, I'd like to write my own letter to put with yours."

"Sure, whatever you like."

There was a short silence, which to Zach felt days long.

"Zach," she said at last, breaking the awkward, uncomfortable silence.

"Yes?"

"You didn't mention anything about the home, you know, the place where I stayed before I had the baby. I thought that would have been your first stop after I gave you the name of the place."

"It was," replied Zach, carefully organizing his thoughts. "I just wasn't sure how you would react to talking about it and since it didn't really figure into what I found out..." He trailed off with a shrug.

"Did you go there?"

"I went. It's closed, Leah, has been for about five years now. It's just a big empty old house overgrown with weeds."

Tears filled her eyes and silently spilled over to run down her cheeks. Zach had never known anyone else who could cry without making a sound. Somehow the silence made it even more heartbreaking.

"Ah, Leah," he said, willing her to stop before touching her became an urge he couldn't deny. "I knew I shouldn't have said..."

"No," she said, her throat muscles rippling as she swallowed to try to regain control. She wiped at her eyes with the sleeve of her sweater, then managed a small smile as she accepted the handkerchief Zach offered. "Thanks. I'm not upset, I'm happy."

His incredulous look prompted another smile.

"Really," she said, "I'm happy that place is closed, that no other girls will be going there and leaving without their babies." She bit her lip, dabbing at the corners of her eyes with his handkerchief. Still the tears came. "Things are much better today. Girls who get pregnant have more choices. They can keep their babies and finish school and there are people willing to help them do it. Maybe even more important, people—society—isn't so condemning of them now."

Zach listened, puzzled. "I thought you wanted to give the baby up?"

"No, I never wanted to do it," she countered quickly. "But I believed it was the best thing I could do for him... and for you..." She shook her head. "Maybe I was wrong. You don't know how many times I thought of changing my mind, of calling you and saying 'Please come get me, marry me, let me keep my baby.'"

"Why didn't you?"

She averted her gaze, staring past him, her arms wrapped tightly around herself. "It was so hard to think clearly there, to make a decision. Every time I'd try to talk to someone about it, they would come back with the standard line about how I was selfish to even think I could provide properly for my baby, that his new parents would be able to give him so much more."

"Damn them," muttered Zach, his fingers curled into fists.

Leah shook her head sadly. "They weren't bad people, really, just convinced they knew what was best. All the rules and indoctrination, I really think they thought it would make what was happening to us easier. And you know, for some people they may have been right."

Zach saw her shudder and his heart twisted in his chest.

"How bad was it?" he asked, his tone unavoidably hoarse.

"I survived," she tossed back, her quick smile brittle.

"How bad?"

"It wasn't a torture chamber, if that's what you're thinking. It was... formal. Here we were, a bunch of kids going through what was most likely the most traumatic and vulnerable time of their lives—certainly it was that way for me—and we weren't even allowed to exchange last names or addresses with the girl sleeping in the next bed. A girl we lay awake half the night talking to because we didn't have any other family or friends to talk to."

"But why? What was the purpose—"

"Secrecy," Leah replied before he finished. "You've seen for yourself how much secrecy can surround the whole matter of adoption." Her sigh raked Zach's senses.

Zach dragged his fingers through his hair, then jammed them into his jeans pockets, anything to keep from putting his hands on her to comfort her. Comfort would turn to something stronger, he knew, and he would never be able to stop.

"I wish you had called me," he said. "I wish to hell I could have been there for you."

"At least they didn't manage to brainwash me entirely. They warned us not to even see our babies, but I couldn't stand the thought of that. I bugged the nurses to see him as much as I could." Her face brightened at the memory. "I held him and sang to him . . ." She glanced at Zach. "I told him all about what a wonderful daddy he had."

A lump the size of Kansas lodged in Zach's throat. He watched Leah's eyes grow dreamy.

"I pretended that he was really mine."

"He was really yours, Leah," he countered, her wistful tone like a knife in his chest.

"I meant mine to keep. Deep down, every minute I held him, I knew it might be the last. That's why . . ." She hesitated, her cheeks growing flushed.

"What?" Zach prodded. "Tell me, Leah."

"That's why I never nursed him even though I wanted to. God, how I wanted to, to feel him so close to me just once.

But I was afraid that I didn't have the right to do it and that if the nurses caught me, they wouldn't let me see him again.''

Zach felt an explosion of heat within and almost wished he hadn't prodded her to tell him. With each new revelation, another window was opened to the past, allowing him farther inside what should have been a shared experience all along, driving home to him exactly how much he had lost.

The image of Leah nursing his son wouldn't leave the front of his mind. He pictured her sitting up in bed, her nightgown open, the baby nestled against her full breast. His blood was pumping furiously. It should have happened that way, damn it. She should have been able to nurse her own baby and he should have been there to see it, instead of having to imagine it fourteen years later.

And imagine it, he did. His vision of the scene was both maternal and erotic. He couldn't help it. At that moment the only thing he wanted more than he wanted to go back and make everything in the past right for Leah, was Leah herself. He wanted her under him, beside him, surrounding him, soft and warm and . . .

"Leah," he said, his voice a raspy intrusion into the silence. She glanced at him, pulling herself from thoughts of her own. "I need . . ."

He hesitated.

"Yes?"

It sounded as if she'd caught her breath. Zach wanted her more than any sane man would allow.

"More coffee," he said at last. "You want some, too?"

Chapter Ten

They heard from the clerk in the Virginia department of records the following day. Leah was both excited and uneasy when the call came. In spite of the snags and regulations that Zach had encountered, it all seemed to be happening unbelievably fast. After fourteen years of hiding inside herself, was she ready to find out that she might have made a terrible mistake?

Yes, Leah decided as she listened to Zach's half of the phone conversation and tried to piece together the rest, she was ready to learn the truth, whatever that turned out to be. She only wished the closeness to Zach, which she was convinced she felt from time to time, wasn't always being short-circuited by him. It would make it easier somehow if she could truly believe that this time they were in this together. Ironic, she thought, last time she was the one making all the calls and shutting Zach out emotionally, and now their roles were reversed.

Leah's complete attention shifted to Zach as he hung up the receiver and turned to her.

"What did he say?" she asked before he had a chance to speak.

"It was the Virginia—"

"I know, I know," she cut in. "I guessed that much. What did he tell you?"

"He said that he checked the records for that year twice and all he could come up with were birth certificates for two of the names on the list." He spoke slowly, as if he was also struggling to come to grips with what might be happening.

"Which two?" she asked.

"He didn't say." Before her spirits could sink, he added. "He's going to fax them to me. The number I just gave him was for the copy shop on the corner. I've had stuff faxed to me there before."

"How soon will he send them?" she asked, thanking heaven for technology.

"Right away." He crossed to the coat tree by the front door and grabbed his jacket. "I'll be back."

"No, wait. I—"

It was too late. She could hardly go chasing after him when she was barefoot, and when he so obviously had no intention of waiting for her to grab her shoes. She had no choice but to wait for him to get back. It was, she discovered, disconcerting to have matters that affected her so profoundly taken from her control. It was hard to stand by while someone else called the shots. Could this crushing sense of frustration be what Zach had felt fourteen years ago?

The minutes dragged by, but Leah knew from staring at the clock that he hadn't been gone even twenty minutes when she heard his footsteps on the stairs and the front door burst open.

She met him at the door. He was panting, obviously having run all the way home, and she was holding her breath in anticipation. His eyes glittered with excitement.

"What is it?" she demanded. "What did you find out?"

"He faxed both certificates," he said, between deep breaths. "One was issued in May."

Leah shook her head emphatically. "The other one... what about the other one?"

Zach lifted his hand and she snatched the crumpled fax sheet he was clutching. Her eyes went first to the name near the top. Ryan Patrick Wayland.

"Oh, my God. Zach, this name... Last night when I read this name I felt something, a sensation... I can't explain it."

He was nodding fiercely. "The date... look at the date."

Leah's eyes scanned the document for the date. When she found it, everything inside her came to a momentary halt. She looked up into Zach's eyes. "December 24."

"And the time? Do you remember the time?"

Nodding, she glanced again at the paper in her hand, already knowing the time—she would find recorded there.

"I remember—7:27 a.m.," she whispered. It was a moment she would remember forever. "Oh, Zach, this is him. Ryan Patrick Wayland." She said it again, learning this new aspect of someone who until now had been only a shadow in her heart. She was laughing and crying at the same time. "We did it—*you* did it," she amended hurriedly. "You said you'd find him, and you did. Oh Zach..."

She lifted her arms, moving toward him instinctively, only to freeze, crashing inside when he stiffened and moved back enough to avert her touch.

"I wouldn't say we've exactly found him," he said, the stiffness in his voice making the moment feel even worse to Leah. "But we're getting closer. I'm going to give my friend a call and tell him what we've got. He's an ace at this. I think the best thing we can do is let him take it from here."

"Sure," agreed Leah, shoving her hands into her pockets to keep from reaching out and humiliating herself again. "You're calling the shots."

It took several more days until they heard back from Zach's private-detective friend. Days that were an eternity of tense silences punctuated by occasional slips into their old easiness, each agonizing moment shrouded in a sexual awareness so thick Leah sometimes had to take a walk just to get a decent breath. Countless times she thought of packing up and going home, but thoughts of her son always held her there. Ryan, she reminded herself over and over, he had a name now . . . She wasn't going to give up the chance to be here when Zach got news of him. And as stubborn and ill-tempered as he was trying to be, she wasn't ready to give up on Zach yet, either.

She spent the time reading and watching old movies, of which Zach had a collection to rival her own. It was strange how alike in some ways they had grown through the years apart. They both liked old movies and listening to the blues and reading late into the night. Leah had a strong suspicion they would both like doing something else late into the night even better, but she had no idea how to get past the wall Zach had put up between them.

When Zach's friend finally called, Leah was in the middle of her morning shower. Zach received so few calls—none from women she'd noted with great satisfaction—that when she heard the phone ring she immediately turned off the water and grabbed a towel. Shoving her still damp arms into the sleeves of her robe, she reached the living room just as he was hanging up.

He turned to her and for the first time in days, a genuine grin graced his face.

"He found him," he told her. "He's alive and healthy and living in what Charlie says is a real decent neighborhood…and he plays football, Leah." Pride widened his grin even more. "And he must be damn good because this Saturday he's quarterbacking his junior high team in a special fund-raising game. And we're going to be there to see it."

"Saturday? Zach, that's tomorrow."

He looked surprised, then ecstatic. "Damn right it is."

She couldn't help grinning along with him. "Just where is this game he's playing in?" she asked, laughing suddenly. "You still haven't said where he found him."

"I didn't? I'm sorry. He lives in Texas, a little town outside of San Antonio." He clapped her on the back, the first time he'd touched her in days. "Pack your bag, Leah, we're going to Satchel, Texas."

They landed in San Antonio midmorning on Saturday. Throughout the flight they talked about what might lay ahead. Leah wasn't sure if Zach was beginning to thaw or if she was simply so full of an anxious need to talk with someone that she gave him no choice. Either way, it was better than the heavy silence typical of late.

She never tired of speculating about what Ryan might look like and which of their assorted relatives he might take after in a particular way. Some of the hypotheses they came up with were so comical they brought tears to their eyes. Zach tried his best to appear cool about the whole thing, one minute cautioning her to be open-minded and not set herself up for disappointment, the next, giving himself away big time by wondering aloud if Ryan might have NFL potential.

Zach's private investigator friend, Charlie Lemarre, had gone out of his way to see that everything went smoothly once they arrived in Texas. He'd arranged to have a rental car waiting at the airport and had reserved two hotel rooms for them in a San Antonio hotel. He'd even picked up their tickets for the benefit game to be played at two that afternoon in Ryan's hometown. He'd left the tickets, along with a map of the area, at the hotel desk. Leah opened the map to find he'd drawn an *X* to mark the Wayland's street and she couldn't help thinking of pirate maps where *X* always marks the buried treasure.

They dropped their bags off in their separate rooms. Leah's room had a queen-size bed and floor-to-ceiling windows overlooking the city. It was decorated in muted shades of coral and green. A very tranquil combination. Unfortunately, she thought wryly, it would take more than a color scheme to calm her nerves today. She was too antsy to even sit and it was a relief when Zach rapped on her door after only a few minutes. He looked every bit as restless as she felt.

"We have a couple of hours before the game," he said. "Do you want to get something to eat? An early lunch, maybe?"

Leah shook her head.

"In that case, want to drive by their house?"

Leah needed no explanation as to which house he was referring to. "Let's go," she said.

The town of Satchel was only a short distance away by freeway. A suburban community, it was laid out like so many new developments, with the forethought and precision that make it easy for even strangers to find their way around. Charlie's map helped even further, leading them through the center of the small town, actually just a string of convenience stores and specialty shops, and past the

Emerald Mall, a high-tech, two-story extravaganza that was no doubt the town's real center.

En route to the Waylands' neighborhood, they passed the Satchel junior-senior high school complex. It was very impressive, the newly built school buildings separate from each other and surrounded by acres of fields, including a football stadium that illustrated how important the sport was in this part of the country. Leah felt a small burst of pride that her son would be playing there in just a few hours. Underlying her pride was a warm sense that, just maybe, his athletic prowess was owed in part to the man beside her.

All these thoughts were a small, private indulgence that she would never dream of sharing with anyone else. Except perhaps Zach. Leah never wanted to take anything away from the couple who had raised Ryan. Full credit for whatever he was went to them, the mother who had been there to teach him to brush his teeth and share his toys, the father who had probably spent Saturday mornings tossing a football to him in the front yard.

Of course she still didn't know for sure that Ryan's young life had been anything like that starry-eyed ideal she wished for him, but Charlie's report had suggested that it was a lot closer to that than to the specter of abuse and neglect that had haunted Leah. And Zach.

"This is the street," Zach announced, drawing her from thoughts of what Ryan's childhood had been like. Had he learned to ride a swing at that playground they just passed? Was that ice cream shop close enough for him to ride his bike to on hot summer evenings? She wanted to know everything.

"Cactus Way. It sounds so...Texan," she remarked, growing nervous as they made the turn. This was a long way from the place she called home.

Zach slanted her a wry look. "I wonder why?" His eyes narrowed. "You okay?" he asked.

Leah nodded. "Sure. Just a little nervous."

"Yeah. Me, too."

"Don't go so slow," she warned. "We don't want to attract attention."

"Why not? We're not doing anything wrong, are we?"

His rough, defensive tone brought to center stage an issue Leah had been doggedly avoiding. How far did he intend to go now that they had actually located Ryan?

"Are we?" he persisted.

"No," Leah replied, a light bulb clicking on in her head. "But I'm sure you wouldn't want to do anything that might upset Ryan before this afternoon's game."

It took Zach only a second to process that information and respond by pressing more firmly on the accelerator. Men and sports, thought Leah with wry amusement. It worked every time.

The question remained however, once the game was over, what would hold Zach back from doing what he'd admitted from the beginning that he might do, confront Ryan directly and reveal that they were his birth parents? Just thinking about it pushed Leah's anxiety level even higher, but before she had a chance to get really worked up, Zach warned her that the Wayland house was coming up on their right.

Theirs was a modern one-story house, alike and yet different from the others on the street in the same way that all the houses here were different. Each was set apart and distinguished by some feature that proclaimed these weren't simply cookie-cutter houses, but real homes to real families of differing shapes and personalities. For one home, a profusion of roses was the defining touch, on another, it was a front porch and colonial blue clapboard that hinted at New England roots.

If Leah had been able to wave a magic wand and create a home for her son, she couldn't have done a better job than Steve and Gloria Wayland had done. The house and lawn were neat and well maintained, but completely lacking in fussiness. A tire swing hung from a tree in the front and above the fence enclosing the backyard Leah spotted the top of a swing set and a pool slide. Here was a yard where a kid could have fun; he could roll on the grass and play ball and shoot baskets at the hoop nailed above the garage door.

The garage door had been left open, revealing a work-bench, a vintage Ford and the usual assortment of garage paraphernalia. Leah craned her neck to see as much as possible as they cruised by, hundreds of questions cropping up along the way. Did Ryan have an interest in woodworking or old cars? Was that his ten-speed bike leaning against the side of the garage?

They drove around the block and back by the house two more times before deciding that was as much as they dared. Leah could have driven past a hundred more times and still not be satisfied. The holes inside her were that deep. She eased her disappointment with the thought that the game—and the chance to see Ryan himself—was only a couple of hours away.

They passed the time until then at a fast-food joint near the mall, neither of them able to eat much. They both scrutinized closely any boys who looked to be about fourteen who happened to come in, always wondering if one of them might be Ryan.

At last they decided it was safe to go to the stadium without fear of being the first ones there. Since the game was between Satchel and a neighboring town, they felt confident they wouldn't stand out as obvious strangers. Still,

Leah couldn't persuade Zach to sit on the opposition's side of the field. She understood that Zach was thinking this might be the only chance he ever got to see his son play, and he was determined to cheer for him.

They found seats about ten rows up in the bleachers behind the Satchel bench. The high school band warmed up the crowd as hundreds of people filled the stadium. Leah stamped her feet in time with the music, both to keep warm and to burn off some of the nervous energy that threatened to mushroom out of control as game time approached. A few rows in front of them a couple in their forties seemed to be having a similar problem with their young daughters. The little girls, whom Leah guessed to be about five and six, squirmed and twisted and demanded to know how much longer until the game started . . . exactly what Leah felt like doing.

Finally the loudspeaker crackled and an announcer with a Texas drawl proclaimed that since this was a special event, they would begin by introducing the members of each team individually. Leah and Zach exchanged grateful looks. This was better than they'd hoped.

He introduced the visiting team first. Leah, her stomach in knots, thought they would never stop calling out names. Finally the last of Satchel's opponents had trotted on to the field and the announcer asked the crowd to welcome the home team, the Satchel Panthers.

Their side of the stadium responded with a deafening roar that continued at only a slightly lower decibel as the announcer again began calling out names. One by one the Panthers, in black and gold, ran onto the field. Leah sat upright, straining to see and afraid she wouldn't hear Ryan's name when it was called. She needn't have worried. A slight lull in the cheering allowed it to come through loud and clear.

"Quarterback Ryan Wayland."

The shouting peaked then, leaving no doubt that Ryan was a big favorite with the hometown crowd. Leah clapped wildly, her throat tightening as all around her people stamped their feet and took up what was evidently an oft-practiced chant.

"Ry. Ry. Ry. Ry. Ry."

And suddenly he was on the field, waving jauntily to the crowd...taller than she expected and impossibly broad shouldered and slim hipped in his uniform and pads. He held his gold helmet under his arm, revealing straight dark brown hair and features that from this distance were so reminiscent of a young Zach that Leah's breath caught in her throat. He was beautiful, she thought, but he was no longer a little boy.

Ryan's was the last name called and the cheering persisted, fading, gradually, only when the band broke into the national anthem. It took the entire "Star-Spangled Banner" for Leah's heartbeat to slow to even near normal. That was as much as she could hope for. Normal itself was not within the range of possibility today.

As they sat again afterward, Zach's shoulder was pressed to hers in a way it hadn't been earlier. He caught her eye briefly.

"Wow," he said.

It was enough. Leah knew that he was feeling exactly what she was, pride and love and regret for everything that might have been, all mixed up in a knot that would stay fixed inside both of them for a long, long time after this game was over.

At halftime, the Panthers were up by three, thanks to brilliant quarterbacking, Zach told her over and over again. They bought soft drinks from a vendor and wandered through the crowd, hoping for a closer look at the boy who was their reason for being there, but the teams remained in their locker rooms.

Before when she watched a football game, even when Zach had been playing—especially when Zach was playing and she knew that later they could be alone—Leah had thought football the slowest, longest game in existence. Today however, the quarters seemed to fly by. Long before she'd even begun to tire of watching Ryan on the field, the game had wound down to its final seconds. She craned her neck for a better vantage point as the Panther offense took the field for the last time.

"I wish I'd thought to bring binoculars," she grumbled quietly to Zach.

He raised his brows, barely taking his eyes off the game for a second. "I thought you were the one who wanted to be inconspicuous?"

"At least I'm not jumping out of my seat every time he touches the ball."

"No, only every other time," he retorted. "But wincing every time he gets tackled isn't a whole lot more subtle."

"Do they have to hit him so hard?"

Zach's jaw squared. "He can take it. He's a tough kid, Leah."

This time he managed to look away from the field for at least ten seconds. Their eyes met and held, silently conveying all the things Leah wasn't sure they would ever find the right words to say to each other. If tough meant strong, Leah agreed with her whole heart. Ryan was strong and fair and patient...and healthy and well liked and everything else Leah had always dreamed he would be. How could she know all that simply from watching him throw a football? She couldn't. She just knew.

Satchel won by thirteen. By unspoken agreement Zach and Leah remained in their seats for the announcement of the record amount of money the game had raised for the scholarship fund and to see Ryan presented with the Most Valuable Player trophy and then be tossed in the air by his happy teammates.

As the capacity crowd began the slow process of filing out, they still lingered, both silently reluctant for the afternoon to end. Around them, Panther fans were celebrating and congratulating each other, gathering in small clusters to rehash crucial plays.

"What a kid," a man in a red parka called to the father of the two little girls sitting a few rows in front of them. "Did you teach him to play like that, Steve?"

Steve? Leah froze, her fingers gripping Zach's forearm tightly. Could this man be Steve Wayland? It would be an eerie coincidence that they had ended up sitting so close together, but then, eerie was an apt description for many things that were happening lately. Like the flutters Leah had felt when she ran her finger over Ryan's name on the list.

"Sure, I did," the man named Steve replied, chuckling. "Taught him everything he knows... you know me, a regular Joe Montana."

Both men laughed in a way that made it clear Steve was far from being a football legend even on the local level.

"Actually I taught him everything he knows," the mother of the little girls chimed in. "Pass, kick... I do it all."

Steve grinned and tossed an arm around her shoulders. "That's Gloria's way of saying she wears the shoulder pads in the family."

His wife elbowed him, drawing a feigned yelp of pain. "Watch it. You happen to be insulting the mother of a genuine town hero."

Every inch of Leah's skin prickled. She felt the muscles in Zach's arm tense sharply and she knew he had made the same connection she had. Steve and Gloria... it was too much to be merely a coincidence. Besides, her crack about being the mother of a town hero gave it away. The couple now gathering their kids and belongings were Steve and Gloria Wayland, Ryan's adoptive parents.

Leah had scanned the crowd several times, wondering who they might be. She had regarded the couple in front with only mild interest, however, and mostly because of their adorable little girls. They were older than she'd envisioned, at least twelve or fifteen years older than she and Zach. But that made perfect sense, she realized suddenly. When she was sixteen, they would have been in their late twenties, a perfect age for starting a family. Perhaps Gloria Wayland had tried conceiving and couldn't. Perhaps she was like so many women you hear of, who have their own children only after adopting a child. Did that explain the spacing between Ryan and the little girls? Ryan's sisters, she thought, swallowing a lump in her throat.

Leah stared at them now with surging interest. Steve was tall and thin, balding on top with a decidedly professorlike air. He looked kind and quiet. He didn't seem to have either Zach's high energy level or his athletic ability and for a reason she couldn't explain, that pleased Leah. It was as if there were ways he hadn't completely taken Zach's place. She was unable to draw as hasty an impression of Gloria Wayland, other than noting that the woman had the patience of a saint in handling her daughters. That and the fact that the laugh lines around her smile were deep, gave Leah a good feeling about the woman who had raised her son.

The Waylands started herding the girls down the steps and Leah was about to push Zach into following them when suddenly Ryan came vaulting over the railing at the bottom of the bleachers and ran up to meet them. Leah froze, gaping at him as wide-eyed and rapid pulsed as a teenager in the presence of a rock star until Zach's none-to-gentle nudge snapped her out of it.

Bending down, Ryan casually ruffled his sisters' hair and tolerated the congratulatory kisses they planted on his cheek, at least three from each of them. When they were through, he straightened, turning to his parents with a wide grin so like Zach's that Leah ached inside. Up close the resemblance was even stronger, right down to the cleft in his chin and the way he tilted his head a little to the side, his square jaw thrusting upward, when he was excited.

"Did you guys see that last pass?" he demanded, reenacting it right then and there in case his folks had missed it. "It was perfect. I knew it the instant it left my fingers. Zowie."

Steve Wayland laughed and slapped his son on the back of his uniform jersey. "Great game, Ryan. I like to see you getting the ball to Scott more."

They launched into a discussion of strategy that Leah could feel Zach was dying to get into and which went on until Ryan's mother broke in.

"It was a great game, Ryan, and you were wonderful, but I have to get these kids home before they do me in."

"Sure," Ryan replied. "I really came to ask if I can go to Larrabee's for a hamburger... all the guys are going."

"By foot?" his father asked.

Ryan nodded. "Yeah."

"As long as you're walking you can go, I don't want you in Duke McLain's car, understood?"

"Understood." Ryan shuffled his feet. "There is one other little thing..."

His father sighed and reached into his pocket. "How much?"

"Five? Just till I get my..."

"Allowance," the elder Wayland finished along with him. "Why does that tune sound so familiar?"

"Thanks, Dad," said Ryan, taking the five-dollar bill his father handed him. "I won't be late."

"Phone if you want a ride home," his mother called after him as he started back down the bleachers.

He'd only gone a few steps when he stopped and bent to pick up something from the edge of the concrete stair.

"Hey," he said, turning with it in his hand. "Look what I found."

Leah nearly gasped out loud as she saw that he was holding the tiger pendant Zach had returned to her. She quickly reached into her pocket, where she had been carrying it ever since, feeling ridiculous as she superstitiously transferred it from pocket to pocket depending on which coat she was wearing. It had been there when they drove past the Wayland's house earlier. She knew because she had curled her fingers around it tightly as they drove away for the last time, drawing some strange sort of comfort from the smooth metal. Her pocket was empty now, and belatedly she felt a small tear in the seam of the lining.

In a split second she realized what had happened. She looked at the tiger swinging from the end of the chain in Ryan's hand and instinctively leaned forward. Immediately Zach's hand clamped on to her thigh, pressing her back. She glanced at him and he shook his head, silently mouthing the word *no*.

Leah was startled. If anything she would have expected him to leap on this opportunity to speak to Ryan and his parents. It was the perfect excuse, the perfect ploy for barging into their serene life and turning it upside down. And Leah's along with it. Suddenly fear that any second now he would do just that rose full force. She felt as if the cement beneath her feet had turned into a sheet of dangerously thin ice as she watched Ryan show the pendant to his parents.

"This is real gold," Gloria commented, cupping it in her hand for a closer look.

"Really?" Ryan countered. "Cool."

"And expensive," his mother told him. "You can't just keep something this valuable."

"But I was the one who found it," grumbled Ryan.

"Doesn't matter. This belongs to someone, Ryan. We'll have to tell Mr. Russo that you found it and see if anyone reports it missing."

"What if no one does?" Ryan persisted, looking as stubborn as Zach could at times, thought Leah.

"Someone will," his mother assured him

"But if they don't? If I report it to Lost and Found and no one ever comes looking for it, then can I keep it?"

"What would you do with it if you did keep it?" asked his father.

Ryan shrugged, another echo of Zach that tugged at Leah's composure. "Wear it. It's cool."

"Yes," his mother said, shaking her head. "If you report it to Lost and Found at school and if no one claims it, you can keep it and wear it . . . or use it to ward off evil spirits, whatever floats your boat, kid."

"Great." Ryan gazed at the tiger one last time, clearly impressed by it, and then with typical teenage nonchalance, tossed it to his mother for safekeeping. "See ya."

In a second he had barreled down the steps and over the railing, disappearing from sight. The Waylands exchanged a resigned look.

"Could be worse," Gloria Wayland said to her husband. "Could be an earring he found."

"I guess." He hoisted the smallest of the two girls to his shoulder and took her sister by the hand. "Come on, gang, let's go home."

Home, thought Leah, feeling a sudden and ominous chill wrap around her. Back to the house with the workbench and the tire swing, where the sounds of the little girls' playing was no doubt a steady hum and where Ryan would be returning later. While she and Zach went back to their empty hotel rooms. Empty and separate hotel rooms. And tomorrow, if by some miracle she survived the night ahead, she would return to her equally empty house.

Zach gently tugged on her arm, signaling it was time to go. Leah was a little amazed that she could actually walk down the steps and to the car. She was numb all over, her muscles operating by rote.

She'd congratulated herself during the game on how well she was managing her emotional reaction to actually seeing Ryan for the first time. She had been overwhelmed sure, but she'd had it under control. Or so she'd thought. Belatedly she realized that actually she had been in a state of emotional suspended animation, with everything her overloaded senses couldn't handle being put on hold until later. Later being right now.

"You okay?" Zach asked as they took their place at the end of the long line of traffic leaving the parking lot at a crawl.

"I don't know."

From the corner of her eye, Leah saw his curt nod. Neither of them was okay and both of them knew there wasn't any way to change that.

Their car inched forward.

"What do you think the odds were of him finding that pendant?" he asked her.

Leah shook her head, beyond even attempting a reply.

"You know," he continued, as if driven to fill the silence, "for a second there I thought you were going to reach out and grab it right out of his hand."

"I almost did." Leah tipped her head back with a sigh, resting it on the back of the seat, her eyes closed. "It was an automatic response, I guess."

"I'm glad you didn't. I like the idea that he has something of ours. Something that meant a lot to us once."

Once, thought Leah. Lots of things had meant something once. This wasn't helping. She opened her eyes to see how far they had moved. Not far enough.

"I know what you mean," she said to Zach. "I'm glad he has it too. It must have been fate that out of all the people at that game, he was the one who picked it up."

"How did you drop it anyway?"

"I hadn't realized," she replied, her tone weary, "that there was a small hole in my coat pocket."

"That raises an even more interesting question...what was it doing in your pocket?"

Leah felt the intensity of his stare and turned her head, unable to resist it. It was a mistake. Something in the dark, wistful way he was looking at her provoked memories of other times and other losses that only added to the weight strapped to her heart.

"I've been sort of carrying it around with me," she admitted with a sheepish shrug. "Don't ask me why, maybe I thought it would bring me luck or something."

He eyed her consideringly, without saying a word.

"For heaven's sake," snapped Leah, "it was no big deal. Haven't you ever done something that you knew was stupid but you went ahead and did it anyway?"

"Yes," he said, his tone laconic. "Twice actually."

Leah stared out the windshield. "Well, that's why I was carrying it around."

"At least it worked. I mean it brought you luck," he explained in response to her quizzical look.

"Really?" countered Leah with a bitter laugh. "Then how come I don't feel lucky? How come I feel like I got run over by a truck and that I went looking for it?"

"What's that supposed to mean?"

Leah rubbed her temples. "I don't know. You probably shouldn't pay attention to anything I say right now. I just feel so..." She paused, at a loss for words to describe the depth of her sorrow.

"It's funny," she said after a minute, "all this time I thought that the reason I couldn't bear to think about my baby, the reason I panicked the way I did when you came back and announced that you planned to find him, was that I was afraid of finding out that what I'd been telling myself for all these years was the right thing to do, was really a big mistake."

"Pretty natural fear, if you ask me."

"But today proved that it wasn't a mistake, at least not in the way I've always worried about... And not in the way I think you were worried about."

Zach nodded in response to the question in her remark.

"Ryan is obviously part of a loving family," she went on, "and from the looks of things, probably as well adjusted as most kids his age."

"I know I'll find it a lot harder after today to picture him as a hoodlum cowering in some dark alley with a gun in his hand."

Leah heard the relief in his voice and she had to fight the urge to touch his leg or reach for his hand. She wasn't sure if it was an urge to comfort Zach, or find some way to stop herself from spinning out of control.

"So he's all right," she said grimly. "I ought to feel relieved and happy."

"And you don't."

"Do you?"

"I'm plenty relieved. But happy?" He shook his head.

"I'm thinking now that, for me at least, it's because what I thought I feared most, wasn't really it at all. I think that deep down, the real reason I never wanted to look for him was because of this, what's happening right now." She turned to look over her shoulder just as they finally reached the front of the line and began to move. "It's like giving him up all over again," she whispered.

It was true, through the sudden blur of her tears, the stadium rapidly disappearing behind her might have been the hospital she had been driven away from all those years ago. The pain ripping through her was the same.

No, it was worse, Leah realized suddenly.

When she was younger, she had believed all those who told her there was no other way. She knew better now. And however good a life the Waylands had given him, Ryan had lost something as surely as she and Zach had.

The enormity of that loss came crashing down on her, turning the ride back to the hotel into a slow-moving nightmare. She found herself gripping the door handle, ready to bolt the instant the car came to a stop, wanting to run away from everything and everyone who wasn't Ryan.

She practically did run down the hotel corridor to her room, Zach beside her all the way. When she fumbled with the room key, he took it from her and opened the door, catching her arm lightly as she stepped inside.

"Look, I know you're hurting.... Do you want to talk or something?"

Leah shook her head.

"No. Me either, really."

He closed his eyes. His sigh had a hollow sound that seemed to echo through the emptiness inside Leah. For years she'd known of the massive hole in her soul, known its exact dimensions so she could avoid it most of the time and never fall too deeply in. But now that hole had a name and a face and an easy laugh that she could still hear ringing in her ears and that made it so much harder.

Suddenly the need to fill the emptiness inside, even for just a little while, was overwhelming.

Surprising him and herself, Leah reached out and grasped the front of Zach's jacket.

"Make love to me," she urged breathlessly. "Please, Zach, even if you can't bear to touch me ever again after this. Please make love to me tonight."

Chapter Eleven

Zach stepped into her room and slammed the door behind him.

"Not bear to touch you?" he echoed, his short laugh low and rough. Not a laugh at all really, but something else, something darker. "You've got it all wrong. Why don't you ask me how I've been able to bear all these days of being near you and not touching you? Especially when touching you is what I think about all day, at night when I'm alone in bed, all the damn time."

"But I thought..."

Leah shook her head, trying to reconcile his words with the way he'd been acting toward her. Was she so emotionally dazed she was misinterpreting what he was trying to tell her? Only one way to find out. She lifted her chin resolutely. "Are you saying that you want me, too?"

"Yeah, I want you," he said, moving closer without seeming to move at all, so close his words caressed her face when he spoke. When he was this close, Leah was always conscious of how much bigger than her he was, and of the raw power of his masculinity. The physical attraction between them was as rampant as ever, and as capable of making her toss caution to the wind. She felt surrounded and overwhelmed by him, even before he laid his warm hand against her cheek and added, "I want you more than I knew could want someone, more than I want to, more than you should trust."

"Then tell me why you've been ignoring me."

"I haven't," he countered, his dark eyes scouring her face as if seeing it for the first time all over again. "I've seen every move you've made, heard every word, every sigh. Sometimes, when I'm sitting across the room pretending to read, I stare at you so hard I swear I can feel your heart beating inside my chest."

"Oh, Zach," she whispered, turning instinctively toward his touch. "Then why..."

"Because I can't," he said hoarsely. "We can't."

But he already was... *they* already were... they were already making love to each other with the questions in their eyes and the yearning heat of their bodies and the hot, intermingled rush of their breath.

Already his hand was sliding from her cheek to her throat, to where her skin was softer than corn silk and Zach knew right then and there that in spite of what he'd promised himself over and over since the day he walked out of her house, he wasn't going to stop.

He bent his head and brought his mouth to within a hairbreadth of hers. He wanted to kiss her, taste her, but he also wanted the sweet, churning pleasure of having it go on and on. And so, instead of claiming the lips she parted in invitation, he kept his mouth where it was, so close to where he wanted it to be, and tantalized them both mercilessly.

Lifting his hands to her shoulders, he slipped them beneath her coat. He painstakingly peeled the garment off first one shoulder, then the other, and let it slide to the floor.

Beneath it she was wearing much too much. Snug black checked slacks and a shirt and another one of those soft, fuzzy sweaters that had been driving him crazy wanting to touch her. This one was black and at that moment black was his very favorite color.

Over and over he'd imagined how good it would feel to rub his hands over this soft material and feel the heat of Leah's skin right through it. But as his open hand roamed freely over her back, Zach realized that when it came to Leah, his imagination, like his memory, was woefully inadequate. The reality of her, the warm, womanly flesh and blood reality, was better than anything his mind could ever conjure or recall.

Much sooner than he intended, the desire mounting inside him, pushed Zach to shove his hands under her sweater and pull it off over her head. Leah was eager to help, arching her neck in a way that thrust her breasts against his chest.

Quickly tossing the sweater aside, Zach sucked in a sharp breath and grasped her shoulders to keep her right where she was. With one hand he impatiently shoved open the front of his jacket so that only thin layers of fabric separated them. His breathing grew heavy as he rocked from side to side just a little, just enough so that she rubbed against him with tantalizing delicacy. Time stopped and his blood raced.

Finally, with a rough sigh, he glanced down, confirming what he'd felt even through their shirts. Leah's nipples were hard and aroused, jutting against the soft material. They presented an irresistible temptation. Enthralled, he leaned back and slid his hands between their bodies, caressing her

reasts with a lazy circular motion that quickly had her
reath coming in short, choppy pants.

Leah raised her hands to encircle his wrists with her long
ender fingers, not to stop him, but to encourage his gentle
inistrations. Zach watched her eyelids flutter and close,
atched her tongue slide unconsciously across her full bot-
•m lip, watched pleasure tighten its grasp on her and he
anked God that this time he hadn't had the strength to
alk away from her. He couldn't offer Leah much, not
·arly what she deserved, but at this moment, tonight, he
uld give her this.

Gradually he broadened the circles he was tracing around
·r breasts, letting his fingers slide from her rib cage to the
p button of her blouse. He paused there to slip it open,
king time to caress the silky skin beneath before moving
n to unfasten the next button and the next.

He had to curb an impulse to rip her clothes from her
ody and crush her against him. That's what it would take
· satisfy the pounding urge to feel her flesh next to his. But
night wasn't only for satisfying those raw urges; it wasn't
night for hurrying or for the kind of fast, urgent loving he
sually succumbed to. Leah needed more.

Zach was determined to give it to her, everything she
eeded. As he patiently undressed her, his hands and mouth
oved slowly and reverently over her body, heeding even
·r softest whispered plea, trying to anticipate where she
anted to be touched, how hard, for how long.

He wanted to awaken the ripe sensuality that he knew was
side her and had been left unexplored for so long. With
ach touch, each time he pressed his open mouth to her
reast, her belly, her thigh, he felt her passion flare higher,
ushing her closer to the outer edge of control. That's where
e wanted her, poised on the brink of madness, ready to
mble with him when the time came.

When he finally kissed her mouth, he did that slowly, too, flicking his tongue at the corners of her lips and sliding it back and forth across them maddeningly until Leah was driven to take control. Holding his head in her hands, she thrust her tongue past his, taking his mouth in a deeply erotic kiss that declared her desire in a way no words could have.

The pleasure she took in her own dominance thrilled Zach. He forced himself to stand still as she tugged off his jacket and then worked her way down the buttons on his shirt. Her eyes glittering brightly, she stripped it off him and dragged her fingers through the dark hair covering his chest. She bent her head and rubbed her face against him, finding his nipples with her tongue and flicking them.

Her pleasured purr caressed his chest, winding itself through and around his heart. Who was he kidding, thought Zach as she undid his belt buckle and worked his zipper down with torturous expertise. He needed this night as much as Leah did.

Once she had opened his jeans, exposing the heat and urgency of his desire, Zach kicked them off along with his boots. He reached for her, drawing her close to at last indulge his longing to feel her against him this way, with no barriers left between them. The contrast between the satin texture of her skin and the roughness of his added to the eroticism of their embrace, their elemental differences sanctifying this most elemental need. Why couldn't it always be this simple, and this good?

Their hands moved over each other, their legs tangled and pressing, but by unspoken agreement they avoided intimate contact, both wanting to make this night, this reprieve from everything that wasn't pleasurable, last as long as possible.

Leah weakened first, sliding her hand down his chest, past his waist, to encircle his rising passion.

"You feel so good," she told him, her voice a raspy whisper. "So warm."

"I'll get warmer," Zach murmured against her hair. "I promise."

"Show me."

"Not yet. Come here."

He led her to the bed and pulled her down, turning on the bedside lamp as he did. The last time they made love it had been in near darkness. This time he wanted the visual memory to take away with him along with the sounds and scents and tastes that were already burning themselves into his senses. He wanted it all.

Gathering both her wrists in one hand, he pulled them above her head and held them there while he looked at her, drinking in the sight of her, naked and open, her skin glowing like gold in the soft light.

"You are the most beautiful woman I've ever seen," he told her. "Your breasts are beautiful, your legs are beautiful, your shoulders, your eyes... You're perfect."

Leah neither preened nor demurred. A small smile curved her lips and her eyes were bright with gratitude.

Bending his head, Zach worshiped her all over again, even more thoroughly than he had before, taking full advantage of her reclining position. He lavished her with kisses, bathed her with pleasure, making her shiver and moan. He sucked her breasts and traced the deep curve at her waist with his fingertips. There wasn't a part of her he didn't adore and desire.

When he ran his tongue along her belly he felt the faintest of ridges. He lifted his head and the dampness from his mouth made the stretch marks she acquired from bearing his child shine faintly in the lamplight. Tenderness welled inside him. These were the outward marks of what she had

been through. How many scars were there that he couldn't
see? He felt Leah's gaze and turned his head to meet it.

Her eyes filled with tears above a trembling smile. "Not
so perfect after all, I guess."

Zach shook his head and pressed his mouth to the marks
on her stomach before lifting his gaze to hers once more.
"You are perfect to me, Leah. Always." He rested his fingertips on her belly. "These marks are part of you, part of
your past, our past really, and they only make me love you
more."

She opened her arms to him, her need obvious, and Zach
reluctantly abandoned his plan to taste all her secret de-
lights. He slid higher, straddling her hips so that he was
poised above her and slowly lowered himself into her body.
Leah drew in her breath and held it as he sank slowly deeper,
until his possession was complete.

He managed a smile. "See? I'm warmer now."

"Mmm. Much."

When he drew back, her hips rose to met him.

"Oh, yeah," he ground out, "like that, just like that."

Usually Zach found it a chore to match his thrusts to his
partner's pace, but not tonight. Not with Leah. Effortlessly they moved together, rising and falling, as if they were
truly one in this.

With each stroke their passion climbed higher, the sensual tension wound tighter until the explosion claimed them
both. And for that second that they came apart in each
other's arms, they were whole at last.

Much later they called room service to order sandwiches
and a bottle of wine.

"I think this is what's known as informal cuisine," Leah
said with a laugh as she lifted the silver domes to reveal their
turkey clubs.

"Actually I think anything you eat while naked is condered informal cuisine," corrected Zach.

"But I'm not naked."

He refrained from pointing out that for all her sheer white ightgown hid from him, she might as well have been.

Over dinner their conversation drifted cautiously to Ryan nd his family. Gradually their hesitancy lessened and they ere able to speak freely, reassuring each other that he was deed all right. Zach didn't ask if he could stay the night nd Leah didn't extend an invitation. After eating, they mply climbed back into bed together and fell asleep in each ther's arms.

Zach woke before Leah did. Before dawn actually. An grained habit, he told himself as he watched the sky righten through a crack in the drapes, the result of all those ears of drawing the early duty. He'd rather chalk it up to at than consider all the other reasons he had for not beg able to sleep.

Rolling to his side, he lay and watched Leah sleep. She oked all smoothed out, the small worried V between her rows, which had seemed a permanent feature lately, was ne. He grew aroused just watching her chest rise and fall ith each slow breath. Unconsciously he reached out to rush the hair from her face and caught himself just in the ck of time.

Uh-uh. Bad move, Blackmore.

Touching Leah was definitely not the way to start this day. would only make things harder, for both of them. He ought about returning to his own room to shower and ress, but before he could move, Leah stirred beside him.

"Penny for your thoughts," she said with a sleepy smile at was like a vice tightening on Zach's heart.

"Save your money," he advised, rolling onto his back to are at the ceiling. "My thoughts aren't worth it."

Leah touched his arm gently. "Everything is going to be all right, you know."

"If you say so."

"I do. Yesterday, leaving that stadium, I didn't think anything would ever be right again. In a way, I was sorry I had ever come here, ever let myself see Ryan. It was as if I'd had this empty place inside me for so long without knowing what was missing, and now that I knew that it was Ryan who was missing, now that I had seen him and heard him and watched him, it made being without him that much worse."

Zach didn't say anything. He couldn't. He had forced this on her, he had brought her here, he was the one to blame for everything.

"Don't scowl," she admonished, an airy thread of laughter in her voice. "The amazing thing is that I don't feel quite that way anymore. I'll always miss him," she said, her voice growing quiet. "I will always mourn for what might have been and I will always, always love him. But I'm not sorry I came."

"That's good," he said gruffly. "I'd hate to think I'm the guy who drops into your life every fourteen years or so just to screw things up."

"You're not that," Leah assured him, resting her head on his chest. "Never that."

She tipped her head up to look at him, studying him with a small smile and a look of such unmasked adoration that Zach cringed inside.

"What?" he asked, uncomfortable with the intensity of her attention.

"I was just thinking how yesterday, when I looked at Ryan, all I could see was you at his age. The resemblance was so strong. And now here I am looking at you, and in you I see so much of him."

"I know what you mean. When I looked at him I saw aces of you, and—don't laugh—my father."

"I'm not laughing, Zach. In his own way, your father oved you very much. I'd like to think that maybe Ryan icked out and got the best of all of us."

Zach gave a short chuckle. "That would be something all ght, the world's first journalist M.D. with a badge."

"Something like that," she agreed, laughing. "Al- hough I'm not sure those are the best parts of us." After a inute, she rested her hand on his chest lightly and said, Can I ask you something?"

"Anything," Zach told her and meant it.

"Why didn't you do what you said you might do... I ean, introduce yourself to Ryan? His finding the pendant ave you a perfect opportunity. I expected you to grab it."

"I expected me to, too," Zach admitted with a rueful ok. "I intended to, right from the start I intended to, right p until we saw him...even after that. I guess all this time ve been picturing myself charging in and rescuing my kid ie way I wished to hell someone had rescued me when I was ourteen, and it suddenly hit me that he doesn't need res- iing."

"That ought to make you feel better, not worse," ad- sed Leah, rubbing his arm reassuringly.

"It does. It just sort of means shifting gears inside." He ared at the ceiling without seeing it, thankful that Leah asn't the sort of woman to drag more out of him than he as ready to give. Except for the one thing that he was ab- olutely sure about, his thoughts at the moment were a ifting, murky mess.

"You know," he said after a while, "once, when Sam and were talking about kids, he told me that the moment he ade up his mind never to have another drink came one day hen he was with Adam and he looked at him and it sud-

denly hit him like a sledgehammer that there was nothing
not a damn thing, in his whole life that mattered to him a
much as that kid's smile. I guess, for me, that moment o
truth happened yesterday after the game. I looked at Ryan
and I knew that the only thing that mattered to me was h
happiness, and if that means holding back until he decide
he's ready to come looking for us, that's what I want to do.

"And I know that's going to happen," said Leah. "I be
lieve with my whole heart that one day a few years from now
I'm going to open my door, just the way I did that night yo
came to see me, but instead of you it will be Ryan standin
there."

Zach heard the quiver of emotion in her voice and fough
the urge to take her in his arms.

"And when he finds me," she went on in a suddenly clea
and determined tone, "I want him to find a whole, happ
woman with a life of her own to share with him if he'll le
her, not a bitter, lonely woman with only regrets...and
string of treeless Christmases."

Zach's mouth curved in an approving smile. "Sounds lik
you've got it all worked out."

"Well, I know the way I want it to happen. The rest is u
to Ryan."

"You're right. We've sent the letters and I've had th
agency contact the Waylands about my family's medica
history. The next move has to be Ryan's." He slanted her
sheepish look. "I guess that's sort of what you've been try
ing to get through my thick head all along, isn't it?"

"More or less. But, like in Sam's case, you have to fin
it out in your own way."

"In my case that's usually the hard way. But not this tim
thank God."

Nuzzling his shoulder reassuringly, Leah asked, "So would this be a good time for me to point out that at least we still have each other?"

Zach squeezed his eyes shut, everything inside him tightening in response to her hopeful words.

"I was just thinking about what we said before," she added when he didn't respond, her hurried tone signaling her sudden nervousness. "You remember, about Ryan reminding us of each other, and of your Dad. I guess that's what they mean about living on in your children. In our case, maybe it could work both ways... maybe by holding onto each other, we can hold onto a piece of our son."

Zach had no choice but to let the silence stretch cruelly. He felt her slowly recoil until they were no longer touching and he just lay there and let her go.

"Bad idea, I guess," she said finally.

"Leah, I'm sorry..."

"No, I'm the one who's sorry. I jumped to conclusions. I just thought..."

"Thought what?" He levered up to lean against the headboard and Leah followed suit. "Thought what, damn it?"

"I don't know," she snapped. "That last night meant something more."

"It did. You know it did."

"Don't lie to me, Zach, I saw your face when I said that we still have each other. I know what you were thinking."

He looked away from the anger and the hurt in her eyes and shook his head.

"No, you don't," he said. "You don't know at all what I was thinking."

"Care to enlighten me?"

"I was cursing myself for at least the millionth time since I woke up this morning, telling myself once again that if I wasn't such a royal screwup I could be doing what I want to do right now, taking you in my arms and telling you that you're right, that at least we still have each other."

"Then do it," she urged. "Just do it, Zach."

"I can't."

Her face went white as she heard the utter finality in his tone. She looked the way he'd seen people look after real bad accidents.

"I don't understand," she said.

"It's not real complicated. Fourteen years ago you didn't want to take a chance on me because I had no job and a shaky future, well that's even more true today than it was then. I can't let you take a chance on me now."

Leah heaved a giant sigh. "Is that all this is about? Your job?" She attempted a laugh. "Do you really think I'd have some objection to falling in love with a cop?"

"That's just it, I might not be a cop much longer. How about falling in love with a convicted murderer, Leah? How does that fit into your plans? You feel like spending next Christmas Eve in the visitors' room in maximum security?"

His words were harsh. They had to be to make her understand what was at stake here.

"If that's what I have to do to be with you, I will."

"That's just it, you don't have to, and I won't let you." He swung off the bed and pulled on his jeans.

Leah rose to her knees on the edge of the mattress. "Don't do this, Zach, don't let this come between us now when it's taken us so long to find each other again. This is coming fourteen years too late, I know, but I love you, Zach. I love you more than anything in the world."

It took a full minute until he felt controlled enough to turn and face her.

"I'm not putting anything between us, Leah. It is already there. Face it. I have."

"No, you just haven't thought this through."

"All I've done lately is think about it."

"But not rationally," she argued as he picked up his shirt from the floor and pulled it on. "You can't have or you wouldn't be willing to throw this second chance we've been blessed with away on . . ."

"What?" he interjected, leaving his shirt unbuttoned as he faced her. "An impulse? That's not what this is. I know all about throwing things away on impulse, believe me.

"In case you never noticed," he continued, his lips curled with self-recrimination, "I've lived my whole life acting on impulse, choosing a college, a career, buying a new bike . . . it's always on impulse. Out on the street," he added, cognizant of the tension that crept into his voice, "we refer to that as instinct, and sometimes that's all you've got going for you."

"Look, Zach, I know you're thinking about the shooting, but you can't compare—"

"No," he said, cutting her off with an impatient shake of his head. "This is about something else."

Leah nodded without saying anything, grudgingly conceding to let him finish.

"On the job, sometimes your instincts pay off, sometimes they don't. But life's not a stakeout." He paused and stared through the crack in the drapes as he struggled for the right words. "Fourteen years ago when you refused to do what I wanted you to do, keep our baby in spite of the fears and concerns you had that we weren't ready to start a family, I walked out on you. And at Christmas, when I wanted you in this with me all the way and you held back, I did it again. Don't you see the irony in that? Here I was always accusing you of having to have things your way, when all along I was the one who couldn't take no for an answer, who could never compromise.''

''You're being too hard on yourself,'' Leah told him gently. ''Nothing is that black-and-white.''

''This is,'' he countered bluntly. ''I've been on my own for years now. I've created life, and I've taken it.'' He paused, his voice cracking. ''But maybe it took seeing the young man my son has become to make me take the final step toward growing up, to finally be able to put something... no, make that *someone*... someone I love, ahead of what I want.''

''No,'' she said, the rapid shake of her head tinged with dread. ''Zach, please, it's not an either-or sort of—''

''Yes,'' he interrupted. ''Yes it is... black-and-white, either-or. My mind's made up, Leah, I won't interfere in Ryan's life, and I won't risk destroying yours.''

Chapter Twelve

"So that's the whole enchilada," Bud Hirsch said to Leah, levering back in his swivel chair and lacing his fingers at the back of his neck. "There'll be a three-month transition period. After that, I take off for my cabin to play fisherman full-time and you take over here. What do you think?"

Leah manufactured a semblance of a smile, something she'd had a lot of practice doing lately, and tried to think of words that would convey the kind of gung-ho enthusiasm that Bud no doubt expected of the newly appointed editor of *Rhode Island Monthly* magazine. There was a time when she wouldn't have had to think, back when she thought that being named editor was all she wanted out of life.

Things had changed. Falling in love with Zach all over again had changed them, and a job—any job—just wasn't at the top of her wish list anymore. She had known for over a week now that the promotion to editor was in the works,

but the official word had just been handed down today.
While she was happy with the promotion, it didn't solve all
her problems.

"I think that sounds terrific," she said finally, cranking
her smile up a notch to compensate for the lack of original-
ity in her words. "I can't wait to get started."

"Yeah, I can tell. If you sounded any more excited you
might fall asleep on me."

Leah dropped the smile and shot him a sheepish look instead. "I'm sorry, Bud. I'm trying, and I really do appre-
ciate all you've done. I know that your recommendation
cinched the deal for me. I won't let you down."

"I'm much more worried about you letting you down."
His big face was scrunched with concern. "How are you
doing anyway?"

"Better every day." She rolled her eyes. "Well, make that
better some days than others."

"That's what it takes to get over something like this,
honey, time. I'll tell you, Leah, I'm glad you finally opened
up and told me about your son and about Zach. No one
should carry something like that around inside of them."

"I know that now. Talking helps, and it's a relief to finally be able to be totally honest with my friends and my
family. If nothing else, this has brought me closer to the
people I care about... Most of the people I care about at
least."

"Yeah, right." His frown was ominous. "I know you said
this Zach character is a decent guy, but I have to tell you,
Leah, nothing would give me greater pleasure than to find
him and scatter him across three counties. Maybe four."

"If it's any consolation, he'd probably stand still and let
you do it. At the moment Zach is doing a better job of
punishing himself than anyone else could possibly do."

"I take it you still haven't heard from him?"

Leah shook her head. "Neither has his friend, Sam. When I left Texas, he told me he was staying behind because he had friends there whom he wanted to spend some time with. I didn't believe him, but I could hardly handcuff him to me and drag him back home."

"I'll bet you felt like it, though," he commented with an affectionate chuckle.

"I still do, but it doesn't work that way. I keep hoping that whoever's handling the investigation will hurry up and clear Zach and that will change his mind about me, about . . . everything. Either that or it will finally sink into his thick head that I love him and want to be with him no matter what the outcome of the investigation is."

Bud smiled at her. "He's one lucky man, I'll tell you that. I'll tell him, too, if I ever get to meet him."

"I'm sure you will . . . tell him, that is," Leah said with a small laugh. "Whether you'll get to meet him before you retire is anybody's guess. Right now it seems that all I can do is sit and wait." She heaved an exasperated sigh. "Wait for Ryan, wait for Zach, is that my lot in life, Bud? To have to constantly wait for the men I love to come to me?"

"Whoa, hold on. That question edges into the territory of love and romance, and if I knew anything about either one, I'd have more to show for my years of marriage than a stack of canceled alimony checks."

"Big help you are," she scoffed, this time managing a genuine smile of affection.

"I could always pour that drink I've been saving for you," he offered, clearly relishing the thought.

"Not just yet. I'll let you know." She stood to leave. "Thanks again, Bud, for everything."

Back in her own office she cleared her desk and got ready to call it a day with little enthusiasm. Here or home, it was all pretty much the same to her these days. Wherever she was, she missed Zach with the same unwavering intensity.

She refused however, to let it affect her work. Never again would she let her feelings simmer until they began to eat away at her inside. She'd meant it when she told Zach that she planned to get on with her life in a way she could be proud of if Ryan came looking for her. With or without Zach, she intended to do just that. It was just that the thought of doing it alone made the road ahead seem like a straight uphill climb.

Crazy as it seemed, she missed Zach more now than she had the first time they parted. Probably because at thirty she had a much fuller understanding than she did as a teenager of how rare and wonderful a thing true love is. It was far too precious to simply toss aside because of circumstances beyond your control. The way she saw it, that's exactly what Zach was doing.

That morning in the hotel, when he had told her that they had no future, Leah had been devastated. She, who was always so pragmatic and analytical about everything, couldn't have reasoned with him even if he had been willing to listen. Which he wasn't. In the two weeks that had passed since then, however, she had thought and reasoned it through plenty.

It was ridiculous for Zach to make their being together contingent on what some committee from Internal Affairs decided. And if she could only talk to him she would tell him so, over and over in her own logical way until he had to agree that she was right. His stance just didn't make sense.

What if they had already been together, perhaps even married, when this tragedy occurred? Would he expect her to divorce him because of it? What if instead of a shooting it had been an accident and he had been permanently in ured? Would he expect her to walk out on him afterward because his "future looked shaky" as he had put it?

It was ridiculous and the more she thought about it the more anxious Leah was to see him so she could tell him so. With every day that passed she compiled more arguments to support her position and decimate his. There were a thousand good reasons she could think of why they should be together no matter what happened, and they all began and ended with the fact that she loved him.

That had been the one single reason she had been able to think of that morning in the hotel room. She loved him more than anything else in the world. More than she ever would love anything or anyone else. More than she ever had. If she hadn't at the time, she understood now that it was more than just her decision not to have children that caused her marriage to Gus to fail. As much as she and Gus had had in common and had enjoyed being together, they had never shared the kind of love needed to build a life together, a love strong enough to endure whatever came their way. She had never loved Gus the way she loved Zach. Beyond reason. So much that it scared her and thrilled her all at once. What more did the man want for heaven's sake?

Leah stopped in the act of tossing some notes into her briefcase. What more did he want? Nothing. Nothing at all. All Zach wanted—all he had ever wanted—was for her to love him enough to put him first in her life in a way that no one, not even his own father, ever had. To put him ahead of her ambition and her other obligations and maybe most important of all, ahead of her fears. He wanted her to love him enough to trust him...enough to make a giant leap of faith even when her common sense was clamoring for her to batten down the hatches.

She may not have been capable of loving that way when she was younger, but she loved him that way now. She'd tried to tell him that, hadn't she? Her mouth curved in a wry smile as it belatedly occurred to Leah that telling him had been her first mistake. How could you tell someone about a feeling so pure and blinding that it transcended any words she knew?

You couldn't, Leah decided, hastily snapping her brief-case shut with half of what she'd intended to bring home still lying on her desk. She flicked off her office light. It was illogical to even try and Lord knows no one would ever accuse her of being illogical. There was a time for words and a time for action...and a time when even a woman of words had to take matters into her own hands.

Zach tipped the driver and swung the taxi door shut behind him. Hitching his duffel bag over his shoulder, he paused for a minute on the sidewalk and stared up at the windows of his apartment. Home, he thought wryly. At least it was home if you weren't too limited in your definition of the word. If on the other hand you adhered to the tradition that home is where the heart is, he was homeless.

He climbed the stairs slowly, the same way he did everything these days. He wasn't in any hurry for anything, not even to find out the results of the investigation, which should be revealed at the meeting with the top brass that was scheduled for Tuesday. The day after tomorrow.

The meeting was the only reason he'd finally ended his solitary tour of the Southwest, a trip he couldn't recall much about other than that every hotel room he stayed in had a phone. He'd spent a good bit of time staring at each one of them, wrestling with the temptation to call Leah, just to see if she was all right, just to hear her voice, just to make what had to be final seem a little less so. It had been like locking an alcoholic up in a room with a bottle of Jack Daniels.

For a while, he'd teased himself with the thought that maybe, if everything worked out the right way, if the investigation cleared him, if he was reinstated to the force, then he would call her and see how things went from there. But the closer he got to Tuesday, the more he accepted that the outcome of the investigation wasn't the only thing involved here. Even if he was in the clear and they handed him back his badge and gun, his future wasn't guaranteed. He still had to carry that gun around with him until some night when he came up against another suspect in another alley and found out if he was still able to use it when he had to.

If not, he'd be not only homeless in a poetic sense, but jobless in an all too real sense. Unemployed with ten years experience in something he no longer had the heart to do. Once the first blush of love had passed, he'd bet that would be something Leah would be real proud to tell her friends at parties.

That's if they ever went to parties at that point. Zach knew himself well enough to know that living with that kind of failure wouldn't make him easy to be around. As he had so often in the past few weeks, he reminded himself that after all she had been through, Leah deserved better odds than he could offer for the fresh start she was determined to make.

Maybe someday things would change, if they cleared him and if he proved to himself that he could still do the job he loved and if Leah hadn't found someone else by then. It was a heck of a lot of ifs, Zach knew, but at the moment it was all he had.

Maybe if he hadn't been so absorbed in his own thoughts, he would have heard the movement in his apartment before he actually reached the door. He froze at the unexpected sound and leaned closer to listen. Someone was definitely in there, messing with his stuff from the sound of it. Zach had a freeze-frame vision of some guy gleefully packing up his stereo and VCR. Punk, he thought, years of habit automatically moving his hand toward the gun in his shoulder holster.

Then he remembered he wasn't wearing it, and as sweat broke out on his upper lip, he realized he was glad. He didn't need a gun to deal with the sort of lowlife who went sneaking into people's apartments when they weren't there.

Soundlessly he took his key from his pocket and slid it into the lock, turning it slowly, silently, waiting until he felt the bolt release. Then, taking a deep breath, his heart pounding with a familiar hard, adrenaline-based rhythm, he shoved the door wide open.

"Freeze. Police," he shouted as he had thousands of times in the past.

From time to time on those occasions when he'd gotten the jump on someone this way, Zach had been surprised by what he found on the other side of the door, but nothing ever shocked the air right out of his lungs the way this did.

"Leah?" he said in a ragged whisper of disbelief.

She turned from the stove where it appeared to his dazzled vision that she'd been stirring something, and smiled at him.

"Welcome home," she said.

She said it all nice and easy and loose, as if she'd been expecting him. As if, thought Zach in confusion, he ought to have been expecting her to be here.

"Who let you in?" he asked.

"I have a key, remember?"

He nodded. The memory of giving her a key immediately triggered all sorts of other memories of the time she had spent here with him . . . the memory of her curled up on his sofa with her book, all long legs and concentration. The memory of her licking maple syrup off her bottom lip the time he'd cooked French toast for breakfast. The memory of the morning he'd accidentally walked in on her as she was drying off from her shower and he hadn't been able to think straight for hours afterward.

"You have a key," he said at last, thinking how ridiculous he sounded. "That doesn't explain what you're doing here."

"I wanted to surprise you," she told him with that same casual matter-of-factness. "Sam told me you'd probably be coming back today for the meeting on Tuesday, so I decided to come up early and fix dinner for you. I know how you feel about airline food," she added, grinning. "Anyway, it was either going to be shrimp casserole or Beef Burgundy and I decided on the beef."

Zach listened in amazement and watched as she turned back to the stove with spoon in hand, a regular Julia Child.

He reached out to grab her and spin her back around, but caught himself in time.

Standing right behind her shoulder, as close as he could manage to get without actually touching her, he asked, "Why?"

"Mostly because the shrimp casserole called for caraway seeds and I wasn't sure if you liked . . ."

"Forget the food," he growled, forgetting as well that he wasn't going to touch her. Hands on her shoulders, he yanked her around to face him. "I want to know what this is all about. What are you doing here, Leah? I thought this was all settled back in San Antonio."

"You thought wrong," she said, her hazel eyes squaring off with his.

She had the look of a woman who knew exactly what she wanted and intended to have it. Inside Zach, bewilderment was beginning to give way to the first stirring of alarm. And, damn it, hope.

"I love you, Zach Blackmore," she said, "and I'm going to go on loving you for the rest of my life. What's more, I know that you love me."

She waited with slightly raised brows for him to disagree. He didn't.

"Now," she continued, "I think that two people who love each other ought to be together however and wherever and for ever long as they can. That's why I'm here."

She paused, tilting her head to the side as if waiting to see if he had any more dumb questions. Zach was struck by a powerful urge to say "Okay" and drag her into his arms to seal whatever sort of bargain she was proposing. Whatever it was, however long it lasted, it was light-years better than what he'd had going for him when he walked in here. Only the fact that he was through acting on impulse held him back.

"What about the investigation?" he asked.

"It doesn't matter."

"What if they decide to charge me."

"That wouldn't matter, either, but they won't."

Her air of utter confidence amazed and thrilled him. Was she for real?

"How can you be so sure?" he demanded.

"Because I know in my heart that you could never hurt anyone intentionally, that what happened that night was a terrible mistake, and I have faith that the investigation is going to reach that very same conclusion."

His eyes narrowed. "What prompted this sudden change of heart?"

"There hasn't been one. I've known that I loved you since you came to rescue me from myself on Christmas Eve... maybe even before that. Long before," she added, the love she spoke of burning warmly in her eyes as she looked up at him. "And I've known from the instant you told me about the shooting that you weren't to blame for it. It was a tragic accident, but an accident just the same."

"I know I should have done a better job of telling you all this that morning in the hotel," she went on, "but you had me so shook up, I couldn't think straight."

"Now there's a first," drawled Zach. There was another first in the fact that for the first time in weeks he actually saw the humor in something. He even felt like smiling.

"Just don't count on it happening again anytime soon," warned Leah.

"Oh, I don't know, if I could figure out another way to shake you up real good it might happen again, and soon."

He saw Leah catch her breath, suddenly not as nonchalant as she had appeared when he first arrived. With good reason. In a matter of seconds the discussion had shifted subtly and ushered them across a threshold that would change the rest of their lives. They both knew it, their understanding of what was happening reflected in their bright eyes and the heightened awareness with which their gazes moved over each other.

A few things were obvious. She wasn't going to leave. And he wasn't going to throw her out. Still, part of Zach needed to hear it all.

"Your faith in justice as meted out by the Department of Internal Affairs is admirable," he told her. "But what if you're wrong about their findings?"

"I told you, that won't change anything. It certainly won't change the way I feel about you."

"Maybe not," he said, her words sending a shaft of pure pleasure moving right through his core. "But the fact is that if they hold me responsible it will change just about everything else. I could go to prison, Leah, for a long, long time."

"I know all about time, Zach. Fourteen years is a long, long time." She reached up and curled her arms around his

neck, pressing herself sweetly against him as she did. "I'l
be there when you get out. Count on it."

Zach's mind was reeling from her closeness. He was
afraid to breathe, afraid to move, afraid to wake up and find
out this was all a dream.

"You mean it?" he demanded roughly, winding his hand
through her hair so she couldn't look away. "You're really
willing to stick by me no matter what happens on Tues
day?"

"No matter what happens on Tuesday or Wednesday or
any of the days afterward. I mean it. For better or worse
whatever comes our way."

Zach peered at her through narrowed eyes. "Is that a
proposal?"

"It is if your answer is yes."

"Yes."

Her smile could have lit up the entire city. "In that case
consider it a proposal. Looks like we're getting married
Blackmore."

"Yeah," he said, sliding his arms down low around her
hips. "About time, too. I couldn't have waited much longer
to kiss the bride."

Bending his head he took her mouth in a kiss that tried to
make up for the lost weeks and years. Nothing ever really
could, of course, but it was a start. He kissed her with his
lips and tongue and teeth and she responded with the same
uninhibited fervor, opening to him completely, melting
against him until he had no sensation of where he ended and
she began.

With every eager touch, each sweet caress of her tongue
against his, she told him again that she was his, completely
and forever. That she was here in his arms was a miracle that
Zach hadn't dared to think about. That she wanted him in
spite of what had happened in the past and whatever the

future might hand them, filled him with the joy that had been missing from his life for so long. And it filled him with love for Leah and with the determination to somehow, no matter what happened, live up to the trust she placed in him.

He kissed her until they were both breathless, stopping only when something stabbed him between the shoulder blades.

His head jerked up. "What the..."

"I'm sorry, it's the spoon," Leah exclaimed. "I sort of got carried away and forgot I was holding it."

"Remind me to make sure you're unarmed the next time I grab you."

"I'll do that." Leah returned the spoon to the pot simmering on the stove. She gave what was in the pot a stir, regarding it quizzically. "You know, the truth is, I never made anything quite this elaborate before. What do you think?"

"My mouth's watering already," Zach murmured, pressing closer to her from the back as he bent to kiss the side of her neck.

"I take it you're hungry?"

"Starving."

"Good. Because it's all ready and—"

"I'm sure it will be delicious," he told her as he removed the spoon from her hand and turned off the stove. "Later. Right now, I'm hungry for something much sweeter."

She smiled, not protesting as he took her hand and led her out of the kitchen.

"Once that's taken care of, we'll have dinner," he said, "then we'll have to talk about this need of yours to always have things your own way."

"Who? Me?" she countered, laughing.

"You have to admit you are one stubborn woman."

"Lucky for you," she shot back.

Zach paused to look at her, overwhelmed by the magni
tude of the truth in her flippant remark. "Yes," he said, as
he pulled her into his bedroom, leaving all the rest of the
world behind. "Lucky me."

Epilogue

he house was quiet and Leah was alone. She wasn't lonely
wever. Her life was very full these days and whenever she
s blessed with a moment to reflect, she usually spent it
nking of all that lay ahead for her and Zach, rather than
iandering precious time and energy on the empty days of
: past. Over the past year or so, she had discovered that
: easy to look ahead when your future is full of love.

There was, however, one small piece of the past that she
alled often, and with great pleasure. Taking a sip of the
ple-cinnamon tea, which in deference to her condition was
 beverage of choice at the moment, she thought of an-
ier cold December night like tonight, this one a year ago,
en she had also been sitting here alone.

The room looked pretty much the same now as it had
n, except perhaps for the addition of Zach's favorite
air from his old apartment and a few issues of *Sports Il-
trated* mixed in with her favorite magazines in the wicker

basket nearby. It was everything else in her life that h
changed so dramatically. Zach's surprise reappearance h
done exactly what she had feared it would do: it had turn
her whole world upside down, and Leah would never st
being thankful.

On that earlier night she had been eating a take-out di
ner alone; tonight she had Zach's favorite casserole waiti
in the oven. The traffic between Boston and Providen
made his arrival time unpredictable, but whether he g
home from work at seven or ten, she always waited to ha
dinner with him so they could talk about the day and so s
could give him the latest report on what their unborn ba
was up to. Understandably, no one else in the world b
Zach was as utterly fascinated as she was by the number
times the baby kicked or hiccuped on any given afternoo

Zach had already expressed frustration that if he stu
with his current schedule after the baby arrived, he wou
get home after he or she was already tucked in for the nig
too late to do more than tiptoe in for a peek and a goo
night kiss. Leah knew that prospect did not mesh w
Zach's vision of the kind of father he wanted to be. She al
knew that Sam had approached him about a partnership
his rapidly expanding business and that Zach was seriou
considering it.

It would please her immensely if Zach decided to ret
from the police force and switch to a less risky career,
pecially one that would keep him closer to home. Howev
she would never pressure him to do it, any more than
would nag her about the hours she spent at the magazi
They trusted each other's instincts and good judgment t
much for that.

Already Leah was scaling back her hours, delegating c
ties she previously thought only she could handle, reord
ing her priorities. It had been a big relief when Bud phon

few days ago and told her he'd decided to accept the ma-
zine's offer to come back as acting editor while she was on
aternity leave.

Leah grinned as she thought of Bud, absently rubbing her
mmy where the baby seemed to be attempting somer-
ults. She had a hunch that her old friend wasn't as smit-
n with the life of leisure as he had anticipated. Privately
e hoped that he might be amenable to handling things
hile she took an extended leave to stay home with the baby.
erhaps she would even be able to work part-time from her
ome office.

If not, Leah thought, she would have to make other ar-
ngements. Only one thing was certain, she had spent most
' her life putting her career first, this time she intended to
whatever was best for her family. What's more, Leah
ew in her heart that in the end, Zach would do the same.
In spite of his passion for his work, she knew that he
ved her and the baby more. The fact that he would even
tertain Sam's offer was proof of that. A year ago, when
e had finally been cleared of any wrong-doing in the
ooting and his suspension was lifted, he had been over-
yed.

In the very emotional aftermath, he had revealed to Leah
at being a cop was such a major part of who he was, that
e had feared losing it much more than he had feared being
nt to prison. Leah had resolved right then and there that
matter how much she worried about him whenever he
as on duty, she would never make him choose between
ving her and being a cop.

For a long time there was no hint that he ever would make
ch a choice. It was as if after what had happened, Zach
d something important he needed to prove, to his supe-
ors and the other guys on the force and, most of all, to
mself. Leah realized that she would probably never com-

pletely understand what that something he had to prove wa
that it was something only another cop could truly unde
stand.

Whatever it was however, he seemed to have handled
okay. After a few months back on the job she noticed th
the intermittent somber moods that had persisted even a
ter they were married were growing less frequent and le
intense, and she could honestly say that since they had d
covered she was pregnant, he'd been just about walking
air.

Truthfully they were both overjoyed and looking fc
ward to the baby's arrival with great excitement. Their lo
for each other had filled the holes in their lives; now th
were ready to share that love. For reasons they both und
stood all too well, neither of them wanted to be a part-ti
parent to this child. They wanted to be there to see his fi
smile, witness his first step, hear his first word. They wan
that for their own sake and for the baby's, and also t
cause in a way it would be like capturing a small piece of
that they had missed out on with Ryan.

Leah smiled at the thought of her firstborn. As she h
since the day he was born, she thought of him daily. Late
however, she was able to smile almost every time s
thought of him. Almost. Automatically her gaze lifted to t
very top of the Christmas tree that stood in the front w
dow.

The tree was, as Zach had tried to warn her when th
were picking it out, much too big for the room. Still, Le
had stubbornly refused to allow him to trim so much a
single needle from it. She needed a huge tree, she had
sisted, to make up for all the years she hadn't had one.

Gazing at it now, she was even happier that she had
compromised. Their rather modest collection of orr
ments, which she had supplemented with red satin bov

were scattered around the tree instead of being crowded and difficult to see. That made it easy for her to locate the pair of crystal angels hung as close to the star at the top as Zach could get them. One was the angel he had given her on that special Christmas they'd shared a year ago. Leah would always think of that angel as Ryan's special ornament. The other Zach had surprised her with only a few days ago, in honor of the baby who would be arriving in just a few months.

Leah had already decided that when her new son—or daughter—was old enough, it would be his task to hang the angels on the tree each year. And when he was old enough to understand, she would tell him about his brother, Ryan, and how if they were very lucky, someday they might all be able to meet him and be friends.

In Leah's heart there was no maybe about it. The adoption agency had been in touch with Zach to tell him they had forwarded the medical information about his father to the Waylands and had received a very nice letter in return asking that their deep appreciation be conveyed to Zach. In their letter they also explained that Ryan was aware he had been adopted—something that Leah had wondered about often—and that when the time came that he expressed a desire to explore his roots, they would do all that they could to help him.

It was going to happen. Not this Christmas, probably not for a while yet, but someday Ryan was going to be a real part of her life. Leah was absolutely certain. When she thought of Ryan these days, that's what she thought of first, the future, and she was filled with hope rather than remorse.

The distinctive sound of a four-by-four Jeep turning into the driveway interrupted Leah's daydreaming. The swapping of his beloved motorcycle for something safer during the bad-weather months had been one of Zach's first concessions to impending fatherhood. He was going to be so good at this, thought Leah, smiling as she hurried to meet him at the front door and welcome him home. They both were.

*   *   *   *   *

MEN MADE IN AMERICA

Fifty red-blooded, white-hot, true-blue hunks from every
State in the Union!

Beginning in May, look for MEN MADE IN AMERICA!
Written by some of our most popular authors, these
stories feature fifty of the strongest, sexiest men, each
from a different state in the union!

Two titles available every other month at your favorite
retail outlet.

In September, look for:

DECEPTIONS by Annette Broadrick (California)
STORMWALKER by Dallas Schulze (Colorado)

In November, look for:

STRAIGHT FROM THE HEART by Barbara Delinsky
(Connecticut)
AUTHOR'S CHOICE by Elizabeth August (Delaware)

You won't be able to resist MEN MADE IN AMERICA!

Silhouette®

SPECIAL EDITION®

WILD RIVER TRILOGY

by Laurie Paige

Come meet the wild McPherson men and see how these three sexy bachelors are tamed!

In HOME FOR A WILD HEART (SE #828) you got to know Kerrigan McPherson. Now meet the rest of the family:

A PLACE FOR EAGLES, September 1993—
Keegan McPherson gets the surprise of his life.

THE WAY OF A MAN, November 1993—
Paul McPherson finally meets his match.

Don't miss any of these exciting titles—only for our readers and only from Silhouette Special Edition!

Silhouette Books has done it again!

Opening night in October has never been as exciting! Come watch as the curtain rises and romance flourishes when the stars of tomorrow make their debuts today!

Revel in Jodi O'Donnell's STILL SWEET ON HIM—
Silhouette Romance #969
...as Callie Farrell's renovation of the family homestead leads her straight into the arms of teenage crush Drew Barnett!

Tingle with Carol Devine's BEAUTY AND THE BEASTMASTER—
Silhouette Desire #816
...as legal eagle Amanda Tarkington is carried off by wrestler Bram Masterson!

Thrill to Elyn Day's A BED OF ROSES—
Silhouette Special Edition #846
...as Dana Whitaker's body and soul are healed by sexy physical therapist Michael Gordon!

Believe when Kylie Brant's McLAIN'S LAW —
Silhouette Intimate Moments #528
...takes you into detective Connor McLain's life as he falls for psychic—and suspect—Michele Easton!

Catch the classics of tomorrow—*premiering* today—
only from ▼ Silhouette

TAKE A WALK ON THE
DARK SIDE OF LOVE WITH

October is the shivery season, when chill winds blow and shadows walk the night. Come along with us into a haunting world where love and danger go hand in hand, where passions will thrill you and dangers will chill you. Silhouette's second annual collection from the dark side of love brings you three perfectly haunting tales from three of our most bewitching authors:

Kathleen Korbel
Carla Cassidy
Lori Herter

Haunting a store near you this October.

Only from ▼*Silhouette*® where passion lives.